DANGEROUS PREY

LINDSAY McKENNA

THORNDIKE
CHIVERS

This Large Print edition is published by Thorndike Press, Waterville, Maine, USA and by BBC Audiobooks Ltd, Bath, England.
Thorndike Press, a part of Gale, Cengage Learning.
Copyright © 2008 by Lindsay McKenna.
The moral right of the author has been asserted.

The text of this Large Print edition is unabridged.
Other aspects of the book may vary from the original edition.
Set in 16 pt. Plantin.
Printed on permanent paper.

LIBRARY OF CONGRESS CATALOGING-IN-PUBLICATION DATA

McKenna, Lindsay, 1946–
  Dangerous prey / by Lindsay McKenna.
    p. cm. — (Thorndike Press large print core)
  ISBN-13: 978-1-4104-1539-4 (alk. paper)
  ISBN-10: 1-4104-1539-2 (alk. paper)
    1. Women helicopter pilots—Fiction. 2. Wildlife rehabilitators—Fiction. 3. Large type books. I. Title.
PS3563.C37525D36 2009
813'.54—dc22   2009000214

BRITISH LIBRARY CATALOGUING-IN-PUBLICATION DATA AVAILABLE

Published in 2009 in the U.S. by arrangement with Harlequin Books S.A.
Published in 2009 in the U.K. by arrangement with Harlequin Enterprises II B.V.

U.K. Hardcover: 978 1 408 44166 4 (Chivers Large Print)
U.K. Softcover: 978 1 408 44167 1 (Camden Large Print)

Printed in the United States of America
1 2 3 4 5 6 7 13 12 11 10 09

DANGEROUS PREY

Dear Reader,

The research for this book hinged on knowing about raptor rehabilitation. The idea for this book hatched (pardon the bird pun) a couple years ago at the Flagstaff, Arizona, Arboretum and Botanical Garden. Susan Hamilton of High Country Raptors (www.highcountryraptors.com) was giving a program along with a number of her students. On their arms were the most amazing group of wild hawks, owls and falcons I'd ever seen. The program consisted of Beau, the Harris Hawk, flying from one post to another in what is known as a "flight oval" — in reality a smooth piece of earth that is oval-shaped, with places for the raptor to land.

I was so entranced by these incredible wild raptors that I thought surely there must be a story in all of it! Well, there was. The information contained in *Dangerous Prey* comes from Susan's decade of experience. I owe this gal, who has a fabulous smile and great sense of humor, a lot. Her love for her raptors, I hope, will be conveyed just as strongly in Sky, the hero of the book.

As I got to put on a gauntlet (leather glove) and Susan had Beau fly to me, I finally understood. There is an electric energy around these raptors. It is palpable. It is awesome and unexpected. The raptors look at you and you become lost in their world and their reality. Truly, there is magic here between raptor and human. I hope I've conveyed all of this in the book. We owe raptor rehabilitators much thanks for rescuing wild raptors who get into trouble and saving their lives whenever possible. And we can thank Susan directly for the wonderful information about her raptors that appears in this love story.

Warmly,
Lindsay McKenna

To a group of friends who soar high in my life and make it a joy to be alive. I appreciate each of you so much. Thank you for being who you are and being there for us: Rose Lipinski, DC; Mary Buckner, RN; Marty Reinstra; Karen David, DD; Linda and Eric Haggard; the Grill Family: Yolande, Paul, Francesca and Manuel; Nina Gettler; Eileen Gardner; Rosemarie Brown; Dick and Mona Stites (Javadog Gallery, Cottonwood, AZ); Mike Smith, PhD; Jackie Dierks, PhD; Linda Skiba; Gail Derin, OMD; Claire and Marshal Klein; Michele Burdet; Grace Verte; Leslie and Patrick Hessleman; Gail Carswell; Michael Foltz; Laura Weigt, RN; Marina and Jean Pierre Jansen; Tricia Speed; Alma Bocanegra and last but never least, JoAnn Prater.

And to Northern Arizona Hospice, Cottonwood, AZ, and in particular, Caroline, RN, who have been so helpful with my mother as she leaves this life for another. Your group is terrific and you've been such a blessing in our lives. Caroline, you're an angel in disguise and my mother loved you and your bright, positive shining light in her life. And thank you to Carl, CNA, who took such good care of Mom on a weekly basis.

And to Cindy and Breck who own Austin

House, an assisted-living center in Cottonwood, Arizona. Thank you for your incredible humanity, your great CNAs who are just the finest, and your understanding hearts. No one could have had better people looking after my mother. And Hazel, you are just the best of chefs! My mother loved your home cooking and she just loved you to pieces. Blessings on all of you for the unsung and heroic work you perform quietly for our elderly every day. I wish there was a medal to give to all of you in recognition for your humanity and care. It gives me hope that this world will not only survive its dark times, but thrive.

CHAPTER ONE

"Hey, Kelly, we got one more run before nightfall!"

Kelly Trayhern was just climbing out of her Sikorsky Skycrane helicopter at the Cottonwood airport when Joe, her mechanic, came running across the tarmac toward her.

"We've made nine drops today," she protested, jumping to the ground and glaring at Joe. She shouldn't be mad. It wasn't his fault. As she glanced over her shoulder toward the north, and Sedona, she saw plumes of grayish-black smoke darkening the Arizona sky. The fire, which had started in Brin's Mesa only a quarter of a mile from the well-known tourist enclave, had been her focus for the past two days. Her job didn't have set hours, but even she needed some rest. The fire had other ideas.

With a shrug of his shoulders, Joe said, "We just got the call from the Forest Service director. They have a hot spot blowing up on them because of the change of wind direction. It's heading down toward Sedona. A lot of homes will burn if they don't stop it. They're evacuating as we speak." He searched her face. "Want me to fill the tanker?"

Kelly winced. "Yeah, go for it. I'm hitting the head."

There were several recreational vehicles within the roped-off area where her crew operated. Even with the obvious challenges, Kelly took pride in her work for Bates International, a well-known fire suppression company. Preparation and readiness were crucial. She didn't have much time, so she picked up her pace, trotting toward the blue-and-white RV. First, go to the bathroom, then glug down a pint of water. She had a few minutes to relax while Joe and her other mechanic, Bob, put twenty-six hundred gallons of water into the tank directly behind the cockpit of the buglike helicopter.

Fighting fatigue, Kelly opened the door and quickly ran up the carpeted steps. No one was in the RV, which was reserved for her and her copilot, YoYo. The mechanics had a second RV. They had been flying dawn to dusk. Nine flights was a lot. It took about forty minutes to turn a Skycrane mission around and get back to the fire to dump another batch of water.

After finishing in the head, Kelly walked out into the kitchen area, opened the refrigerator and grabbed a small bottle of cold water. Twisting off the cap, she drank deeply. After wiping her mouth with the back of her hand, she sat down to examine a group of topographical maps of the Brin's Fire area. Frowning, she searched for the location of this last-minute drop.

"Hey," YoYo called as he opened the door, "Frank, our Forest Service advisor, just said we are going into very dangerous territory."

Her copilot, a twenty-eight-year-old from Daytona, Florida, leaped into the RV, grinning as he sat down across from her. YoYo was married and had two kids. He'd come out of the U.S. Army to join the fire service, after flying Apache helicopters over in Afghanistan. She and YoYo were a team and worked well together.

"Show me," Kelly said, taking another sip of water.

YoYo turned the map around and punched his index finger at a spot with a lot of contour lines. "Right here. A hotshot crew in there will get trapped if we can't drop a suppression load on top of them. It's their only escape."

"Damn," Kelly muttered, studying the steep ascent of the canyon walls in the area. "That's tough flying even under good conditions."

"I know," YoYo murmured worriedly. He stood up, grabbed a bottle of water from the fridge and sat back down. Giving her a searching look, he asked, "You okay? You're looking real tired. Got dark circles under your eyes."

Kelly shrugged it off. "Nothing I can't handle."

"You didn't sleep well last night."

With a twist of her mouth, Kelly gave him a chagrined look. "When do I ever sleep well, YoYo?"

"Yeah, not since Afghanistan," he said sympathetically.

"I'll be okay," she told him gruffly. YoYo knew what combat duty was like. While flying the Apache in that country he'd gotten into plenty of scrapes. She had flown CH-47s there for the Marine Corps. That was two years ago, and still at night her dreams were filled with the reason why she'd left the military for the civilian world.

Lifting her hands, Kelly made sure her hair was still caught up in a ponytail. She had to wear a helmet and her shoulder-length red locks sometimes got in the way. Tugging on the rubber band, she anchored them firmly against her neck and down the back of her dark green flight suit.

"You want me to fly this load and you play copilot?" YoYo asked.

It wasn't unusual for them to switch off every other load. YoYo, whose real name was Cody Stark, had been in fire suppression for a year and was a damn good helicopter pilot. And she trusted him with her life. He was steady and reliable, unlike most of the men in her life. "No . . . I'll take it."

Still concerned, he glanced out the window of the RV. "Looks like Joe is getting the water pumped into our helo. He's got the tanker up alongside it now."

Kelly smiled and nodded. "He'll get us out of here as fast as he can. They know the drill." She studied the sky, which was turning a muddy red color from sunset. Normally, they never flew in half-light conditions because their helo wasn't equipped with radar. After dropping nine loads, everyone in the crew was dog tired, Kelly knew. All she wanted to do was go to her motel, fill the large bathtub with hot water and sink into it, shaking off the nerve-racking tension that inhabited her.

She didn't want to acknowledge that

tonight she'd take a sleeping pill; otherwise, she'd never get to sleep. Flying the Skycrane into steep, rugged canyons where the winds were quixotic at the best of times, not to mention during a violent forest fire, she had to be alert, her hands steady. After two nights of nightmares, she was feeling raw internally. Why wouldn't the memories of those two days in Afghanistan go away? Why the hell wouldn't they leave her alone?

Kelly had her answer: the ten-man Special Forces team she'd ferried into a hot spot. The engine of her helo had been shot out by Taliban, and she'd made a crash landing on the side of a barren mountain. She and her copilot had ended up grabbing rifles to fight off wave after wave of the enemy, who were determined to kill them all.

Rubbing her eyes, Kelly sat back and tried to shake off the memories, but it didn't work. They were there, always there. When her group had finally been rescued, she and two Special Forces men were the only ones left alive. Before another CH-47 had picked them up, and two other Special Forces teams arrived, Kelly had thought she was going to die, like everyone around her. But she had lived.

Pushing strands of hair off her brow, she frowned. So they'd awarded her and the other two men silver stars. So what? She was just glad to have survived.

Because of her hand wound, the military wouldn't let her fly anymore. They'd cited nerve damage. Angered, she had left the Marine Corps, but hungered for more service missions. She found them in fighting forest fires across North America in her Skycrane helicopter. Bates International had given her a flight test, and were not worried about the minimal nerve damage in her left hand. They felt, rightly, that she could fly for them. It had been a marriage made in heaven for Kelly, and she'd more than proved they could count on her. She had a spotless flight record.

As she flexed her left hand, the one that had taken a bullet from the Taliban, she felt it cramping up on her. That wasn't unusual at this time of day, after twelve hours of flying in rugged mountain conditions. She eased the cramp by running her fingers across her left palm. Glancing up, she noticed YoYo studying her, his dark brown eyes filled with worry.

"Just a cramp. Nothing much, so stop giving me that moon-eyed look," she growled.

"I can take this last load, Kelly."

With a snort and a twisted grin, she said, "You didn't sleep well last night, either. I heard you screaming through the walls of the motel." They had rooms right next to one another.

YoYo forced a laugh. "Oh, and never mind it was your screams that woke me up around 3:00 a.m. That's the pot calling the kettle black."

Kelly felt very close to her copilot. He'd been fired at and shot down in Afghanistan, as she had. There was an unspoken camaraderie between them because they'd been in the military, experienced the worst of combat — and survived. They were protective of one another and their secrets created by war.

"Yeah," she groused good-naturedly, "you're right." Looking out, she noted, "Joe's giving us the high sign. Come on, pardner. One more drop and then we can haul our sorry asses back to the motel."

With a groan, YoYo stood up and rubbed his jaw, covered now by a five o'clock shadow. "Yeah. I dunno about you, but I'm taking a sleeping pill tonight. I can't keep this up, and this Brin's Mesa Fire is gonna go on for a few more days."

"I agree." Kelly opened the door and stepped down onto the tarmac. Joe was driving the water tanker away from the ungainly, ugly Skycrane. It was painted a

16

bright red-orange to stand out for Forest Service spotters below, calling in directions for where they should drop the water. The second mechanic, Bob Johnson, did a quick walk-around check of the Skycrane. The U.S. Forest Service man who regularly came on their flights, Paul Warfield, had already climbed into the cockpit and settled into the jump seat at the back.

As she glanced around, Kelly grew worried. The wind was blowing hard one minute, changing direction the next. This made flying dangerous, especially in an unforgiving canyon with steep, jagged walls. There was no room to maneuver, no room to make a mistake. This drop would be a challenge, but someone had to do the job. Giving Bob, who was in his forties, a nod of thanks, Kelly hoisted herself up to the rear of the Plexiglas bubble and eased through the narrow cockpit door.

"Ready for one last drop?" Paul asked as she slid by him.

"No choice," Kelly answered. The U.S. Forest Service advisor would be in touch with the ground spotter, helping to coordinate the drop. It was one more element of safety in the perilous world of air tanker crews who fought wildfires. Tonight, they were going to need Paul's eyes and ears.

"I know," he muttered, strapping in. "Where we're going, Kelly, is very dangerous. I've been in radio contact with the spotter. She says winds are erratic in the mesa."

Settling into her seat, Kelly nodded. She picked up her white helmet and put it on. After tightening the strap beneath her chin, she pulled the radio microphone into place, less than an inch from her lips, and flipped on the switch. This would keep her in contact with Paul throughout the noisy trip.

"Nothing new there, Paul. All drops are dangerous in this fire."

As YoYo came in and shut the rear door, Paul spread the topo map across his lap. "I wish we didn't have to drop this load," he said to no one in particular, studying the contours with drawn brows. He reminded Kelly of a lean wolf with his sharp features and gray-black hair.

YoYo began running down the preflight list with Kelly. They worked together seamlessly, going through the necessary checks on the helo. In no time, they were ready to get the Skycrane airborne. Kelly turned to make sure Paul had his helmet on, and YoYo gave her a thumbs-up. They were ready to go.

The engine growled to life. Within moments, Kelly felt the familiar vibration as the rear rotor on the tail spun in synchronization with the main blades.

The Skycrane always reminded her of a big, unwieldy praying mantis. The front was box-shaped, with rounded Plexiglas windows. The water was carried in a tank right behind them, with the rest of the bird thin and long. Though ungainly looking, the Sikorsky could drop the most water of any helicopter, which made a life-and-death difference to the crews fighting below. Because of this, Kelly loved the homely helicopter more than any other.

As she watched YoYo flip switches and check instruments, reaching with knowing ease around his station, her stomach tightened. Usually, she wasn't frightened like this. Maybe it was the lack of sleep for the past two nights, or that so many drops today had frayed her already taut nerves. Grimacing, she kept her hands firmly around the cyclic and collective, which controlled the chopper's flight. Moving the rudders, she coaxed the trundling, heavily loaded craft toward the center of the tarmac as YoYo called the tower for permission to take off. Kelly heard the conversations, thanks to the speakers in her helmet, but her focus was now on flying.

Within a few minutes, they were lifting off from the small regional airport for the tenth time that day. The helo shook as it gained altitude. They continued upward steadily, climbing to two thousand feet. In the distance, about eight miles to the north, thick plumes of roiling dark smoke snaked upward in columns against the fading red of sunset. Kelly didn't like it.

A hotshot crew was trapped, the fire closing in from all sides, she reminded herself. If they could dump a load of water in just the right place, it would create a safety corridor for the crew to escape. Ten lives were in jeopardy. Just as they had been in the Tora Bora cave region of the White Mountains of Afghanistan. This time, it wasn't the Taliban coming to kill these courageous fighters, it was fire. No less a threat, Kelly thought, as she felt the comforting vibration of the Skycrane reverberating through her.

The prospect of saving lives made this last flight worth it to Kelly. Normally, the Forest Service would not allow such a maneuver to take place this close to dark. The Skycrane did not have fancy computers and state-of-the-art instrumentation to "see" through smoke and gauge their proximity to a canyon wall or a tree.

Tonight they only had their eyes, and the

ground observer leading them in with verbal directions.

As they drew closer to the canyon, Kelly began to ease the Skycrane downward. The flames were a lurid red-orange, shooting skyward amid the billowing smoke. The thermal columns rose ten thousand feet into the air above the Brin's Mesa catastrophe, and as they approached, erratic and powerful winds began to jostle them. Kelly tightened her hands around the cyclic and collective. Her feet dancing on the pedals below the instrument panel, Kelly kept her bird on a straight course, heading toward the center of the fire.

"The spotter says the wind is shifting again," Paul warned her through the radio. "To the northwest."

"Roger that," Kelly said, her voice cool and clipped. If the smoke came their way, they'd have to back off. Since they had no radar, carrying on would be a recipe for disaster.

"Wind's erratic," YoYo agreed, his voice grim.

They had reached one thousand feet, and the canyons around them rose upward, their steep sides fashioned out of white dolomite and black volcanic rock beneath the limestone formation. Trees clung to their flanks, like green spears jutting skyward. Suddenly, a gust of wind struck the helicopter. Kelly quickly compensated, pulling the helo back on course, toward where the spotter was ordering them to drop their vital, lifesaving load.

YoYo switched on a device that would lower a ten-foot-long, flexible line through which the water would shoot to the ground. Once it was in place, Kelly could bring the bird down even closer.

Eyes straining, she saw how the winds moved the smoke in their direction. She dropped the Skycrane down to four hundred feet. Below, the forest was still green, but the fire had entirely encircled the target area. She noted the corridor on which the spotter wanted the water dropped. Straight ahead, the flames roared a hundred feet high, their tongues red, yellow and orange. She and her crew were literally flying toward a wall of fire. The unburned island where the hotshots were trapped grew smaller by the minute. Kelly understood how important this drop would be.

"Ready to begin?" YoYo asked her, grasping the handles that would begin the pumping action.

"Ready," Kelly rasped.

"Paul?" YoYo called.

"The spotter says to begin the water drop," he reported.

The helicopter bounced suddenly upward, pushed to one side by an unexpected gust. The flames licked underneath them. She heard and felt the pumping begin. The helo quivered.

"Water releasing," YoYo crowed. "Right on target, Kelly."

Her job was to hold the bird just above the flames. Her left hand ached as she gripped the cyclic hard. The bumpy air threw them around, and Kelly had to steady the unwieldy helicopter, right above the necklace of flames.

A minute later, the tank was empty.

"Good job!" Paul crowed. "You did it! We got a corridor! The spotter just reported the hotshot crew is escaping right now! Well done!"

There was no time to celebrate as the smoke suddenly shifted. Kelly reared back on the controls and tried to avoid the gray plume.

YoYo gave a yelp of warning, and Paul also cried out in alarm.

A split second later, the smoke enveloped them completely. It was unexpected. Blinding. Suddenly disoriented, Kelly had no idea of which way was up, and her gaze shot to the horizon indicator. The wind grabbed the straining helicopter, shoving it sideways once more, with surprising speed and power.

Within seconds, Kelly corrected their position.

But not fast enough.

The helicopter's six blades were long and broad, and one struck the canyon wall with a shattering screech. The bird wobbled drunkenly. Kelly swore and tried to pull the wounded Skycrane away from that rock wall hidden by smoke.

But it was too late.

Her world came to a frightening halt as the helicopter slid downward. At least one of the blades had been broken. Kelly used every skill she possessed to save them from the downward rush. It was no use. They catapulted earthward, the blades screaming and the helicopter listing more and more, tilting dangerously.

And then the ground became visible. Through the darkness, Kelly saw the gray shapes of rocks and trees. They were falling into the fire break they'd just created. With a grunt, she tried again with all her might to right the helicopter, to crash-land on its three wheels and not its side.

Impossible! As she wrestled with the sluggish controls, her life paraded before her eyes. She knew then that she was going to die. They were all going to die. The feeling was one of anger mixed with utter helplessness. Hissing out a curse, Kelly watched as the ground leaped up at them. The last thing she remembered was YoYo screaming in desperation. And then her world went black.

CHAPTER TWO

Screams. Someone was screaming above the deafening screech of metal. Kelly felt the scorching, withering heat of fire. Smoke clogged her lungs, making her choke repeatedly and gasp for breath as she was tossed one way and then another. Pain arced through her shoulders where her harness bound her against the seat.

She had crashed!

Opening her eyes, Kelly saw flames and thick, blinding smoke shooting across the top of the cockpit. YoYo's screams brought her to full consciousness. Instinctively, she tried to reach in his direction, only to have flames hiss between them, a burning barrier. Fire was everywhere.

Save YoYo!

Dizziness swept over her. With shaking fingers, Kelly somehow found the release mechanism on her harness and got free of it. Now she could turn and help YoYo with his. But when she leaned toward him, she suddenly found herself tumbling through the wall of fire and smoke. A second later she hit the earth and, with a groan, started rolling down a steep, rugged incline, feeling every jab of the sharp lava rock until she finally came to a halt. Disoriented, she tried to get up and run back to the helo to help YoYo, but through the smoke and fire, saw the broken Skycrane on its side, engulfed in flames.

With a cry, Kelly lurched forward, only to fall with a thud against the rocks and pine needles. For some reason her left leg wasn't working. But she had to get to YoYo!

Dazed, Kelly stared up at the burning helo, realizing with horror that his screams had stopped. What about Paul, their passenger? She hadn't heard him cry out once. . . .

On her belly, she tried to crawl forward by reaching out and grabbing at rocks.

Voices. Many voices. . . . Was she hearing things over the roar of the forest fire? This was the mountain crash she'd experienced in Afghanistan all over again. A terrible déjà vu. Sobbing, she clawed her fingers into the hard, dry earth and tried once more to stand up, and collapsed once more.

Out of the smoke belching around the

Skycrane she saw a crew of hotshots in yellow gear and hard hats appear. Some tried to get near the burning chopper, but the flames pushed them back.

Kelly's mind was clouded by shock and pain. Her left leg was limp and wouldn't follow her directions. A woman hotshot, her face blackened with smoke and streaked with sweat, raced over and knelt down beside her.

"Don't move. You've crashed," she said. "We've got another helo coming in to medevac you out."

"YoYo, Paul . . ." Kelly cried, her vision dimming. "Get them! Get them out of the helo! They're trapped in there!" Her voice cracked and she began to sob.

"We're doing all we can. Just lie still," the firefighter soothed, pressing Kelly to the ground when she tried again to move.

Pain worse than what was shooting through her leg engulfed Kelly. YoYo and Paul were trapped inside the Skycrane, which was blazing like a funeral pyre. With a cry, Kelly collapsed, and again lost consciousness.

"Kelly Trayhern? Can you hear me?"

A bright light surrounded Kelly. She heard a male voice and felt a hand gently squeeze her shoulder. Though pain was traveling in waves up her left leg, she struggled to lift her lids. It took a gargantuan effort.

A bald man wearing gold-framed glasses was peering down at her. He had on a white coat, and she was in a bed. Confused, she searched his kind brown eyes.

"Ah, good, you're coming out of the anesthesia, Kelly. I'm Dr. Bennett Goodman. You're here at the Flagstaff Medical Center hospital. How are you feeling? Are you in pain?"

It took too much energy to assimilate what he was saying. Feeling nauseous, Kelly gulped several times. And then the horrific crash of her Skycrane came slamming back to her, paralyzing her. Closing her eyes, she moaned.

Again, the physician squeezed her shoulder. "Kelly? You're going to live. Your parents were called after you arrived at the hospital, and they're on a flight to Phoenix right now. They'll be here in about an hour. We just performed surgery on your left leg. Are you in pain?"

Pain? Hell, yes, she was in pain! Opening her eyes once more, she felt hot tears trickling from the corners of her eyes and down her cheeks. "YoYo, my copilot? Paul? Where are they?"

The doctor shook his head regretfully. "I'm sorry, Kelly. They didn't make it. They died in the crash. Their families have been contacted."

Kelly blinked, her vision blurring again, this time with her tears. YoYo and Paul were dead. . . . And she'd caused it. The crash was her fault. She'd killed more people. . . . "Oh, no . . ." she groaned. Lifting her hand, she realized there was an IV in her arm.

"Kelly? How is your leg feeling?"

Overwhelmed by the terrible news, she found she couldn't concentrate on the doctor's words. Her mouth contorted with agony and, gripping the bedclothes, she wept uncontrollably. Oh, God, why hadn't she been more careful? She remembered the blade striking the sheer canyon wall, recalled the ominous shudder that had raced through the Skycrane. . . .

Dr. Goodman was patting her shoulder. "I'm sorry for your loss, Kelly. Your parents will be arriving shortly. That should be of some comfort to you. They know you've just come out of a successful surgery. If you're in pain at all, please let the nurses know. We want to keep you comfortable."

Kelly didn't even feel the doctor's hand leave her shoulder. Wrapped in anguish over the loss of YoYo, of Paul, she bitterly berated herself. Right now, she didn't care if she lived or died.

And once again she was alone. Just as she'd been in Afghanistan. Mercifully, she felt that familiar dizziness descend.

The next time Kelly awoke, the sun was slanting through the window blinds, and the room was quiet. She could smell the antiseptic odors of the hospital, and felt nauseous. But at least there was no physical pain. Looking down, she saw that her left leg was suspended by a series of pulleys and nylon straps from the ceiling.

What time was it? What day? she wondered. Then the deaths of her teammates filtered back into her groggy consciousness, and agony seared her chest as she started remembering the crash all over again. Every excruciating detail . . .

The door quietly opened.

"Ah, you're awake," Morgan Trayhern said. He smiled tiredly.

Seeing her father, Kelly automatically tensed in terror. He would judge her actions. After all, she had killed two of her men. Yet as he moved toward her, his gray eyes dark with worry, the fear dissipated and she was glad to see him.

As usual, he was impeccably dressed. But

it wasn't the dark brown executive suit, pink silk tie and cream-colored silk shirt that gave him that undeniable air of authority. Kelly studied his square, clean-shaven face, his military-short salt-and-pepper hair. To her, he was the epitome of power and success. Her father was in the spy business. He owned Perseus, a supersecret agency that worked with the CIA on missions that the U.S. government couldn't touch.

As he smiled down at her, reaching for her hand and giving it a paternal squeeze, Kelly held his gaze.

"I killed two men, Dad. My copilot, YoYo, and a Forest Service advisor. I just can't live with it. I can't . . ." She turned her face away and fought a sob.

"Kelly, that's not true," Morgan rasped. "Hey, look at me. Come on . . ."

Hesitantly, she did as he asked. "There's nothing you can say, Dad. Nothing. It was all my fault. I should have been more careful, more —"

"Nonsense." Her father gently brushed strands of hair from her brow. "The firefighting crew escaping through the corridor you created saw it all happen. They told us the winds were wildly erratic there, and that after you'd dropped your load, a violent gust enveloped your helo in smoke and pushed you into the canyon wall. You have ten witnesses, Kelly. Right now, the National Transportation Safety Board is investigating the crash, but given the eyewitness reports, I'm sure you'll be found free and clear of any pilot error. Honey, you did not cause that crash. You hear me?"

The urgency in her father's voice couldn't touch the guilt she suffered over the loss of those men. Kelly closed her eyes with a ragged sigh. She was feeling disconnected and disembodied, probably from the pain medication. "But I let them down . . ." She almost said, *Like I let down my men in Afghanistan.* Eight of the ten Special Forces troopers were dead by the time the U.S. Army was able to expedite a rescue mission. . . .

Her father's hand was gently stroking her shoulder, as if he was trying to take away her pain. But even her parents didn't know the whole truth of her Afghanistan experience. Kelly was too ashamed ever to speak of it.

"How's your leg feeling?" Morgan asked. He drew over a chair and sat at her bedside. "They put you under for five days, did you know? Your leg was broken in seventeen places, Kelly. But you were lucky. Dr. Goodman, the surgeon, was able to pin it together, though it was touch-and-go for a while. He was afraid he was going to have to cut it off."

Opening her eyes, Kelly stared at her dad, noting for the first time how exhausted he looked. Five days. She'd been out cold for five days! "My leg?"

Nodding, Morgan pointed to her limb, suspended by the pulley system above the bed. "Yes, you nearly lost it. It was badly shattered in the crash. You have some first- and second-degree burns on the back on your neck, and a lot of your hair was singed off." The look he gave her was full of love and concern. He squeezed her hand again gently. "Your hair will grow back, though, and the burns will go away with time."

Slowly, Kelly began to orient herself. "Dad, can you find me a phone? I need to talk to Debbie and Colleen. I have to tell them I'm sorry. Can you please get me their phone numbers? They were in my purse in the RV."

"Of course," he said. "Your mother has all your belongings, and she'll be by soon. In the meantime, are you hungry? Thirsty? Is there anything I can do for you?"

Yeah, rip out my heart. It hurts so damn bad. Shaking her head, Kelly whispered brokenly, "No . . . nothing. Just get me the phone numbers. I have to speak to the wives of these men. I have to tell them how sorry I am . . ."

"They buried YoYo and Paul two days ago," Morgan said quietly. "Their families know what happened, and they don't blame you, Kelly. Please don't blame yourself. Don't do this. You had such terrible depression after what happened in Afghanistan. It took you nearly a year to climb out of it and start living again."

"It *was* my fault, Dad. I ought to know! I was the pilot handling the controls on that flight. If I hadn't been so tired, not sleeping well for days beforehand, maybe I'd have been quicker with my reflexes. Maybe I'd have seen through the smoke . . ."

Her father's expression grew grim and his gray eyes narrowed. "You were sleep deprived? But I thought —"

"I'm sorry I said anything. Just get me the phone numbers, please? That's all I care about. I have to apologize to Colleen and Debbie."

"Okay." Her father seemed to lose his usual ruddy coloring as he got to his feet, and his eyes were melancholy. Going to the phone near the bed, he dialed a number and was soon having a short conversation with her mom. After replacing the receiver in its cradle, he turned and studied Kelly.

"She's coming right over and will bring your purse with her. Everything you want is in there," he reported. "The two of us have been here with you for the past five days, honey. Your mom scarcely left your bedside, but I just persuaded her to take a break."

Her dad looked so helpless in that moment that Kelly hated herself. She'd been through this once before, coming back from Afghanistan. "I'm sorry to hurt you like this all over again, Dad. I know I'm causing everyone so much pain."

"Listen, baby girl, that's what being a parent is all about. You love your kids through thick and thin." Morgan forced a game smile, stepped back to her side and slid his hand into hers. "Don't think for a moment that we'd want it any other way, because we don't. I'm so grateful you survived. The hotshot crew leader said the crash was very bad. Your chopper fell four hundred feet onto the side of that canyon. By all rights, Kelly, you should be dead. But you're here with us, and that's a miracle."

Tears glimmered in her father's eyes, which caused a lump in Kelly's already tight throat. She squeezed his hand weakly. "I'm still sorry. I've caused so much pain for you and Mom, for YoYo's and Paul's families."

She wanted to say, *I wish I had died in the crash. That way, I wouldn't have to feel this horrible guilt and pain. . . .*

"Nonsense, baby girl. We're overjoyed you're alive. Our children live in dangerous times and have dangerous jobs. Your brother Pete builds power plants in wartorn countries. He and Cali are always in harm's way. And Jason paid dearly over in Afghanistan, suffering traumatic brain injury. Thank God Annie, his wife, has helped pull him out of a lot of it. You're no different, Kelly. We're a military family. Our roots go back to the time this country was born, and our people have done their patriotic duty in just about every major conflict since then. We know the sacrifices, the pain, the loss. And now, unfortunately, it's your turn — again." He gave a shrug. "Maybe if our children all had 'safe' jobs in this world, life wouldn't be like this, but your mother and I know that you carry Trayhern genes, and will always be in the thick of things. That's just the way it is."

And now Kelly had a terrible emotional dilemma. After her rescue in Afghanistan, she had wondered why she'd survived when so many others had died. It was the same thing all over again. Only this time, the tragedy was clearly her fault. The forest fire hadn't been a combat situation in a foreign country. No one had been trying to shoot down her helicopter.

She'd done it all by herself.

But no way could she divulge her real feelings to her father. She could see the love and concern shining in his eyes, could understand his need to fix things for his daughter, to help her. But Kelly knew there was no outside help for her. There hadn't been the last time, and there wouldn't be now.

"I'm tired," she murmured wearily, half to herself.

Morgan Trayhern had been a Marine Corps hero until he'd lost a company of men in Vietnam. And then, through governmental foul play, his stellar reputation and the Trayhern name had been smeared. Morgan had been branded a traitor to his country, something Kelly couldn't imagine. Yet her strong, resilient father had somehow weathered that awful storm. With the help of Laura, he'd gone on to clear his record. And the Trayhern name once more shone in the military world, the bright star it had always been.

"You've got to be exhausted," he said now. "Why don't you rest? Your mother will be here shortly." He looked at his watch. "I've got some calls from Perseus coming in soon.

Mike Houston is running the show back in Philipsburg while we're down here with you. I need to check in."

"Go ahead," Kelly urged. She knew her powerful and influential father could move mountains if needed. He was well-known to the cloak-and-dagger community, a kingpin among kings who, for the past two decades, had used his company, Perseus, to save many lives.

As he leaned down and planted a gentle kiss on her bandaged brow, Kelly hungrily absorbed his love. She felt like such a failure in comparison to her father, to the rest of her siblings, she almost wanted to die.

"I'll be back tonight," Morgan promised as he walked to the door and opened it.

"Okay. Thanks, Dad."

Morgan met his wife near the bank of elevators. Laura was getting off just as he was about to get on. "I'm glad to see you first," he told her, taking her arm and leading her aside for a moment.

Laura had Kelly's leather purse in her hand. His wife's shoulder-length blond hair curled softly around her slim shoulders. Morgan could smell the jasmine perfume she preferred. He admired her pale green linen pantsuit and the fuchsia top she wore beneath. Her face, softly lined and barely showing her fifty-plus years of life, looked beautiful and young to him.

"How is she, Morgan?"

Grimacing, he said worriedly, "Not good. She's taking on the blame for the deaths of the two men who flew with her."

Laura groaned. "Oh, no. Did you tell her what happened? Does she understand it wasn't her fault?"

"Yes, I did, pet, but she's not hearing it." Morgan kept his voice low as a group of hospital staff and visitors left the elevator. "It's Afghanistan all over again, I'm afraid. Last time, she had that year-long depression neither of us thought she'd pull out of."

Rubbing her brow, Laura gazed into her husband's dark gray eyes. "Oh, God, Morgan. I was so worried Kelly would kill herself. She was practically suicidal last time. What are we going to do?"

Morgan heard the anguish in his wife's soft voice. He saw the strain in her expression. "I don't know. We've got to think outside the box on this one, pet. Last time, Kelly basically stayed in her bedroom for a year. She refused psychiatric treatment, but by the grace of God, pulled out of it on pure guts alone."

Laura shook her head and slipped her arm around her husband's waist. "No, Kelly never did fully recover, remember? The therapist we consulted in Anaconda said Kelly had post-traumatic stress disorder. You don't just get up and walk away from that. You should know, and so should I. We've both had PTSD because of our kidnapping by that drug lord years ago. I know I'm still jumpy, but I've worked out most of the other stuff with a lot of help from you and my therapist. Kelly needs help, Morgan. This time, for sure."

"I agree, pet," he said, giving his wife a warm look. Laura might be petite, but she had a mighty heart and was one of the most courageous women he'd ever known. He could see the gleam of challenge in her blue eyes, and the determined set of her full mouth. His wife was committed to helping their wounded daughter.

"What's worse," he confided, "is that I couldn't tell Kelly she isn't ever going to fly again, because of the massive injury to her leg. She knows it was broken in seventeen places and had been put back together with steel pins, but she wasn't even fazed, Laura. Her heart, her mind, her guilt and pain are all focused on the loss of YoYo and Paul, the two men she flew with on that mission."

With a moan, Laura looked down at the white tiled floor, which shone with a fresh coat of wax. Pale pink walls livened up the place, making it seem less like a hospital to her. "Then let's not go there with her right now. We have to focus on what she's focusing on. I think it's important to fly her home to Anaconda for the next stage of her recovery. After that, whenever the doctors release her, she'll recuperate at home in Philipsburg with us. I don't want her left alone, Morgan. I'm afraid. In my gut, I feel like Kelly might be giving up on life for good this time."

Morgan knew better than to ignore his wife's powerful intuition. "I understand. But you know she'll refuse help from every quarter, like she did last time. She's stubborn just like me. Internalizes everything to such a degree that she allows no one to reach her."

Laura smiled gently and caressed his cheek. "But you let *me* in, Morgan. You allowed me into your dark, wounded world, and look what happened. It got resolved and you healed."

Picking up his wife's hand, he turned it over and kissed the back. "That's because I fell hopelessly in love with you, pet. It was easy to let you in because I trusted you."

"Well, we need to find someone who Kelly will trust, darling. Let's put on our thinking caps. There's got to be someone out there she might open up to." Laura frowned thoughtfully. "I have an idea — but let me talk to Kelly and see if I can help her at all. Will you be back at the hotel?"

"Yes." He eyed his watch, then pulled the cell phone out of his pocket. "I have a lot to discuss with Mike about certain missions. I'll be at the Marriott."

Reaching up on her toes, she pressed a kiss on his jaw. "I'll see you back there, then."

He nodded and gripped her hand again. "I hope you can reach Kelly better than I did. She just clammed up with me."

"She did that last time," Laura whispered in a pained voice. "And she did it to both of us, Morgan, not just you. So don't blame yourself, okay?"

Shaking his head, he muttered darkly, "Dammit, I wish Kelly hadn't inherited my ability to suppress my emotions."

"She also has your courage. And my bet is when it gets really dark, she's going to reach out for help. We just need to find someone she trusts — with her heart and with her soul."

"A tall order," Morgan stated, rolling his eyes.

"But not an impossible one. Like I said, I have an idea. I'll talk to you after I see Kelly."

CHAPTER THREE

The unexpected knock on Sky's cabin door startled him. He had been settling Bella, a Harris hawk from the Arizona desert, on her bow perch in the small living room when he heard the sound. Frowning, he quickly double-checked the long jesses of fine kangaroo leather leading from the hawk's yellow leg to the arched stand. When she was thirsty, Bella could leave the perch and walk over to a large pan of water, or hop around on the white terry-cloth towels that surrounded it. After straightening the plastic underlay, Sky stood up and turned toward the door.

Who could possibly be dropping in? Few people knew he lived up here, off a logging road thirty miles west of Philipsburg. Sky wanted to stay hidden, for good reason. Rubbing his hands on his jean-clad thighs, he crossed the room to the cabin door, his well-worn cowboy boots thunking on the cedar floor.

Peeking through the peephole, Sky felt his dread and terror turn to surprise. Laura Trayhern? What could she want with him? Instantly, images and memories of Kelly Trayhern, her daughter, deluged Sky as he reached for the brass knob and opened the door.

Laura was older now, her face softly lined, her hair drawn back into a tasteful chignon. She wore a white blouse, a pink cardigan and dark green cotton slacks.

"Mrs. Trayhern?" Sky said gruffly. He couldn't disguise the shock he felt at seeing her here. It wasn't unusual for him to bump into her at the local grocery store, where they sometimes shared pleasantries, but he'd never in a million years expected her to show up at the cabin.

During a terrible incident and trial he'd been through as a child, the Trayhern family had offered him unwavering support. At the time, he'd had his heart cut out of his chest — his family had been forced to move out of Philipsburg when he was eight until he was twelve years old, his puppy love for Kelly Trayhern aborted in the process. But Sky had never forgotten her. He was thirty years old now, with a long road behind him. But he still felt that stretch of time as a teenager with her contained all his happiest memories. Whenever he encountered her in town, he'd catch up on Kelly's news, find out where she was in the world.

"Hello, Sky." Laura tried to smile. "I'm sorry to bother you, but you don't have a listed phone number and I had to see you. May I come in for a moment?"

Angst gripped Sky momentarily. As much as he admired Laura Trayhern, he didn't want her in his cabin. He wanted none of his past returning.

"Come in," he said, stepping aside despite his discomfort. Laura Trayhern was clearly upset about something. He saw it in her large blue eyes, in the way she seemed to struggle with her emotions. And as she walked into the spacious rectangular room, he felt unparalleled dread — just as he had the day Kelly had saved his life.

Turning, Laura noticed the raptor on the floor near the wall of the cabin. "Oh, my! What kind of bird is that, Sky?"

He walked over to where she stood staring in awe at the magnificent hawk. Sky's world was one of secrets. Even though he would chat with Laura in the store maybe two or three times a year, he revealed little of his own private life with her.

"I'm a raptor rehabilitator, Mrs. Trayhern." He tried to curb his impatience, especially since the woman hadn't come to see his birds. "Meet Bella. She's a Harris hawk that was found near Phoenix. I got her just a few days ago. Right now, we're beginning to get acquainted. She needs to know my schedule and all the sights and sounds of this environment so that she isn't upset and nervous here. Pretty, isn't she?"

Laura sighed. "Oh, yes, she's beautiful, Sky. I didn't know you did this for a living." She looked at him with real respect. "You always loved animals, and this is the perfect calling for you."

"My Native American blood came out, I guess," he responded.

He saw her eyes lighten with understanding. It had been his half-breed status in grade school that had been the core of his problems.

"Your Navajo blood is a gift, Sky. I knew that someday you would allow it to filter into your life." She studied the large hawk. "And what a wonderful way you have employed it." She turned to search his face. "May I have a few minutes of your time, Sky? Something important has happened. Morgan and I need your help."

Problems. He was always dealing with problems. Did they ever end? Suppressing a scowl, he gestured toward the kitchen. "Of course. Come on, I just made some coffee."

It was easy for him to trust Laura Trayhern. Her entire family had been a bulwark against the attack he'd experienced as a sixth grader at the Philipsburg school. If it hadn't been for Kelly's quick intervention after he'd been stabbed in the hand by Billy Jo Talbot, he'd have bled to death. And at the trial, the Trayhern clan had paid for his lawyer and defense, since his own family was dirt poor.

"Thank you, that would be great," Laura murmured. She entered the sunny, cedar-paneled kitchen. Sitting at the small round wooden table, she set her purse aside and watched Sky walk to the Formica counter and pour each of them a cup of coffee. "I'm here to ask for your help, Sky."

He brought the mugs over and set one down in front of her, then glanced into her eyes. "What exactly do you want from me?"

"It's complicated," she said, pausing to take a sip of her coffee. Sky looked so strong and fit. He'd grown into a handsome and confident-looking man, a far cry from the shy boy he'd once been. Laura had ached for him as a child. His father had been an abusive alcoholic, and his mother finally divorced him. But not before Sky became a quiet, withdrawn child that bullies loved to taunt. If it hadn't been for Kelly, who became his champion and protector at school, Laura wondered if Sky would have made it at all. His painful shyness was still evident. He didn't have good eye contact, but as a child, he'd had none. No child should have suffered as he had.

"It's Kelly," she began in a low, strained tone. "Let me tell you what happened. . . ."

Sky sat there for the next forty minutes listening to the story of Kelly's helicopter crash three months ago. Laura was obviously stressed and nervous. Her flighty gestures and restless shifting reminded him of a high-strung falcon whose nest was being threatened by a predator. And no wonder. His heart twinged as he listened to the tragic story. Sky had known about Kelly's crash in Afghanistan. At the time, he'd wanted to visit the family and offer help, but he'd been going through a rough time emotionally himself, and couldn't pull it off.

"Right now, Kelly's at home with us, back in her old bedroom. For the first month, the death of her colleagues darkened her life, Sky. When it finally sank in that she would never fly again, the realization broke her in a way we can't fix. Right now, she's so depressed she's hardly eating. She lies in her bed and refuses to do much of anything, especially exercise her leg. The doctors say that with work and rehabilitation with a physical therapist, she could regain the use of it, though it will never be strong like before."

"This must be rough for her," Sky said, finishing his coffee. "I'm sorry." He felt bad that the tragedy had happened to the spunky girl he used to know. After all, Kelly had saved his life.

But Sky hoped that, whatever her mother wanted, it wouldn't be asking too much of him. He had to remain in hiding, a hermit on a mountain slope, living far back along a rutted logging road. His life took place in the shadows, and he intended to keep it that way.

"You can help Kelly by visiting her." Laura clasped her hands together and looked deeply into Sky's large glacier-blue eyes. They were just as alert as those of the hawk in his living room. "Morgan and I both felt you're someone who had a positive influence on Kelly. You had that teenage crush going, remember? We're hoping that some of that connection, the friendship the two of you shared, is still there. Right now, Kelly needs an advocate, someone she trusts and cares about. Someone who can give her hope, and maybe make her want to live."

Sky considered Laura's words carefully. It was very true he and Kelly had loved each other. As a child, he'd openly worshipped his red-haired, green-eyed classmate. As a hormonally driven teenager he'd ached for her. It never entered his consciousness that she was white and he was Indian. Until Billy Jo Talbot and his gang of bullies made it clear that he was a half-breed "Injun" who had no business making eyes at the beautiful, smart and very rich Kelly Trayhern.

"I can't do it," he growled. "The past is the past. I have other obligations." He hardened his heart over the shock on Kelly's mom's face.

"Listen," Laura begged softly, "could you just come down and see her one time? Kelly needs help. She rejects physical therapy. A friend of ours who is a psychotherapist said Kelly has PTSD from both incidents, and has never worked through it. She's just buried the memories deep down inside herself."

Sky knew that reaction himself, and understood only too well what Laura Trayhern was describing. After Billy Jo had sliced open his right hand with the knife he'd wielded that fateful afternoon on the playground, Sky had gone into denial, too. But despite his compassion, he couldn't extend himself as Laura asked.

"I can't do it, Mrs. Trayhern." Sky lived in utter seclusion because his life depended on it.

After he turned eighteen, he'd lived in Blackfoot, Idaho, trying to get a job. His dream of a military career had been ruined because of his injured right hand. He had sustained considerable nerve damage, and the military had turned him down.

And when Sky was nineteen, Billy Jo Talbot had murdered Sky's parents to get even with him for sending him away to juvenile hall.

Sky had had to come home and face a second trial. A trial that had indicted Talbot and sent him away to prison for twelve years. The sentence was too light, and Sky suspected the jury and judge were prejudiced against Indians, but he could never prove it.

After that, Sky had remained in Philipsburg, and tried to start his life once more. But he wanted nothing to do with the past or with Kelly Trayhern. That chapter in his life was too painful to reopen.

Her mother reached out and gripped his

hand. "It would mean so much to Morgan and me if you would. I — I don't expect you to commit to anything long-term, Sky, but if Kelly responds, if she reaches out to you . . . could you help her?" Laura's voice cracked with emotion. "We love her so much, but we feel so powerless. Nothing has helped. Kelly's slipping away from us, has become a ghost of herself. She's lost thirty pounds. I'm so afraid."

Didn't Laura Trayhern understand the word *no?* And couldn't she understand why he couldn't fulfill her request? "I'm sorry, I'm not the right person to do this, Mrs. Trayhern."

Withdrawing her hands, Laura shakily brushed away the tears from her eyes. "We're at our wits' end. She's disappearing a little more each day. It's so painful to watch. We don't know where else to turn."

Sky tried to take the steel out of his tone as he stated, "Time has moved on. I don't want anything to do with my past. It's hard enough to forget, and I don't want to be dragged back into it."

Laura's mouth fell open and then she snapped it shut. "We've never asked anything from you before," she quavered, gripping the dampened tissue in her hand. Her voice lowered with anguish. "Please, Sky.

We need you."

"I'm not the guy you're looking for," he rasped. "Hire a therapist to help Kelly."

Rearing back in the chair, Laura studied him in the tense, deepening silence. "We paid for both your trials because we knew your family couldn't afford it."

Emotion rippled through Sky. He cleared his throat. "It's true. You folks backed me and my mother, and paid for a lawyer when we needed one. You put Talbot in juvenile hall for us. Later, when he burned down my parents' house here in Philipsburg, and — and did what he did, your husband hired the best attorney in Montana, and put Talbot into prison. I had no money. I was like a tumbleweed blowing around, unsure of what to do with my life now that my mother and stepfather were murdered . . ."

"I know how awful that was for you, Sky. You lost everything." Laura choked back a sob. "So you should understand how we feel now. We could lose our daughter."

Sky tried to deflect the emotional impact of her words. "I never made enough money to ever repay you the hundred thousand dollars it took to put Talbot away that second time. I know my folks paid you back for the first trial, but the second . . ." He looked away, feeling ashamed. "Right now, I live on the edge of poverty." He shrugged. "Raptor rehabilitators don't get paid to rescue injured birds. It all comes out of our own pockets, and from donations." He lifted his right hand. "With this nerve damage, I can't do a lot of things I'd like to, and that's stopped me from getting jobs that would earn me more money. I do have a night job as a security guard down in Philipsburg to stay afloat."

"Don't worry, Sky. We'll pay you any amount of money — for your gas, your time — to help Kelly. You'll have whatever you need."

Sky knew the Trayherns were very rich. "This isn't something you can buy from me, Mrs. Trayhern. I don't feel I'm the right person to help your daughter. I'm not trained for it."

Leaning forward, her eyes bright with unshed tears, she insisted, "I don't give a damn about that, Sky. You owe us. And now I'm asking you to pay us back. I can see you don't want to do this. I'm shocked that you're so unwilling. But we need you to try to help Kelly. You're our last chance." Her mouth went grim as she glared across the table at him.

Tightening his jaw, Sky pushed back his chair, the noise startlingly loud in the kitchen as he rose to his full height. "I can't do it."

Laura Trayhern stood in turn, her voice steely as she stated, "You will, Sky, or else. I'm not going to let our daughter die just because you don't think you can do this."

Though he'd never seen the woman so angry and dogged, Sky held her stubborn stare. "And if I do it and she kills herself?" he retorted, his own voice deep with anger. "What then? Will you blame me for that? I'd have to live with it for the rest of my life. Frankly, I've got enough to live with from my past."

Visibly shaking, Laura said, "No, we won't blame you. But you're going to help us, Sky. I want you down there. I *need* your help. Just this one time."

He heard the threat in her husky tone. This was a side to Laura Trayhern he'd never seen. To survive the past, Sky had had to wall it off. By forcing himself to live strictly in the present, he could manage to forget the past darkness. Until now.

His conscience niggled at him. Laura was right: he owed them, big time. But what could he possibly do to help Kelly? His heart twinged with pain. He'd given up on Kelly Trayhern a long time ago. She no longer existed. But now . . .

"No guarantees . . ." he growled, like a cornered wolf.

"We know that." Laura grimaced. "Maybe Kelly will get out of this depression that's killing her day by day. We can only hope . . ."

"She needs a reason to live," Sky agreed. He felt the terrible weight of expectation settle heavily on his shoulders. "Doesn't Kelly have a man in her life? Is she married? Have kids?"

Shaking her head, Laura murmured, "She has no relationship with anyone right now. She never got married and has no children."

Sky drew a careful breath. "Listen, I have to feed my raptors." He looked at his watch. "Morning feeding."

"May I expect you sometime this afternoon?"

There was such determination in her tone that Sky had to relent. "Yeah, I'll be there. But just this once."

"Thank you so much," she said fervently. "I won't tell Kelly you're coming. You can walk into her room and announce yourself. That way, she won't have time to think of why she doesn't want to see you."

Sky walked his visitor to the door and opened it. "Don't expect much to happen from this, Mrs. Trayhern." Out of habit, he scanned the area. There was a wooden fence four feet high around the small front yard of the cabin. Wild native columbine grew along the rails, adding color. The logging road was about a hundred feet away, and trucks lumbered by daily with their cut timber. He noted the sunlight lancing through the branches of the tall Douglas firs covering the slope that led up to a snow-capped peak.

Laura gripped his hand. "Thank you, Sky. You remember where we live?"

"Sure I do." There had been many times when the Trayhern family had invited him to dinner and he'd sat at Kelly's elbow. They'd accepted him fully, so much so he'd almost felt like a member of the family. Never once had they made fun of his coppery skin, his different breeding the way Billy Jo and his gang of bullies had. Sky had often thought back to those happy moments he'd shared with the Trayherns. He'd valued them deeply, and after he lost his own parents, those memories became even more important to him. As rich and powerful as the Trayherns were, they had always treated him with respect and welcomed him into their large brood. The joy, the laughter and fun he'd found with Kelly and her family were priceless jewels in the dark fabric of his life.

In some deeper part of himself, Sky fought that reality. He had no idea, now, if he could help his old friend at all.

"I'll be down to see Kelly this afternoon," he promised gruffly.

Battling a fresh round of tears, Laura whispered brokenly, "Oh, Sky, I pray this works. We're losing her . . ."

CHAPTER FOUR

Sky tried to steel himself emotionally as he stood outside Kelly's bedroom door. Laura Trayhern had left after escorting him up to the second floor of the massive cedar home.

His stomach was tied in knots. He owed the Trayhern family, and being so in debt to them, in so many ways, left a bitter taste in his mouth. Sky hated to admit he was also afraid of Kelly's rejection.

His shyness was a painful reality. That was why kids in school had picked on him, called him names. Why Billy Jo Talbot's gang of bullies had relentlessly hunted him down. Well, the taunts had worked. Sky was happy living alone, being a hermit. His raptors were his family, and he accepted that. Unlike human beings, they were honest and clear in their signals with him.

Wiping a hand down the side of his jeans, he stared at the wooden door. His heart pounded in his chest and his mouth was dry. What to say to Kelly? How to begin? What would her reaction to him be? It had been so long since he'd seen her. Sky understood that she had a full and fascinating life far from Philipsburg, Montana, and that he'd never be a part of it.

He hadn't expected Kelly to come home for a visit and renew what they'd shared as teens. She'd been home many times on leave, but she'd never tried to reconnect with him. What they'd had was in the past. Kelly's mother sensed there was still something between them, but was there? Sky felt sweat collecting beneath the band of the dark brown cowboy hat he wore, felt his nerves jangling. Curling his hand into a fist, he gave two sharp, almost angry knocks on the door. He wanted to get this confrontation over with.

There was no answer.

Sky stood in the hall, unsure what to do next. He glanced over his shoulder, toward the other bedrooms on the second floor of the rambling, two-story log house. Classical music wafted from somewhere below, soothing his fractious state.

Sky wondered if Kelly might be asleep. It was 3:00 p.m., but Laura had said her daughter would stay in her room for days at a time. Her left leg was in an inflatable cast, and she had crutches, but she refused to come out. There was no television in her room, apparently, only her computer.

Laura had assured him Kelly was up. Maybe he hadn't knocked loudly enough? That was part of his learned behavior: to walk without being heard; be a shadow; keep to the periphery, where no one could find him.

Upon his sentencing, Billy Jo Talbot had promised that, when he'd served his twelve years in federal prison, he would come back to Philipsburg. That he would hunt Sky down and kill him, thereby completing his revenge on him and his family. It wasn't a threat Sky took lightly, but he was no weakling or coward in the face of it, either. As Dirty Harry from the movies had said, "Make my day." Sky intended to do just that when Talbot came calling.

Flexing his right hand once more, the one that had been stabbed by Talbot, the one Kelly had held tightly to stop the bleeding resulting from the cut artery, Sky knocked again, much more emphatically.

"Go away!"

Brows raised in surprise, Sky took a step backward. Kelly's voice. He'd recognize it anywhere. Low and husky, it riffled through him like a forgotten summer breeze. And even through the door, he could hear the anguish in her tone. His heart contracting with some unknown emotion, Sky frowned. Kelly was hurting, there was no question.

What should he do? He wanted to leave, but he owed the Trayherns. He stepped forward with determination. Hopefully, Kelly was dressed . . . Wrapping his hand around the knob, he opened the door and entered.

Kelly was sitting on the edge of her bed, dressed in a black T-shirt and jeans, staring at the curtained window. Shock riveted Sky when he saw her. Her once glorious red hair was cut short.

An old memory hit him as he stood paralyzed beneath the cold green glare she turned on him. Kelly had always had long, flowing red locks. As a child, she used to gallop around like a wild mustang, saying her long hair was her mane. She'd felt it was her greatest attribute.

"Kelly?" he said gruffly. "It's Sky."

Kelly gasped, suddenly recognizing the man who filled the doorway. He was dressed in a gold shirt, boots and jeans — true cowboy garb. He stood tall, his strong legs slightly apart, as if ready to fight. His square face had grown even more handsome with age, and his sharp blue eyes were trained on her. He lifted his right hand toward her, a sign of peace.

"Sky?" she said in disbelief, as impressions flooded her. Every time she'd come home on leave, Kelly wanted to contact Sky, but had no idea how to reach him, because he had an unlisted phone number. She had given up hope of ever seeing him again. A lump grew in her throat as she gazed at him, absorbing every detail.

He was six feet tall, with a medium build and proud, broad shoulders. His clothes did little to hide his deep chest, narrow hips and long, powerful legs. Was this really her childhood friend and sweetheart from so long ago? Ruthlessly, Kelly searched his face. The copper color showed his mother's Navajo heritage. His blue eyes had come from his alcoholic father. Sky looked so ruggedly handsome, so pulverizingly male, like a cover model in some slick magazine ad.

And he seemed angry. As if he really didn't want to be in the same room with her.

Shaken, Kelly turned toward him awkwardly, her movements hampered by her left leg. She noticed he carried a rectangular cardboard box with holes in the sides.

"It's been a long time. May I come in?" he asked. Sky tried to swallow his shock.

Once vibrant and full of energy, Kelly was gaunt and thin now. He noticed the dark smudges beneath her lifeless green eyes, the pallor of her skin, and felt terror over her precarious health situation. Now he understood why Laura Trayhern was so anguished about her daughter. Kelly looked like a skeleton. Literally.

Her full lips thinned and her arched brows flattened as she growled, "Did my mother and father hunt you down and insist you come and visit me?"

Unexpected anger bubbled up within Kelly, warring with the joy she felt over seeing him once more. She watched her bitter words strike home when Sky flinched.

"Your mother did come to see me," he admitted quietly. "I didn't know what had happened to you in Sedona, Kelly. And I'm sorry about the helicopter crash." And then he lied to her. The words came rushing out before he could stop them. "I wanted to come see you. Find out if there was any way I could help you."

"Really?"

Wincing inwardly, Sky felt the scorching tone of her question, the anger radiating from her narrowed eyes. "All that you did for me as a kid, well . . ." He was stunned by his response to her. Why the hell was he

66

saying that? She was staring at him so suspiciously . . .

Rubbing her eyes, Kelly couldn't stand his pitying look. No question, this was Sky, just a grown-up version of the boy she had been hopelessly enthralled with as a child. He'd obviously aged in the best possible ways.

But she still needed to deal with this on her own. "I don't want any visitors," she told him irritably. "I want to be left alone, Sky. Do you understand that?" She tried to convey her defiance so he could turn around and leave.

To her surprise, he came into the room, shut the door behind him and set the box he was carrying down on the floor.

"Sometimes when we're hurting the most, the best thing that can happen is to be wanted," he told her gruffly. Taking off his cowboy hat, he set it on the floor near the door. "After my parents were murdered, I really needed somebody."

Sky didn't say that he knew Kelly needed someone now. Not him, of course. But he was here to fulfill a debt to the Trayherns. He'd just play the game and leave.

Crouching, he gently eased open the green cardboard box. "Well, the Great Spirit answered my call. There was an old man,

Frank Edwards, who lived thirty miles up an old logging road out of Philipsburg. He took me under his wing and taught me falconry and raptor rehabilitation. He and the raptors saved my life, literally and figuratively."

Kelly watched, mesmerized by the way his masculine hands moved with such grace as he handled the box. What was inside? Stymied, she saw him pull two leather gloves from his back pocket. "What are those?"

Sky rose and handed her one of them. "Here, put this on," he ordered. "It's called a gauntlet." He slipped the other glove onto his left hand. "I'm going to share my world with you."

Her anger dissolved as Sky walked back to the box and carefully opened the lid all the way. Inside was a large bird. Kelly wasn't sure what kind, but before she could ask, he pulled a small piece of meat from a leather pouch he wore around his waist. He gave the treat to the bird, which grasped it in its large yellow beak, then swallowed it down as he spoke softly.

"Now, Bella, I need you to be a lady here for Kelly's sake. Let's give her a welcome to the world of raptor rehabbing, shall we?"

Gripping with her long yellow toes, Bella stepped from the perch inside the container onto his gloved hand, which rested on the perch. Gracefully, he eased the hawk out of the box and stood.

Kelly could only stare at the animal's beauty, at the dark brown plumage, the patches of bright cinnamon on each of her wings. The bird seemed to be assessing the room, her hazel eyes missing nothing.

"This is Bella," Sky announced. "She's a two-year-old Harris hawk. As a baby, after she fell out of the nest on top of a saguaro cactus, she was taken home and raised by people who lived near Phoenix. They didn't know what to feed her, so she grew up on the wrong foods, like hamburger and chicken meat."

He pointed at her bright yellow, scaly legs. "Raptors need special types of nutritious meat from the wild, and her rescuers, although they meant well, didn't give her what she needed most, which was calcium. The bones in her legs are not as strong as they should be, as a result of her poor diet that first year. If those people had turned her over to someone like me, we would have put her back in her nest, or at least fed her the right foods. I could have shown her how to hunt, and survive in the wild. After that, I could have released her back to the area she'd come from, where she could fit into a social network, lead a normal life. Sadly, none of that happened."

Hypnotized by Sky's low, husky voice, Kelly felt her depression momentarily lift. Nearly two and a half feet tall, the hawk was gazing about in an animated manner, and Kelly watched in fascination. "What did happen to her?"

Heartened that his old friend's anger had disappeared, Sky continued, "Arizona Game and Fish stepped in and removed Bella from the family. By federal law, it's illegal to own a wild raptor of any type, whether a falcon, owl, hawk or eagle. They sent Bella to me through another rehabber, located in Flagstaff. She had too many raptors to deal with, but I was able to take Bella and care for her. We have a nationwide network of about twenty-five hundred licensed rehabbers who do this work."

"But you said this hawk couldn't be released back to the wild. So what are you going to do with her?" Kelly couldn't stand the thought of that beautiful, elegant bird being imprisoned.

Sky melted inwardly as Kelly focused on him. His heart swelled unaccountably, with emotions he couldn't name. And then more words came flying out of his mouth. "Well, that's where you come in. I need someone

70

to come to my cabin, where the mews, or cages, are kept, and help me out."

He gulped and clamped his lips together. What the hell had just happened? How could Kelly give him one sad look, and his brain turn to mush?

"How could I help you?" she asked, frowning.

His heart beat faster, and again he couldn't censor himself. "I could train you on how to handle raptors. Bella was raised by a girl, so she's more responsive to women than men. Hold out your gloved hand so that your thumb is on top." He gazed into her eyes. "When I transfer Bella to you, Kelly, watch what happens."

He came over and set his glove next to hers. And when Bella politely stepped off his wrist and onto her gauntlet, amazement shot through Kelly. The hawk then turned around, shook herself and started making soft croaking and grumbling sounds.

Kelly watched the hawk roll her feathers, fluff them up and let them resettle smoothly against her sleek form. Bella eyed Kelly and made more of those rumbling sounds that reminded her of gravel being crunched by car tires. "Why is she making those noises?"

Sky frowned, fighting his reaction to Kelly's nearness, and the crazy things meeting her gaze was doing to his heart. "Bella loves women. She was raised by a woman as I said. When she rolls her feathers, it means she feels at ease with you. She's relaxed. She trusts you, Kelly. And those sounds she's making means she wants you to feed her. Bella was imprinted on humans and she thinks you're her mom." He reached into the small pouch hanging off his leather belt. "Here, hold out your right hand. I'm going to put some jackrabbit meat on it."

Without thinking, Kelly complied. Everything was so surprising, she followed Sky's direction automatically. Bella watched the transfer with great delight. The Harris hawk grumbled some more, excitedly opened her wings and then folded them back against her body.

"Okay, now put the morsels where your thumb meets your index finger. Bella will lean over, peck it off and eat it. She's gentle. She won't hurt you."

Kelly did so, then gingerly held out her hand. Bella was surprisingly light for her size. She moved deftly along the leather sleeve of the glove protecting Kelly's forearm, then, with a dainty dip of her head, quickly gobbled the proffered jackrabbit meat. "Oh, gosh . . ." Kelly whispered, stunned. "She's hungry."

Sky fought to bring his armor back into place, to remain immune to Kelly. "Any raptor will make a pig out of itself. They survive by making a kill and gorging themselves, then not eating for two or three days." He gave Kelly more meat. She placed it exactly as he'd instructed earlier.

A thrill ran through Kelly as she watched Bella politely peck the red meat from her gauntlet. "She's no pig. Look at her, Sky. She's very delicate about it." Kelly managed a small smile. "I'd say she has hawk manners."

Seeing the wonderment of discovery in Kelly's eyes, he felt his soul bound with an old yearning — for things that he'd fantasized about in the past and could never have. Now, so many years later, here she was: beautiful, pathetically thin and needing his help. Sky could feel the wounds in her. The two of them had always had an unspoken connection. As children, he'd always known how she felt, even when she said nothing. He just knew. . . .

A new feeling, strong and catalyzing, soared through him. Kelly had helped him so much when he'd been wounded, body and soul. And now she was the one isolating herself from society, shattered and hurting. He watched her admiring Bella, who was now preening her dark brown feathers. In such a short time, Kelly had bonded with the hawk. This was a new beginning.

"Bella's real pleased with you, Kelly."

"This is incredible. I — well, I just never thought about wild raptors needing our help."

"Some of them do. And taking care of them . . . it's another way to fly," Sky suggested.

He saw pain flitting through her green eyes before she looked away.

"Your mother told me that because of your shattered leg, you can never fly again. At least not commercially. Your sole source of income has been ripped away from you, and I'm sorry for that." This was the sad truth, but he wanted to lift her spirits. "Remember when you were a kid, how you used to run with your arms outstretched? Like you were an eagle, flying around the playground at school."

Kelly smiled at the memory, but then felt renewed anguish. She'd forgotten about that time in her life, but now was not the time to rehash history. She focused on Bella, perched placidly on her arm. The large bird eyed her again, ruffled her feathers and smoothed them down once more. Kelly almost thought she saw the happiness radiating in the hawk's alert gaze. Or maybe she felt it. "I guess I'm sort of like Bella, relegated to obsolescence. I'm no longer of use. I feel trapped. She lives in a cage and so do I."

Sky stood quietly, hearing the suffering in Kelly's strained voice. "You know what? In many cases, these raptors can be given back their lives. People find injured birds that hit power or telephone lines, or fell out of the nest. If they're given to us, we can nurse them back to health and, many times, return them to their world of freedom and flight."

"There's no such possibility for me," Kelly said bitterly. Her frown deepened, and she stared down at her encased leg. The late afternoon sunlight had shifted, but the reddish-gold cedar floor still shone. "I'll never fly again. My wings are clipped. The life I love is gone for good."

Sky wanted to say he understood how she felt all too well. That he had shadows in his own life that never went away. But he didn't want to mention Talbot's threat to find and kill him. As soon as he was released from prison, his old foe would hunt him down, Sky knew.

"Listen, Kelly, you're not finished with your life," he said instead, his tone harsh. "Okay, you have a broken leg, but it's going to mend. You're not obsolete."

Something inside Sky dissolved when she looked up, her eyes glimmering with unshed tears. His mouth opened and, instead of his mind taking charge, his heart overwhelmed him. "I could really use your help. Your mother said you had at least nine more months of recouping before getting back into the mainstream. If you have nothing else that interests you until then, please consider working with me at my cabin. It's only thirty miles away, just ten miles from where your brother and his wife live. It's on the same road."

Kelly hadn't realized that. Jason and Annie visited her weekly with their children, and that always lifted her dark mood. "Do they know you live so close to them?" she asked.

"No, they don't. I sort of keep to myself. You know, my Indian blood and all," he joked.

"You liked being alone because you were shy," Kelly said. "I don't think it's an Indian thing. You're an introvert by nature, and there's nothing wrong with that."

"And you were always an extrovert when we were growing up," he muttered, suddenly restless. He had to get out of here. He was saying too much. "You didn't mind if I hung back, was quiet or uncomfortable in a crowd. You always accepted me just as I was."

"I liked you," Kelly said, holding his gaze. She felt a new, gentle sensation flow through her and wrap around her heart. So many wonderful memories of her past with Sky were surfacing, flowing like a healing unguent through her damaged spirit. "I still do," she added, giving him a game smile. "And I'm glad you came. I'm sorry I was so rotten to you when you opened the door. It was just such a shock, seeing you. School was so long ago . . ."

Nodding, Sky rasped, "We did try to stay in touch, but it just didn't work out."

"I know. Now, I wish I'd put more of an effort into it. You lead such an interesting life. It would have been nice to share that with you over the years."

Heat and longing filled Sky as a spark of life came back to Kelly's emerald eyes. He could barely keep his joy in check. "Let's share our lives now, then. All we have is today. Do you feel up to it?"

What was happening to him? he wondered. He recalled the puppy love he'd shared with Kelly. But not until this moment had he suspected any of it had survived. Had it? Did this explain his behavior?

"How will I get up to your place? I can't drive yet."

"Your mother said she would drive you up daily and come get you. Would you like to help with Bella? I'm pretty overwhelmed with raptors right now, and I could use another pair of hands, especially from someone who loves them as much as I do. What do you say?" he pressed.

He was sweating, he realized. What would it be like to have Kelly near him once more? The thought was so foreign, it left him stunned and unable to think clearly.

Moistening her lips, Kelly searched Sky's eyes. "What could I do? I have to use crutches to get around. I'd be in the way, wouldn't I?"

"No, there's plenty to do, Kelly. I'm always needing new leather hoods made for my raptors. There are lots of small repairs on my falconry equipment. I need someone to cut up the meat and create diet plans for the incoming birds. You can go out to the cages on crutches without a problem, and feed them. They don't care if you hobble around." He smiled. "Later, as your leg gets better, you can help me teach them to fly, and train them to work with a lure."

Sky saw her considering his offer. He continued, secretly hoping she'd take on the challenge. "Once you're free of your crutches, you can go out in the field with me and scare up rabbits for the raptors, so they learn how to hunt again. After they've learned how to feed themselves, we'll release them back to the wild." He held her eyes, which sparked with interest now. "It's a wonderful way to work with nature and give back to her. And to them." He pointed to Bella.

And this was a way to pay back Laura and Morgan for all the money and time they'd put into him, he told himself. Still, he was reeling. Spending time with Kelly scared him on a deep level. And her sad-eyed look tore him apart.

Being near the hawk thrilled Kelly as nothing had for ages. And Sky, a known quantity in her life, wanted her help. She knew he was trustworthy. And reliable. Already, with him here, she felt more emotionally stable and hopeful. That surprised Kelly most of all. Nothing in the past three nightmarish months had given her hope, only a spiraling sense of despair.

"Well, I don't feel good every day, Sky. Sometimes I am pretty exhausted, and all I want to do is sleep. I probably won't be as reliable as you need me to be."

Sky was resigned by now to obeying his

flapping jaw and sawdust-filled mind. "Just give it some thought," he told her. "I could use whatever help you can provide, Kelly. I expect nothing, receive everything."

Sky saw a flash of recognition in her gaze. That was a saying his parents had raised him with, promoting a Native American way of life. It involved a surrendering of self every day, and an understanding that doing so brought new learning. A person had to be flexible and accept the day as it was presented by the Great Spirit.

"I remember you sharing that saying with me long ago," Kelly whispered, a sudden catch in her voice. She lifted her gauntlet. "Are you ready to take Bella back? My arm is starting to tremble a little."

Kelly had always worked out in a gym, run two to three miles daily. All of that had been taken away from her. Now, she was a weakling, and shame flowed through her. She didn't want Sky to see her like this.

"Sure, no problem." Sky stepped forward and placed his gauntlet next to hers. He liked touching her like this, and it raised another fond memory from their teenage years. How many times had they walked hand in hand? And just before he'd moved away, he'd kissed her cheek. . . .

Bella chattered in protest at leaving Kelly's

glove, but when Sky insisted, moved with aplomb back onto his arm. He walked her over to her cardboard box and gently set her down on the perch, which was covered with Astroturf for good purchase. When Bella turned around, Sky gave her a little meat as a reward.

"You can't force a hawk into a traveling cage," he confided to Kelly. "They have to want to go into it. So you always give them a reward, and they eagerly look forward to getting into it, despite the confined space."

Kelly watched, fascinated. It was true; Bella seemed fine with being in the container. There was about six inches of space on either side of her and plenty of room for her tail, which she waggled back and forth after receiving her prize.

Kelly's lips started to curve upward. "What's it mean when she wiggles her tail like that?"

Sky gently closed the traveling case and pressed the Velcro straps back into place. "Harris hawks use a lot of feather language. More so than some other raptors," he told her, the gruffness coming back to his tone as he set the case near the open window. Turning, he said, "Waggling the tail means she's happy and satisfied with the status quo. No upsets. She's relaxed."

"So food makes a raptor happy," Kelly concluded, meeting his hooded stare. An unexpected heat flared in her body as she studied his weather-worn features. Sky had turned into a gorgeous man. There was nothing soft about him. If anything, he was the consummate outdoors person. Kelly assumed that what he did while helping raptors probably accounted for that. But even in childhood, Sky had been a child of nature. He'd fished with his stepfather, hiked and hunted with him in the Rockies to provide meat for their table.

"Well? Would you consider part-time work with me? When you feel up to it? I can't pay you anything. A raptor rehabilitator gets no money from the state, unfortunately, so I'm more or less living on the edge of poverty. I have a second job as a night watchman at a concrete plant just outside Philipsburg. I took it to cover the expenses of caring for the birds I rescue."

"How often do you work?"

"Five nights a week." Sky gave her a penetrating look. How beautiful Kelly was, but how ravaged and wounded, too. He knew his raptors had helped him heal. And he knew in his heart they could help Kelly as well. She was a stubborn person and took after her father, who Sky knew was a bulwark of stability and calm no matter what storm enveloped the family. Kelly had Morgan's genes, that was for sure. Would she leave this room? Take a chance on life again? Helping her to do so would be a way to pay off his debt.

Nervously running her fingers through her short hair, Kelly muttered, "Let me think about it, Sky, okay? I don't know. I feel so helpless. I'm of no use to anyone right now."

"And yet, you did something for Bella. You made her happy, Kelly. You made her day."

"I'm so wobbly on crutches . . ."

He knew she was throwing up obstacles. "Then talk to your physical therapist about doing more exercises to get strengthened," he suggested. Sky knew she wasn't going for therapy at all, which was part of the problem. Kelly had given up living. Given up trying.

Watching her face closely, he saw her weighing his words.

"Well, I guess I could . . ." Kelly stared down at her hand and slid off the russet-colored gauntlet. She held it out to him.

"No, you keep it," Sky urged. "Bring it back to me once you've made up your mind — one way or another." He reached down and grasped the handle of Bella's carrying case. "I have to go now, Kelly. My birds will be having temper tantrums in their mews because it's past their feeding time."

Sky forced himself to move toward the door. He could feel Kelly's eyes on his back. She was like a wounded raptor, someone who had loved to fly but had had her wings broken by the terrible crash she'd experienced. Without a doubt, Sky knew he could help Kelly rehabilitate if she'd just give herself permission to do that.

From handling so many injured raptors over the years, he knew that some flourished and were able to resume a normal life, while others never did. It was a matter of character, of personality. He hoped that if Kelly did decide to help him for a while, she would not only flourish under his tutelage and support, but learn to fly all over again.

"Sky . . ." Kelly said as he reached the door. He turned toward her, Bella's traveling case in hand. "Thank you for visiting me. It was really nice to see you again. I never expected this . . . or you . . . I'm still in shock, I guess." Opening her hands, she whispered, "Can I call you with my decision?"

His mouth hitched into a slight smile. "Sure. I have an unlisted number. I'll leave it with your mother. Fair enough?"

There was that word *fair* again. Kelly hated it. Nothing in life was fair. Ever. "Yes. I'll let you know in a week or so."

Nodding, Sky scooped up his hat and settled it on his head. Then he frowned as a ball of unsettling emotions rolled through him. Kelly was beautiful. She was unattached, with no man in her life. . . . He savagely squelched his longing. He'd purposely remained free of relationships, because he could never put someone he loved in Talbot's vengeful line of fire. And Talbot was going to hunt him down once he was released from prison. . . .

No, Sky would never do that. Especially to Kelly.

"That's fine," he told her. "Bella and I will be happy to see you again. Stay well, Kelly."

The door closed as quietly as it had opened, and Kelly was alone once more, feeling suddenly bereft.

CHAPTER FIVE

The more he thought about it, the more Sky realized he'd lost his mind for even asking Kelly to help him. Sure, it would be payment to the Trayherns. Yet as the week went by, he became hopeful that she'd decide against his offer. Then his debt to Laura and Morgan would be paid once and for all.

Sky didn't want to compromise Kelly's safety. Talbot *had* promised to find him, stalk him and kill him; he'd made no bones about it that day the jury had found him guilty. Billy Jo was incarcerated in a federal prison in Washington State, but that wasn't far away. Sky hoped he'd covered his tracks enough to stay off Talbot's radar once the man was released, a year from now.

Sky would then institute his plan. This time, their encounter would be on his terms and turf, not Talbot's. Sky was determined not to let his nemesis set the agenda, as he had twice before.

Sky refocused on his work with a beautiful European eagle-owl, Luna, affixing shorter flight jesses around her strong, feathered legs. As he handled the huge, six-month-old raptor in her open-air enclosure, a June breeze brought in the soothing scent of pine. Inhaling deeply, he tried to calm his worry.

"There," he told Luna. "All done. Okay, it's your turn. Let's go to the perches in the back and see if you'll fly from one to another."

Luna made soft noises, like the rough purr of a tomcat. Sky grinned at the owl, admiring her mottled brown-and-golden plumage. She looked a lot like the great horned owls of the Americas, but was even larger and more commanding. Luna weighed four pounds now. When she was a year old, and fully mature, she'd weigh seven. Eagle-owls were the largest owl in Europe, which was why they'd earned the name. Luna had been purchased and allowed in the U.S. by special permit. She had been too much for the amateur falconer and had been transferred to Sky's care.

Offering his left hand, covered by a thick, protective gauntlet, Sky wrapped Luna's flight jesses around his fingers as she stepped willingly onto his forearm. He was carefully teaching the young bird to follow him from perch to perch. Each time Luna performed the movement, he would provide her with food. In this case, nutritious mouse meat. Because she'd been imprinted by a human, Luna could never be released back to the wild.

Sky was just leaving the mews behind his cabin, with Luna on his arm, when he heard a car approaching on the logging road. Few people, except for lost tourists, ever came this far up on the mountain on the deeply rutted, narrow dirt road.

Sky had nightmares about Talbot finding his home. This could be a freed convict that Billy Jo had sent to track Sky down. Whoever it was might take the information about his whereabouts back to Talbot, who would start plotting his revenge once he was released. Sky didn't want his home to be the battleground this time, and had plans of his own to make certain it wasn't.

Swallowing hard, he stepped quickly around the log cabin that had been his home for so many years. A black Toyota Forerunner was pulling up in front. His heart started to pound as Kelly Trayhern got out of the passenger side of the SUV then reached for her crutches, and the gauntlet he'd left with her. Laura came around the vehicle, allowing her daughter to get clear of the door before she shut it.

What had Kelly decided? Sky saw her frown as she hobbled forward with the help of her crutches. She wore a removable cast from midthigh to her ankle, and a thick sock on her injured foot.

Trying to squelch his anxiety, Sky quickly came forward. "Good afternoon," he called, raising his right hand in greeting and trying to sound a lot cheerier than he felt.

Luna flapped her wings when he made the sudden movement, displaying their nearly four-foot span, and brushing Sky's cowboy hat in the process. He saw Kelly look up with wonder in her expression as she watched Luna showing off. The owl was a big ham around people.

"Hi, Sky," Laura Trayhern said, smiling tensely as she opened the gate for her daughter. "What a beautiful owl! Is that a great horned?"

"No, ma'am." Sky explained Luna's lineage, and what she was doing in Montana. But he kept his gaze on Kelly. Today, she seemed slightly better. There was a little pink in her gaunt cheeks. Her hair was combed, and she wore a bright pink tank top and a pair of loose-fitting, white cargo pants, with the left leg slit to accommodate her cast.

"Kelly? How are you?" he asked as he gestured for her to climb up on the wide porch of the cabin, which had several straight-back chairs and a round, wooden table. Balancing Luna on his glove, he quickly brought over a chair.

"Okay, I guess, Sky. Phew! This is work! Thanks for the chair. Time for me to sit down."

Sky brought over another chair, for Laura. Then his gaze went to the glove Kelly still clutched in one hand. Would she help him? Take him up on his offer to teach her about raptors?

Emotions warred violently within him. His silly, irrational heart wanted nothing more than Kelly's presence in his life. His mind, however, screamed that he'd be putting her in jeopardy if he allowed her to stay around. If Talbot found him, she'd be in danger. Sky knew the man would kill anyone he loved. Sky wanted to remain hidden until Talbot came after him, and then he'd fight for his life. But he'd do it alone, not with Kelly there.

"Can I get you some iced tea? I just made some about an hour ago. It's pretty hot out here for this time of year."

Kelly frowned. "Uh, no, thanks, Sky. I just came to give you back the glove." She offered it to him. "We're not staying long."

Taking the gauntlet, he searched her green eyes. "Thanks." He saw Kelly looking at Luna. The owl was incredibly regal and beautiful. "Have you thought about my offer, Kelly?" Inwardly, Sky prayed she'd say no.

She shrugged. "I don't know yet. I'm torn. I'm so weak and out of shape."

He nodded, feeling a twinge of relief. "That's a good reason to say no."

Laura cleared her throat. "I've been doing reading on falconry, Sky." She gestured toward the cabin. "Despite Kelly's weak condition, couldn't you bring some of your gear out here on the porch and teach her to do the repairs? Her muscles might be weak right now but her mind is working fine. What do you think?" She drilled him with a look.

His relief dissolved under Laura Trayhern's stubborn glance, and silent message. "Well," he muttered, looking at Kelly, "I guess you can put eyelets in kangaroo leather, and make new flight jesses for me. That would sure be a help." Though Kelly was tentative, Sky understood that her mother was desperate to get her out into the world, to start living again.

"I went for physical therapy again," Kelly stated, giving her mother a look that spoke volumes. "It showed me just how much muscle mass I've lost." She pointed to her leg, encased in the white-and-green removable cast. "I can't do much yet. The bones aren't knitting as fast as they should. I'm on antibiotics and I feel like crap because of the drug. I'm lethargic, irritable and snarly."

"How about pain?" Sky asked. He brought over another chair and set it opposite her. The whole time, Luna was happy to sit on his glove, her huge orange eyes trained on their visitors, her head swiveling often to face one or the other.

"Even on a bad day," Laura interjected, "wouldn't you rather be doing something to help these birds than sitting in your bedroom feeling alone and miserable?" She gave her daughter a searching look.

"I don't care if you feel snarly or snappish, Kelly," he said. "These raptors have their fits, too. It's just part of life. I can handle it." Sky knew he had to act as Laura's advocate. This was payment time, and he had to play his part whether he wanted to or not.

Kelly tried to calm her racing pulse. Just seeing Sky again made hope burn like a brand in her chest. Since his unexpected visit, she found herself wanting to get well — well enough to work with him and his hawks.

She couldn't explain why she felt such a change, except that Sky had been her childhood sweetheart. They'd had a connection. Maybe they still did. He was honest and trustworthy, and perhaps that was what she needed right now. The depression that gripped her was so dark that she felt numb most days, and detached from life. Except around him.

"Life isn't a bed of roses," he was saying gruffly. "I have my own moments, Kelly. We all do."

As she gazed into his eyes, trying not to drown in their vivid blue depths, a kernel of optimism sprang to life within Kelly's heart once again. He looked good in that dark blue cowboy shirt, the sleeves rolled up to his elbows, and old, threadbare jeans that outlined his hard, long thighs. He was in such great shape. . . .

Compressing her lips, Kelly muttered, "Okay, I'll try. But I don't know how often I'll feel like coming up here. I can't drive yet, and don't like having to ask other people to take time out of their day to get me around."

"We all need help from time to time," he stated carefully. Laura Trayhern seemed relieved, he noted. Turning his attention back to Kelly, he asked, "How do you feel today?"

"It's a good day for me, compared to how I usually feel," she admitted. "Why?"

When Sky reached up and stroked Luna's sleek feathers, her heart contracted. She wondered what it would be like to be touched like that by Sky. The thought was unexpected, and she suppressed it instantly. Touching and being touched had no place in her life right now.

"If you want, you can come with me. I was going to work with Luna out back, training her to fly from one perch to the next. After that, I was planning to drive into town for my weekly supply of groceries. I could drop you off at your home on the way down the mountain." He glanced at Laura. "If that's all right with you, ma'am?"

"Of course," Laura murmured, a smile blossoming on her face. "Kelly? You okay with that?"

"Sure," she said. "I just feel like such a burden to everyone. I know you have a lot to do, Mom."

Laura rose and patted her shoulder gently. "I will always have time for you, Kelly. More than anything, your dad and I want you to get well." She turned her attention to Sky. "Don't forget that Kelly tires very quickly."

Nodding, Sky said, "I understand that, ma'am. When she's ready to go home, I'll take her down the mountain. No problem."

"Okay." Laura pressed a kiss on Kelly's short red hair. "I'll see you later, honey."

Relief flowed through Kelly as she watched her mother drive away, the Toyota disappearing in a cloud of yellow. She turned to Sky, feeling suddenly like an awkward teenager. "Are you sure you don't mind doing this? I feel like you've volunteered to be my new babysitter and you really don't want to be a part of it."

Sky stroked the owl again, and Luna responded by ruffling her feathers and making those purring sounds. Sky's conscience was pricking him. Kelly was right, but he wasn't going to admit it. He stood up and balanced the owl on his glove.

"I don't see you as needing a babysitter, Kelly," he said tersely. "Feel like following me? It's about a hundred feet around the cabin to the training oval, where I teach birds how to fly to me and retrieve food."

Sky tried to wrestle with his reactions over the fact that Kelly would be coming up here. Payback was a son of a bitch sometimes. Swallowing his frustration, he tried not to take it out on her. She was the innocent in this situation, and didn't know about her mother's pressure on him. And he would never tell her. He cared about her, and she'd been through enough.

"Sure, let's go." An infusion of excitement flowed through Kelly as she awkwardly got to her feet. She had to hold her broken leg up to keep her foot from scraping the ground. Fortunately, the brick path around the side of the house would make it easier for her to navigate. Being on uneven ground could spell disaster for her and her crutches.

Sky picked up a chair in his right hand and, carrying Luna on his left, moved ahead of Kelly. "I'll get you set up at the flight area," he told her, trying to keep his voice even. "You can sit and watch. I'll show you some of the basics I'm teaching Luna."

The pine-scented air, the warmth of the noonday sun, all conspired to make Kelly feel better. Despite the sense of darkness, of hopelessness that always hung around her like a suffocating blanket, she set off willingly. Being here with Sky, working with him, seemed to break through that never-ending gloom. Watching Sky walk, his shoulders thrown back proudly, the huge eagle-owl riding on his gauntlet, made Kelly smile. He reminded her of a lordly crusader with a falcon on his glove, a chivalrous knight.

"Here we are," he said, situating the chair near the flight oval. She gave him a nod of thanks and sat down. He could see perspiration dotting her brow, and realized moving was still quite an effort for her. He'd remember that in the future.

The training area, raked clean of pine needles and other woodland debris, was about four hundred feet wide and encircled by tall, stout Douglas firs. Luckily, the sun was at an angle, so Kelly was in the shade. An unexpected happiness filtered through Sky as he passed her a baseball cap to block the glare.

"Thanks," she said, settling it on her head.

Sky opened a large cedar trunk, which contained falconry gear. He then reached into a small ice chest and handed a bottle of water to her. "It's easy to get dehydrated out here. I'm often so caught up in what I'm doing, I forget to drink for an hour or more. And with this heat and sun, it's not a good idea."

His thoughtfulness warmed her. "Okay, okay, you've taken care of me enough, Sky. Now I want to learn. Teach me about Luna here, so I can understand better what you want from me."

His heart flew open as he saw her full lips curve in a smile. Sky could tell she was in pain. The tension was still there, too. He ached to see Kelly's eyes filled with life once more. When they were young, her eyes had reminded him of sparkling emeralds caught in sunlight. He had always been mesmerized by them. Sky used to tell her that, and she would blush fiercely, her freckles turning a dark copper color. Knowing now that he'd always been a romantic, Sky sensed he was like a safe harbor for her. Now more than ever, Kelly needed that. And he would give it to her.

Sky's spirits lightened as he crossed the training area and placed Luna on a metal T-perch. Made of sturdy, lightweight steel pipe, it had been specially welded, and thick Astroturf wrapped around the crossbar, where the owl could easily grasp it. Sky released the short flight jesses from the fingers of his glove.

"I'm teaching Luna not only to fly, but to know that where I point my glove or click this clicker —" he held it up for her to see "— that she will be rewarded by being fed. Right now, she's just learning how to fly. How to handle her growing body and bulk." He grinned as he saw Kelly focus on the owl. "Luna's a teenager, agewise," he told her. Walking to the other side of the clearing, he placed a bit of mouse meat on the perch he wanted her to fly to.

Then, he drew Luna's attention with the clicker, and pointed at the meat. "Now, Luna is an owl, which means she's going to take her time, think about all this, wait, watch and consider. A hawk, eagle or falcon would go for it in a split second. But an owl looks at the world differently than his or her raptor cousins. An owl usually flies from dusk to dawn. Sometimes they'll hunt during the day if they're really hungry. I train all raptors during daylight hours because I don't have the night vision they have." Sky placed his hands on his hips and watched Luna, who was craning her neck, looking around and then back at the meat. "I'm asking her to fly two hundred feet."

"Why is she looking around so much?" Kelly wondered aloud.

"Her hearing is so acute that she can detect mice scurrying beneath the pine needles of the forest floor. That's triggering her instincts to go fly off and find one."

"So what stops her from doing that?"

Sky liked that she was asking questions. Kelly looked involved. The murkiness was gone from her wide green eyes, and she was leaning forward, excitement written across her pale features. "Absolutely nothing except her trust in me."

"Trust. Seems to be a big word for raptors and their trainers."

"Trust is something two-leggeds need in another person, too," he said, disgruntled. "Yes, you're right. I'm counting on the fact that I've hand-raised Luna from three months old. She was imprinted with another falconer, but now she's transferred that imprinting to me. She sees me as 'Mom,' and so I'm hoping that as I use the clicker to tell her food is here on this perch, she'll override her wild, natural instincts. I'm hoping she won't fly off and find those critters under the pine needles, but come to me instead."

Kelly was about to speak when, suddenly, Luna opened her wide wings and took off. With a few strong, silent flaps, she crossed the training field, nearly overshooting the landing. Beating her wings wildly, the young owl finally righted herself on the perch and quickly gobbled up the choice piece of mouse meat. Kelly could swear she saw pleasure in Luna's round, feathery face.

"Wow! That was something! I didn't hear her flying."

"You won't," he said, pleased with her

observation. "They fly on silent wings. The Cherokee people call owls the queen of the night. I like that symbology." Sky reached up and stroked Luna's breast feathers again, and rewarded her with another tidbit of meat. Then he prompted her to step onto his gauntlet, which she did. After placing the eagle-owl on another perch, about a hundred feet away, he walked toward Kelly.

"Okay, we're going to get Luna used to working with you." Sky handed Kelly the glove. "Put it on and then raise it, about head high." He positioned her in the chair so her back was slightly angled toward the owl, then placed the meat in the crotch between the thumb and index finger of the gauntlet she'd slipped on. "Now, what I'm going to do is ask Luna to fly over to you from that perch. I'll stand behind you and use the clicker to get her attention. A raptor will rarely fly directly toward someone. If they see your eyes, they feel challenged, and won't fly to you. Instead, we present our back, or the side of our body, so they feel safe flying in."

"But . . ."

"It'll be fine," Sky said, and without thinking, he patted Kelly's shoulder. His fingers tingled as soon as he'd touched her. He didn't want to admit just how much he'd wanted to do so.

As he stepped behind Kelly, Sky raised the clicker and pressed it three times. Luna turned her head and stared at Kelly's raised gauntlet, and the red meat visible there. She made soft, purring sounds.

"What's that?" Kelly asked excitedly.

"It's the way a baby owl tells its parents that it's hungry. Can you turn your head and see how Luna is studying you? She has to deliberate over whether to trust you, because you're new to her. You can see how she's memorizing your face and checking out the gauntlet you're wearing. She knows if it's at head height, that means, 'fly to me.' "

"Has she ever flown to anyone but you?" Kelly asked, her gaze riveted on Luna, who was now looking around. She was considering all those hidden mice beneath the pine needles, Kelly was sure.

"I have no helpers." Sky tried to suppress the thrill he felt, sharing his knowledge with Kelly. As children, they'd been inseparable. Their families would often go on picnics together, fishing the cold trout streams nearby, or taking a day hike up some trail that would lead to a flower-strewn meadow. Those times and memories had helped keep Sky sane through all the terrible trials of his young life. "Luna's looking at you again. Seriously now. Do you see her orange eyes? Look at her pupils. They're widening and then dilating. She's thinking about you and that food on your gauntlet."

The huskiness of his voice behind her made Kelly feel equally excited. She noted how Luna unfurled her large, rounded wings. In a heartbeat, the owl was flying toward her. She felt the sweeping rush of air around her head and shoulders, and then Luna's large, feathered legs and big yellow feet settled lightly on her gauntlet. The owl weighed much more than Bella, Kelly found. Still, though large, she was extremely light. "Ohh . . ." Kelly whispered. "She's so beautiful. So strong and yet feminine."

Luna reached down and quickly took the meat, gobbling it down in one gulp.

"Okay, slowly lower your arm so you can hold her comfortably. You might want to plant your elbow into your waist in order to rest your forearm. More than anything, we want to keep Luna calm and stable on your gauntlet." Sky started to reach out to give Kelly's shoulder a gentle squeeze, but stopped himself. "You did well. Luna landed without a problem because you were holding your hand and arm in the correct position," he said.

Amazement shimmered through Kelly. As Luna watched her, studied her, she felt the bird's incredible energy. "She's so big, Sky!"

He came around to the perch across from where Kelly sat. "She's a baby weightwise. Right now she's about three feet tall, with a wingspan of four feet, and later will weigh around seven pounds at maturity." He rose up on his toes and placed more mouse meat on the perch. How he wished he had a camera. Kelly's face was flushed pink, her copper freckles visible. Her green eyes were wide with awe as she studied the owl. "Raptors have a way of stealing your heart and opening you up," he confided. "Do you feel her energy?"

"I do, Sky. She feels so . . . maternal. So strong and feminine. I can sense what she's thinking." Kelly raised an eyebrow. "Am I making all this up?"

He shook his head. "You're not. Raptors are very psychic, as far as I'm concerned. They are wild and have natural instincts they've honed for hundreds of thousands of years in order to survive as a species. For example, if you presented a quiet, calm exterior, but were really upset or emotionally charged about something, Luna or any other raptor would sense that."

"Really? What would they do?"

"They'd get restless. Flap their wings a lot. When a raptor sits quietly on your glove, ruffles and fluffs their feathers or waggles their tail like Bella did, that means they trust you and are relaxed in your company. If you're calm, the bird will be, too. They mirror and reflect how we really feel, despite what we're showing to the outer world." It was a good thing Luna wasn't on his gauntlet, Sky realized, given his churning emotions. The owl would have been fidgety and upset.

Chuckling for the first time, Kelly gave Luna an appreciative look. The owl was considering the food Sky had placed on the perch. "Then I guess I can't come up here when I'm in a snarly, irritable mood. She won't want to be anywhere near me."

Sky tipped his cowboy hat slightly with his thumb. "I've found that on bad days, working with the birds soothes and heals me. It brings me back to my core. I forget my worries, my anger or problems. They have a magical way of making it all go away. You feel so vital . . ."

That was true. Kelly was amazed all over again. "Just getting to hold Luna makes me feel good, Sky. I can't explain it. I was depressed, but now I don't feel numb. I feel more alive. The thrill of holding Luna, of just having something this wild and beautiful on my hand is, well, like Cinderella going from pumpkin to princess."

Sky nodded and raised the clicker, drawing Luna's attention with the snapping sounds he produced. "The raptors here at my rehab center make you feel like part of them, their family. Most hawks and owls have a much better life in some respects than we ever will. They can fly free. They're a part of the fabric of nature, while two-leggeds have lost that sense of play, of freedom and wildness."

Saddened by his words, Kelly nodded. Luna was peering at the perch next to Sky. The owl seemed very content on Kelly's hand, yet when Sky clicked a second time, she unfurled her wings and took off with a rush of air. The raptor was so fast, so silent, that Kelly was amazed once again. This time, Luna landed squarely on the perch. She gulped down her meat and then ruffled her feathers, expressing her contentment. As a reward, Sky handed her another tidbit from his leather pouch.

"Well, that's all for Luna today," he said. "She's only six months old, and flying her too much at this age will stress her out. I've been building her up to daily flights, and she's covering a little more distance each day." He lifted his glove near the owl and she stepped onto it willingly. Sky gave her another treat.

Kelly watched as he went toward a large group of dark green metal cages among the trees. The first mew was Luna's, and he opened the door and carried her inside. Carefully closing the door, he put her on a substantial wooden perch set diagonally in one corner, then gently removed the flight jesses from the owl's thick, feathery legs. Luna was now free. He gave her one more treat of meat, and left.

"That was really spectacular," Kelly told him as he approached her. "Thank you so much. It's such a thrill to hold Luna. I can't believe it." She handed him the gauntlet.

"Keep it. Just bring it with you when you come. We'll work with you and the raptors." He tried not to notice how his heart skipped as he gazed at Kelly. Her upturned face was pink with excitement. How badly he wanted to stare down at her parted, full lips. The sudden thought of grazing them with his own mouth startled the hell out of him. What was he thinking? There was no way he could let Kelly know how he'd felt in his youth. The yearning was even more intense now. Stymied by all he was feeling, Sky said, "Are you ready to go? Exhausted?"

"Tired but exhilarated," Kelly admitted, getting up on her crutches once more. She took an awkward step and started to fall. Instantly, Sky was there, his arms, strong and caring, reaching out to her.

"Oh!" Kelly cried as one of her crutches fell to the earth. She gripped the front of his shirt with her outstretched hand. Pain ripped up her leg as she stumbled forward.

"Easy . . . I've got you, Kelly," he breathed, his mouth tickled by her short red hair. "It's all right." Sky carefully helped her upright. Leaning down, he retrieved the crutch and gave it to her, noting how she avoided looking at him. Resting his hand on her shoulder, he waited until she had the crutches settled in place. "Okay now? Can you make it back to the front yard?"

"Yeah, sorry. I lose my balance all the time. I hate it. I hate these damn crutches." Her left leg ached, but she knew it wasn't serious. In a few minutes, the pain would lessen, her nerves calm down. Kelly cast Sky a quick glance and saw concern in his eyes, along with some other indecipherable emotion she couldn't name. His mouth was thinned, as if he were experiencing her pain, her discomfort. She laughed, embarrassed. "Having your hand on my shoulder is like having Luna on my gauntlet. You make me feel calmer. Not so irritated or ashamed, as I normally would." She added, softly, "I don't like appearing weak to anyone, Sky. I don't want handouts. I can't stand people pitying me."

Sky squeezed her shoulder gently. "I understand, Kelly. Come on, I'll walk you to the gate, and then I'll bring the pickup around. It's time to get you home." How could he lose control around her like this? His heart was ripping apart inside his chest, and his vulnerability was maddening.

Looking around at the beautiful forests, the secluded cabin and mews, Kelly whispered, "This feels better than home."

CHAPTER SIX

"Dammit, Harve, I want the goods on Mc-Coy!" Billy Jo Talbot sat with his childhood friend in the visitors' area of the penitentiary. Jabbing his finger at the paper Harve had given him, he snarled, "I'm allowed to use a computer, but the prison officials block certain sites from us. You've got to do better than this!"

On Saturdays the visitors' center was always crowded with prisoners' loved ones. The noise level was high, but Billy Jo was careful to keep his voice low enough that only Harve could hear.

Shifting nervously on the picnic-style bench, Harve pushed his fingers through his thinning, light brown hair. "Look, Billy Jo, I've done the best I can. McCoy is a shadow. I've tried for years to find him. Believe me, I have." He gave his friend a pleading look. The rage banked in Talbot's brown eyes frightened him. "The only thing left to do is hire a private investigator to locate him. I've searched his name on Google and nothing comes up. Nothing. He's got an unlisted phone number, but I can get it."

"He's back in Montana," Billy Jo growled, folding his large, square hands on the table in front of him. "That son of a bitch Indian isn't going to leave the land of his birth. They're all like that. They live where they're born." Compressing his thin lips, Talbot rasped, "And he's gonna die on the very same land that birthed him. I've got one year to go. Next June, I'm out of this hellhole."

Harve Gunnison nodded and looked around. The place was a beehive of activity, with so many spouses and children visiting. Guards in blue shirts, badges and dark blue pants, with weapons at their sides, stood around the periphery, watching and listening. "Did you hear me? I said you need to hire an investigator."

"Like I have the money . . ." Billy Jo craved a cigarette, but smoking had been banned in public areas of federal prisons. He snorted. As if living with violent offenders wasn't dangerous to one's health. What was wrong with this picture? Once he got back to his cell, he couldn't smoke there, either.

"What about your mom? I know your dad passed on, but did he leave her any cash?"

Talbot shrugged and scratched his square chin. When he got out he was going to grow a beard, because he didn't want McCoy to recognize him right off. He had lots of time to plan and plot how he would stalk him, watch him, learn about his habits. He wanted to learn what McCoy liked or loved. And then he planned to take it all away from him before he pulled the trigger and blew off the Injun's head.

A feeling of satisfaction rolled through Billy Jo. Just thinking about killing the last of the McCoy family gave him pleasure. It would be a just revenge for McCoy killing his father, who had suffered a massive heart attack midway through Billy Jo's murder trial. If McCoy and the Trayherns hadn't brought in investigators, who'd found his fingerprints on some window glass the police had overlooked, he'd have never been caught. And now McCoy was going to pay. Pay big time. Flexing his fist, Billy Jo smiled at Harve.

"Yeah, my ma may have a stash," he told him. "I keep needlin' her about it. I ask her to come visit, but she says she can't. Living back in Philipsburg and all, she don't wanna travel out here to see me." Billy Jo knew his mother had come down with chronic fatigue syndrome shortly after she'd lost her husband to that heart attack. Lena was in her fifties now, and although she could drive, run her daily errands, she was pretty much housebound, and dependent upon the state of Montana. Meals on Wheels volunteers often brought her dinners, which she was grateful for. She used to love hiking in the mountains, but lately, her physical strength was limited. Most of her energy was devoted to tending a small vegetable garden at the back of her home, and some flowers in front.

Talbot could forgive his mother, considering her circumstances. But they only fueled his hatred for Sky McCoy, the cause of all his family's suffering.

"How big a stash?" Harve demanded. "Maybe I could persuade her to hire an investigator."

"Yeah . . . that might work. I know you have a drywall business in Lewiston, Idaho. Do you get any vacation?"

"I do. But my missus and two kids have to go with me. Why?"

"Take them to the local sapphire mine near Philipsburg — that's a good vacation spot. And then sneak off and see my mother.

Persuade her to pay for a P.I. I know she's got a chunk of money somewhere. She don't want to admit it, 'cause the state pays for her doctor bills. If they knew she had dough, they'd stop helping her, so she's keepin' her mouth shut."

"Maybe it'd help if you call her?"

"I can, Harve, but I can't mention too much. The jerks here listen to every phone call we make. We'll coordinate a date and time for your visit, and I'll tell her to hand over a couple of hundred bucks to get that investigator." He pointed his finger at his friend. "Don't you *dare* tell her why I want a private eye. If she asks, tell her it's to look for new evidence for a new trial to get me out of here sooner. She'd buy that explanation."

"Don't worry," Harve promised fervently, "I won't tell her the truth."

With a smile, Talbot sat up and moved his thick shoulders. He worked out in the weight room every day, and his six-foot-five-inch frame was solid muscle. He wanted to be in damn good shape when it came time to hunt down McCoy. Billy Jo knew his enemy wouldn't go down easy. No, the bastard would fight back just as he had as a kid.

Instinct told Talbot that he was probably

stupid enough to live in the same area where he'd been born. And that suited Billy Jo just fine.

Sky tried to ignore his worrisome thoughts. Since her first visit, Kelly had not returned.

The morning was young, with pinkish clouds in the sky as he scooped out the scat from the ten mews his raptors occupied — part of his morning routine. Using a dustpan and small rake, he squatted in Luna's mew. She looked wise and owlish on her sturdy perch in the corner of her large, airy home.

"Do you miss her, Luna?" Sky asked the European raptor as he scooped up her castings. When they ate their prey, owls swallowed everything — fur, bones and all. Whatever wasn't digested was vomited back up in a thumb-size grayish pellet. Sky studied Luna's latest casting, to make sure it looked natural and normal. It did. As he dropped the dried pellet into his dustpan, he heard Luna purring.

Sky smiled and acknowledged the truth. "I miss Kelly. I shouldn't, but I do. It's been two weeks. Maybe your flight antics scared her. What do you think?" He gazed up into Luna's huge orange eyes.

The owl ruffled her soft, tawny feathers

and continued to purr.

"Yeah, that's what I think, too. But she looked pretty happy with you on her gauntlet. You were a very good girl and didn't go flapping around and scaring her to death." Sky straightened and went over to put fresh water in Luna's steel bowl. "I've got a helluva lot of mixed feelings about Kelly. I never thought she'd be a part of my life again. And now she is. Sort of . . ."

The owl began rumbling deep in her throat, an owlet's way of begging for food. Sky had just fed her, so he knew she wasn't hungry. "I wonder if there is such a thing as a piggy owl?" he teased, and left the cage. After making sure the door was locked, he dropped the pellets into a lined garbage can.

At 7:00 a.m., the day was already turning warm. The sky was a porcelain blue above the pointed tips of the Douglas firs surrounding the mews. Sky was always afraid of forest fires. He'd built the wire enclosures over time, as money became available. Each one cost around a thousand dollars, made of lightweight steel with a wooden door frame. Each raptor had to have its own cage. They didn't do well living together, being highly territorial.

As he sauntered down the concrete walk, Sky's thoughts returned to Kelly Trayhern.

Should he go visit her? Find out for sure she wasn't coming back? He wanted to find out if his debt to the family was paid off. The core issue was Kelly's depression, and while he tried to resist his attraction, he cared about her healing.

Gazing at the fir trees, he made a decision. This afternoon, he would drop by the Trayhern place unannounced. Maybe he'd find out the reason for Kelly's disappearance. And then talk to Laura, to make sure he was off the hook, though his conscience was chewing at him over his attitude.

As he entered the cabin, Sky took off his cowboy hat and hung it on its wooden peg. His heart pounded briefly as he reviewed his decision. Those erratic beats had happened the first time he saw Kelly a few weeks ago, and again when she'd left his cabin.

Absently rubbing his chest, Sky sauntered into the sunny kitchen to pour himself another cup of coffee. Sipping it, he leaned against the counter and frowned. His life would be in danger once Talbot was released from jail, so he couldn't cultivate any long-term relationship with Kelly. He had to take the threat seriously. If his old enemy ever found him, it would be a fight to the death, only one survivor. And Sky knew that eventually Talbot would locate him.

Glancing toward the bedroom, Sky thought of the pistol in the drawer of his bed stand. He was licensed to carry it, but didn't like the thought of even having it in his home. It was there because of Talbot. Sky struggled to understand all the karma between him and the bully from his childhood. And how Talbot, even though in prison, still cast a threatening shadow over his life. In a way, Sky felt imprisoned by the man. Because of him, he'd never had a normal life.

Sighing, he took his coffee over to the table and sat down. Though he tried to focus on the work he wanted to accomplish that morning, he couldn't stop thinking about Kelly. How was she? Something drove him to find out.

Stupid or not, Sky would drop by to see her after he'd completed his errands in Philipsburg.

With a triumphant cry, Kelly slowed the stationary bike she'd been pedaling in the family's gym. Grabbing a white towel, she wiped the perspiration from her face, neck and arms.

Sunshine poured through the floor-to-ceiling windows, making the red-gold cedar floor gleam. The spacious room held a treadmill, a complete Nautilus workout center and the cycle. At her request, her father had had the left pedal modified so that she could put her slipper-clad foot into a larger stirrup. The doctors said cycling was a great way to recreate lost muscle mass, and Kelly was determined to get into better shape.

She removed her iPod earbuds and let them dangle down her gray T-shirt, darkened now with splotches of sweat. Wiping her flushed features once again, she thought she heard the doorbell ring, but wasn't sure. She finished up her workout by wiping off the handlebars.

"Kelly?"

Turning on the seat of the bike, she couldn't contain her surprise. "Sky!" Her heart thudded in reaction to seeing him. He stood, hat in hand, dressed in a light blue shirt, jeans and his cowboy boots. She grinned and waved him into the large, spacious gym. "Good to see you. I haven't called because I was going to surprise you."

Shooting her a guarded glance, Sky walked across the polished cedar floor. "I guess I don't like hearing my phone ring. There's something peaceful about hearing the wind in the pines and the birds calling. Ringing telephones jangle my nerves." In reality, he chose to have an unlisted phone number so Talbot couldn't trace him. But Kelly would never know that. As he drew closer, he could see her face was flushed, her once muddy-green eyes now lighter-looking, and clearer.

"You always were close to Mother Nature." Wiping her neck again, Kelly reached down and grabbed a bottle of water from beside the exercise bike. "I'm sorry I couldn't divulge my plans to you." She took a quick swig as she saw surprise flare in his blue eyes. How handsome Sky was. Kelly found herself looking at him again through a woman's eyes. Though his hair was cut military short, a few black strands drifted across his deeply tanned forehead. She liked his broad shoulders. She liked everything she saw. Maybe too much.

"What plans? The surprise you mentioned?" Sky gripped the brim of his cowboy hat and swung it casually.

"Well," Kelly murmured, "that day I was up at your place, I realized just how far I'd sunk. I was so weak. I fell, and if you hadn't caught me, I'm sure I would have reinjured my leg here." She patted the cast gently. "To tell you the truth, I was mortified with embarrassment, Sky. You don't need a cripple up there helping you."

He opened his mouth to speak, then closed it.

Holding up her hand, Kelly said, "And it made me realize how far I'd gone. When I got home, I talked to my mom about working with my physical therapist and getting serious about rehabilitating this leg of mine. And I've been on a grueling routine, doing just that." She gently removed her left foot from the stirrup of the bike. Placing her feet on the floor, she set the towel and water bottle aside. "Watch this . . ." She gripped the handlebars and, putting all her weight on her right leg, stood up. "And this . . ."

Sky watched Kelly lift her left leg, which didn't bend well due to the removable cast. She slowly turned and held on to one of the handlebars. "No more dizziness. I had a lot of it before. My P.T. told me that not doing any activity before was the reason for my instability." Kelly grinned. "See any crutches?"

Sky noticed them leaning against the wall near the door. "Over there." And then he said, with surprise in his tone, "You *walked* to this cycle?"

Kelly could feel his amazement and pride in her. Joy rushed through her and settled into her skipping heart. "Yes. Every day, I work out on the bars over there." She pointed to the twenty-foot-long wooden rails spaced about one and a half feet apart. "I can't put a constant amount of weight on my left leg, but I can put some. Watch this."

Sky stepped aside as Kelly hobbled slowly but surely toward the wall, where her crutches rested. He saw the pain in her face, at the tight corners of her mouth as she put weight on her injured leg. Still, she persevered. And he saw in her eyes the dogged determination to reach her goal.

Kelly looked ravishing in the skintight gray sweatpants and body-hugging T-shirt. And Sky ached for her, because she was still so gaunt.

"Success is taking baby steps," she told him, placing the crutches beneath her arms. Turning, she looked into his eyes. How she wished he would smile. That touched her as nothing else ever had. Sky's smile always reminded her of the sun coming out after a dark, rainy day. Kelly felt hungry to see it, but his expression remained somber, his frown in place.

"The reason I'm doing this," Kelly confided, a little out of breath as she hobbled back to him, "is that I wanted to return to help you, but not be someone else you had to care for. I wanted to walk that distance from your cabin to the training area with you. I didn't want you worrying I might get vertigo and fall."

His heart sank. So the debt still had to be paid. What the hell was he going to do?

Just looking into Kelly's warm green eyes, he found words flying out of his mouth yet again. "I wouldn't have minded helping you," Sky told her gruffly. He moved the cowboy hat between his fingers, feeling awkward. "You seem better, Kelly. There's more life in your eyes. But why aren't you eating better? You look like one of the birds I rescued, a red-tailed hawk. He was a youngster, less than a year old. About eighty percent of all raptors die of starvation in their first year because they don't learn the tricks of how to hunt. When I got this red-tail, you could feel the bones protruding beneath his feathers. He was so close to dying. If the woman who rescued him didn't see him drop off the telephone line to the ground below, and stop, he'd be dead. Luckily, she cast the hawk, which means she wrapped him in a small blanket that keeps raptors calm and motionless, so they can't hurt themselves. And she knew where to take him, which was the Fish and Game Department here in Philipsburg. They brought the hawk up to me, for care and feeding."

"Did you save it?" Kelly asked, enthralled with his story.

"I did. And in four months, he was back to full weight. I kept him for another year, teaching him how to hunt. He still hangs around the cabin. I'll see him every now and again. A real success story."

"It sure is. Eighty percent of the babies born in a year die?"

"Nature is ruthless in culling out weaklings," he answered. "And that's one reason raptor rehabbers are so important. If we lose hawks and owls, rodent and rabbit populations explode. Raptors keep things in check. If you've ever had mice inside your house, you probably don't have a hawk or falcon around. We often take a rehabilitated raptor to an area with lots of rodents, to help keep the numbers down."

"You do so much valuable work," Kelly said, then watched as Sky's cheeks turned a dull red. As a child he'd been very shy. She knew better than to call attention to his blush. "And as for your question, I am eating more. My parents are thrilled that I'm cleaning up my plate. My physical therapist said I can't build muscle back without a lot of food, especially protein, so I'm forcing myself to eat, whether I feel like it or not."

Sky frowned. "You still don't have an appetite?"

"No, I don't." Kelly hobbled over to a bench nearby and sat on it. She leaned down and took off her tennis shoe, then the soft slipper from her left foot, letting her sock-clad feet air.

He sat at the other end, his elbows on his thighs. "Why do you think that is?"

Kelly shrugged. "I've had my whole life, my career, shattered, as well as my leg, Sky. I'm scared. All I knew how to do was fly. I don't have any other skills." Kelly held up her hands. "I can't stay here in my parents' home, expecting them to keep me forever. I have to find a way to earn money, and I don't know how I can do that just yet. I sure don't want to be on welfare."

"I think it's too soon in your healing to be thinking of those things," he counseled her quietly, looking down at his hat. "Sometimes, Kelly, you just have to sit back, in blind faith, knowing that the Great Spirit will open up a door or opportunity when it's right."

"How do you mean?"

"Well," he said, straightening his spine, "after Billy Jo Talbot murdered my family, I was lost. I was unsure what to do with my life, didn't have a clue where to go."

"Anyone would feel like that," Kelly murmured sympathetically. She recalled that terrible day when his parents had been burned alive in their home. The fire had been set in the early morning hours, while they were asleep. Kelly had been eighteen, a recent graduate from high school and on her way to the U.S. Naval Academy for four years, to become a Marine Corps pilot. "And I'm sorry I couldn't be there for you, Sky." She reached out and gripped his hand, which rested on his thigh. "Mom kept me informed about the investigation and trial. I tried to stay in touch, writing letters to you, too."

"I know you did," he said, his hand burning like fire from her gesture. Just as quickly, she released his hand, much to his relief. "I wasn't any good at writing."

Kelly's mouth quirked. "I know that."

Tucking his lower lip between his teeth, Sky felt his stomach clench. "You had your life to live, and I understood. So it's okay. I didn't expect you to stay in touch." He looked up to gauge her expression.

"I've always felt guilty about how we lost touch. Thanks for letting me off the hook." Kelly glanced at her watch, hoping she could entice him to stay a little longer. "Have lunch with me, Sky. It will be just you and me in the house. Mom's out for the afternoon, visiting some people up at the Anaconda veterans' hospital. I've got ingredients for tuna fish sandwiches, and some fresh lemonade made. How about it? You and me. Like old times."

Rising, Sky knew he should leave, but he'd painted himself into a corner he hadn't seen coming. Being around Kelly again was infectious. It made him feel giddy. Scared as hell. "Well . . ."

Reaching out, Kelly gripped his hand, her voice pleading. "Please? For me, Sky? You're a bright spot in my very dark world. Can I guilt you enough to stay? You can tell me why you disappeared like you did."

CHAPTER SEVEN

"What happened to you after the second trial was over?" Kelly asked Sky as she sat down in the breakfast nook. The big bay windows were on the north side of the large two-story home. Through the glass Kelly could see the tall Douglas firs beyond the rustic rail fence surrounding the yard. Inside the fence, colorful and bright columbines, indigenous to the mountains, waved their frilly heads in the breeze.

Sky busied himself at the counter fixing the tuna sandwiches. He'd insisted that Kelly sit down and rest after her workout. It would be hell to run around on a pair of crutches, trying to get things out of the fridge, to the counter, and then stand on one foot to make sandwiches.

His nerves clenched in reaction to her casually asked question. With his back to her, he stated, "I needed to get away. To grieve, I guess." That wasn't a lie. He quickly cobbled the sandwiches together, adding tuna, slices of dill pickle, lettuce and tomatoes. He grabbed an open bag of corn chips nearby and arranged a handful on each brightly colored plate.

Kelly watched as Sky turned around, plates of sandwiches in hand. She noticed the turmoil in his eyes. He refused to look directly at her most of the time. She knew part of that was his upbringing in the Navajo world. She'd learned a long time ago that Navajo people considered it rude to look directly into someone's face.

"Thanks," she exclaimed. "Looks great. A new spin on tuna sandwiches. Mom never puts lettuce or tomato in them." Their fingers brushed as she took her plate.

"I guess I got carried away," he said. A big part of him wanted to run away from Kelly. She was too warm, too friendly. Too . . . *tempting* was the word that came to mind. Sky stopped in his tracks, stunned by the fact that more than a decade had passed and yet their old camaraderie had returned. How could that be? Stymied, he set the plates down, went to the fridge and got each of them a can of V8 juice. Opening them, he set one before Kelly, along with a glass.

"My mom used to make them like that," he told her, sitting down opposite her. The nook was small and cozy. Sky tried not to appreciate the natural intimacy between them. "In fact, she used to throw a square of cheese on it, too, but that might be a bit much." He bit into his sandwich and began to chew. Sky had lost his appetite because of the nature of Kelly's questions, but forced himself to eat.

"I like it," Kelly said between bites. She actually felt like eating, for the first time since the helicopter crash. She wondered if Sky's confident, strong presence had inspired this change. For now, she would just enjoy. "I'm sure that trial was exhausting for you. I wanted to be there so badly to support you, but I was at the Naval Academy. As kids, remember how we used to hug each other? Cry on one another's shoulder when things got bad?"

Sky nodded and picked disinterestedly at the corn chips on his plate. "Yeah, I remember." He'd forgotten those times until she mentioned them. "It was lonely in that courtroom. And I was angry throughout the trial. Every time I saw Talbot, all I wanted to do was kill him, for killing my parents." His mouth flattened. "Your mom and dad were strong and caring. I had no place to live, and they let me stay here, in Jason's old bedroom. That year was hell. Your mom and dad became like parents to me."

He didn't mention his present arrangement with the Trayherns. Sky was still angry about it, although he understood Laura's desperate request. But he was in disarray over Kelly's unexpected reentry into his tidy, well-ordered life.

"They care for you, Sky. Very much. And I'm glad my mom and dad could offer you a home. All your relatives are in Arizona, as I recall. Is that where you went after they sentenced Talbot?"

"It is. My mother's parents were devastated by the whole thing. I went out to the Navajo reservation to try to screw my head on straight after the trial. I was filled with so much hatred and rage toward Talbot. My grandmother, who was in her eighties, really helped me get more in balance with that aspect of myself. Later, when I was twenty-one, I moved back here."

"You were only nineteen or so at the time," Kelly said sympathetically. Shaking her head, she muttered, "Bullies. They should be seriously reprimanded by the school. It's so sad that it took the awful shooting at Columbine and other school incidents to shed light on disturbed kids." She cut him a glance. "Back in our day, school officials often turned their heads and

131

ignored the bullies."

Finishing his sandwich, Sky picked up the paper napkin and wiped his mouth. "Yeah. Too little, too late. I keep asking myself what would have happened if the school officials had gotten involved. My parents complained to my teacher, as well as the principal, many times over. They told them how Talbot stalked me and beat me up, out of sight of staff, but they turned a blind eye. Sometimes I think school officials were prejudiced against Indians, just like Talbot and his gang."

Hearing the sadness in his voice, Kelly reached over and patted his shoulder. "I know. My parents were very upset." She grinned slightly. "Of course, that day in the school yard when Talbot and his gang were beating you up, and I saw it, all hell broke loose. I went screaming into the fray, using the judo I'd learned."

"And you didn't know at the time that Talbot had stabbed me with his knife." Sky held up his right hand to show her the scar between his thumb and index finger. "You didn't know he had a weapon. I was flat on the ground, under the pileup, with a broken nose and bleeding hand. I couldn't warn you to be careful."

Kelly stared at the white, thick scar. "I

just remember kicking butt, screaming and taking names. When I got all three of them off you, and saw how bloody you were, I was shocked. I'm so glad I turned around and noticed Billy Jo with the knife in his hand."

"Yeah," Sky said, admiration in his tone as he held her gaze. "You whirled around, lifted your foot and swung your leg, striking his hand and sending the knife flying. Good thing a teacher came around the corner and saw it all happen. She was a prime witness at Talbot's juvenile court hearing. It helped put him in detention until he was eighteen."

Having finished her sandwich, Kelly wiped her mouth with her napkin, then drank the V8 juice with relish. "I've always wondered if I'd have been so bold that day if I'd known Talbot had that knife."

"I know you would have." Sky folded his hands around his drink. "We were close, Kelly. We always looked out for one another. Always stood against Talbot and his gang, our backs together. You could almost sense when Billy Jo was stalking me. And usually, you were there to make the difference." His mouth curved faintly as he stared down at his juice can. "I wasn't very strong or confident back then."

"How could you be? Talbot had been picking on you since the first grade. By sixth grade he got to thinking you were his personal punching bag. And you *did* fight back, Sky. You didn't just fall to the ground and wave a white flag."

"I know. My parents didn't believe in fighting back. They believed in peace and harmony."

"I can respect their belief system," Kelly muttered, "but it left you prey to Talbot."

"Well," Sky sighed, "one good thing came out of all of that — my parents sought out the principal and teachers about those attacks. Their visits to the office were all part of a log that was presented in court, and helped put Talbot away."

"And then he got out and went after your parents. That was so tragic," Kelly said, shaking her head. "I was shocked by it. Devastated. I didn't think Talbot would extract revenge like that."

"I'm sure my folks didn't, either." Sipping the last of the vegetable juice, he set the can aside and gazed into Kelly's face. The way her red hair dipped across her smooth brow, the clear green of her eyes, made him ache.

When his eyes dropped to her lips, he noticed a crumb at one corner. Without thinking, he cupped her chin with his hand and wiped it away.

"Just a crumb," he told her. Touching Kelly like this made him feel euphoric, like an eagle soaring high. Sky wasn't prepared for the shocked expression that flooded her face. Instantly, he dropped his hand, embarrassed by his unthinking actions. "Sorry," he muttered, avoiding her huge green eyes. "I guess . . . well, childhood . . ."

It was a lame excuse but true. They would often sit together and eat their lunches. If a crumb dropped on his lap or stuck to his mouth, Kelly would wipe it away with her napkin and then giggle. And he'd do the same for her. At that age, Sky hadn't analyzed their innocent, joyous gestures. Once more, he wasn't thinking, just blindly reacting to her.

A prickle of pleasure danced along Kelly's never endings. Sky's move was so unexpected, and she reacted automatically, feeling a wave of desire stealing through her, like an incoming tide. How long had it been since she'd felt so aroused, experienced such desire? As she studied Sky, she noticed his flushed complexion. He nervously got up, took the empty plates to the counter and tossed the wadded-up napkins into the trash can beneath the sink. While he walked soundlessly around the kitchen, she realized the pleasurable sensation was still with her, that her body was still eager for Sky's grazing touch. Blinking, she looked away and tried to dispel her confusion. Having Sky touch her had felt so right, so wonderful. How could that be? And now, of all times?

"Hey," she called, "don't worry about what happened, Sky. We have a strong connection between us from childhood. Don't be upset about it, because I'm not." She wondered what he would say if she told him just the opposite. That she craved the contact again.

Rinsing off the plates and putting them in the dishwasher, Sky didn't dare look at Kelly. He could hear the unsteadiness in her husky voice, the note of bewilderment. Well, he was just as confused. Admitting that he'd consciously wanted to feel her flesh beneath his fingertips, he told himself he'd have to watch himself around her. "We used to be so close," he muttered, folding the washcloth on the rim of the sink.

He forced himself to look her in the eye and saw that her cheeks were flushed. Had his unthinking touch been upsetting to Kelly? Sky gulped inwardly over the realization that he saw something else there. Something familiar. When they were racing around on the playground, pretending they were eagles flying, Kelly often had that same look in her dazzling green eyes: the gold color of pure joy. Had she wanted his touch as much as he'd wanted to touch her? Now it was his turn to be stunned.

"Listen," he said hurriedly, rubbing his hands together, "I should go. I need to get over to the grocery store and post office."

"Sure." Kelly heard the sudden tension in his voice. It was obvious Sky was ashamed of their unintentional intimacy, and she searched frantically for some way to ease his discomfort. "Hey, before you leave . . ."

Sky halted in the doorway and turned on his boot heel. "Yes?" All he wanted to do was run away. Like he always had when things got bad at school. As a little boy, he'd learned to run from the bullies. After Talbot had set the fire that killed his parents, he'd learned to hide. Of course, as he matured, all that had changed. His fear had turned to raw anger toward Talbot. Sky was now a hunter waiting for his quarry to appear.

The same couldn't be said for his emotions. His carnal need of Kelly had erupted out of nowhere. And the urge to flee had come back with a vengeance. More than anything, Sky had to protect her. Talbot couldn't go after her or her family. It was better that Kelly didn't know about Billy Jo's threats and what he planned after his release. She had enough on her plate.

"I was thinking, Sky," Kelly said in a breathless tone, "that if it's all right with you, maybe I could stay at your cabin. It would be temporary, of course, until I can drive again. The doctor says it will be another three months before my leg is up to that kind of activity. But if I could stay up there, I could help you. I really like the raptors. And you may not realize it, but since you came back into my life I've been wanting to live again."

Taking a deep breath, Kelly rushed on. "My parents would pay you to put me up. I could rent the second bedroom from you." She held up her hands. "At least these and my brain work well. I know I can assist you in many ways, small as well as important ones. And to tell you the truth, I have to get out of here. My mom and dad, bless them, mean well, but I feel suffocated being with them every day. They're so worried about my depression, about me . . ." Her voice trailed off.

Looking down at the table, Kelly felt her heart pumping as if she'd run a marathon. Once she mustered her courage, she glanced up at Sky, whose expression was filled with surprise. "I know this is asking a lot of you, Sky. I've been wanting to come clean, to tell you that you give me hope. That's a lot to put on your shoulders. And if you don't want me underfoot for three months, I can understand that. I might be a third wheel. You may have a girlfriend . . ."

Swallowing, Sky opened his mouth and then shut it. In his dreams the other night he'd been welcoming her into his cabin. He'd awakened the next morning snorting over that impossibility. Yet here she was, asking for that very thing. Rubbing his chin, he glanced down at his scarred, well-worn boots. "I don't have a relationship at the moment," he told her gruffly.

"Oh . . . I see. Okay . . ." Why was she so ecstatic that Sky was single and available?

Hearing the desperation in her tone, Sky couldn't tell her no. He reminded himself of all he owed her. Had her mother put her up to this? Something in his gut said no, that this was Kelly speaking.

She had helped him so much when he was a shy schoolboy, a beleaguered child. She'd stopped him from bleeding to death on that playground after Talbot stabbed him. How could Sky turn her down now? After three months, she would be gone. And Talbot wouldn't be out of jail until next June. What would it hurt? Sky asked himself.

Lifting his head, he saw the raw pleading

in Kelly's eyes.

"I imagine living here with your mom and dad can make you feel pretty closed in," he said, the corners of his mouth quirking.

"It does, believe me. I'll be a good roommate. You'll see."

"You can help me with the rehabilitation of my raptors," Sky rasped. "As long as it's only three months. After that, I have to get on with my life. I have things I need to do." He hated to say it, but he forced out the words. "Then it would be best that you either move back here or maybe live in one of those condos your father has in town." Six months before Talbot's release, Sky had a number of projects to put into place, as he waited for the bastard to come home to Philipsburg. And he didn't want anyone around at that time. This was the shoot-out at the O.K. Corral, as far as Sky was concerned, and he sure as hell didn't want anyone in the line of fire. Especially Kelly.

"Sure, that would be fine. I promise, I won't be a problem, Sky."

He looked around. "You'll need your exercise cycle up there, to keep up with your workouts. I can load that in my truck this weekend. That will give you the rest of the week to prepare your parents, and pack. I'll come down Saturday afternoon and we'll move you up into the mountains."

Relief surged through Kelly. "That's great, Sky! Thank you . . . thank you so much! You have no idea how this will help me."

He saw gold flecks dappling her green eyes, and drew in a deep breath. "You saved my life once, Kelly. If I can do this for you in return, it's not a problem. Then we'll be even. I want you to get better. I know your parents are worried sick over your depression. They feel helpless, and I understand their worry." Sky wondered if Kelly knew that her mother had forced the duty issue with him. Was this why she was asking to move in with him? His stomach sank with dismay at the sudden situation he'd been tricked into. Where did duty end?

"I think they'll be happy with my decision," Kelly stated, with a catch in her voice. Her eyes blurred with unshed tears. "I don't know how to repay you, but I'll try."

He saw her eyes glistening with moisture, and held up his hand. Tears were his downfall. "Sometimes duty has to be paid, Kelly. I'm willing to do my part." Sky had to get out of here or he was going to take swift strides across the kitchen, gather her up in his arms and hold her. Simply hold her, and give her the sense of protection she so badly needed right now. Sky could see the vulnerability in her face and hear it in her husky voice. Even worse, he realized just how fragile she was emotionally. Every shred of him wanted to fiercely protect her. Something told him Kelly's request was spontaneous, not her mother's idea at all.

Kelly shakily brushed strands of hair away from her brow. "Duty it is. Payback, I suppose. I helped you, and now you can help me. That's a good way to look at this. Thanks for letting me rent a room for three months. I think being around your birds and having my own space will help me a lot."

"I'll see you Saturday at 1:00 p.m. Unless something changes," Sky promised her darkly. Unable to stand the grateful look on her face, to see her lower lip trembling with emotion or the tears glimmering in her forest-green eyes, Sky forced himself out of the kitchen and out of the house.

What the hell had he just done? As he settled his cowboy hat on his head, walked down the path to the gate and then to his beat-up old Ford truck, he found his world spinning. His hand shook as he slipped the key into the ignition. His heart thundered in his chest, and not from fear.

He backed out of the parking space and drove toward town in the valley below. Rubbing his brow, Sky muttered, "You stupid fool! Why are you letting her come home with you?"

And yet he knew he couldn't say no to Kelly's request. He owed her too much, and his heart ached at her fragile state. Her depression was so deep and pervasive that she wouldn't eat, or engage in life, Sky knew.

Asking to come stay with him meant she *wanted* to dig herself out of that dark, bottomless pit, with his help. With the help of the raptors.

Well, he'd gone to her with Bella, who had worked her magic on Kelly, all right.

Sky just hadn't figured the magic would include him and his cabin — or Kelly staying under his roof. What was he going to do? With a muffled groan, he drove down the dirt road. Somehow, he had to ignore Kelly. Keep his hands off her. Stay at a distance. But how?

CHAPTER EIGHT

"Hey, sis," Jason Trayhern called from the entrance to Sky's cabin, "we did it. We're done." He grinned and held up his hands.

"It was fun sitting here on the couch watching you two ripped hunks move my stuff in," Kelly kidded her oldest brother. Mac, her sister Kathy's husband, appeared at Jason's shoulder. He was smiling, too. Kathy and he had flown in two days ago for a month's leave from their drug interdiction assignment in Peru. Both were Marine Corps Blackhawk helicopter pilots.

Kelly pushed aside her sadness at the thought that she'd never fly again. "Thanks, Mac. You didn't know you'd have to work like a dog on your vacation, did you?"

He laughed shortly. "No problem, Kelly. I'm glad to be active. Flying over the jungles of Peru gets me a lot of butt time, but no real exercise."

Kelly understood that only too well.

She sensed more than heard Sky coming from the kitchen. Glancing to her right, she saw he carried a huge plate of barbecued chicken. Earlier, he had set up a picnic table in the front yard, beneath the boughs of the huge fir tree there. "Looks like enough meat to feed ten starving men," she teased him.

Sky was so good-looking. Clean-shaven today, with his hair neatly combed, he wore a short-sleeved red shirt and jeans. Her heart thudded with happiness over being in his home. The more she was around him, the more he lifted her mood. That fact amazed her.

"Come and get it," Sky told the men. Jason and Mac stepped aside to let him set the platter of chicken on the table.

"Jason? I know Sky was boiling some corn on the cob," Kelly told him. "Can you retrieve it from the kitchen? He could probably use some help."

"Right, sis." Jason moved through the doorway, and Mac followed him around the couch and into the kitchen.

After finding her crutches, Kelly stood and put a little weight on her broken leg. The only way she would strengthen it was to use it. Pain engulfed her limb, but she ignored it and hobbled toward the door. The screen was propped open, so she had clear access to the table near the sidewalk. The warm summer breeze was filled with the sweet aroma of pine, and she drew the scent deep into her lungs. As she approached the wooden table, she noticed that Sky had thoughtfully placed a chair at the end for her. He seemed to think of everything that would make her life easier. What other man had ever done that except her father?

"Come sit down," Sky urged, as he walked up with a platter of steaming corn. "All we've got to do is get the baked beans and rolls." He set the platter on the table and pulled out the chair for Kelly. It was impossible to ignore the pink flush in her cheeks, the light in her eyes. *Three months.* He had three months of heaven and hell with her under his roof. To be honest, she was more heaven, and he couldn't deny his own excitement when she was near him. His hell was going to be keeping her at arm's length, treating her as a duty to be fulfilled, not as a dear friend from his distant past.

Sky tried to tell himself this arrangement would work out. He didn't need to worry about Talbot sneaking up on him, with murder on his mind. The prison officials would notify Sky when Talbot was about to be released. Then the nightmare would escalate, until he could confront the killer once and for all.

For now, he didn't have to focus on that aspect of his life. He had Kelly to look forward to, and her presence felt like sweet light pushing away his dark future.

"Thanks, Sky." Kelly sat down and leaned her crutches against the edge of the table. "Are the guys getting the baked beans for you?"

"Yes, they are." He reached out and patted her shoulder. "I'll be right back . . ." As he lifted his hand, Sky chastised himself for his spontaneous gesture. What was he doing? There was no such thing as a casual touch with Kelly. He wasn't thinking, and that was dangerous. Lips thinning, he headed back into the cabin. His fingers tingled from the contact, and he realized that old childhood actions and reactions were surfacing. How many times had he and Kelly touched one another? Gripped hands in play?

Before his thoughts could snowball, Sky saw the two men coming with the rest of the meal.

"Only thing left is the lemonade," Mac called as they passed him in the living room.

"I'll get it," Sky told them. The men of the Trayhern family were hard workers, not shirkers. Sky had more or less grown up with Jason, though Kelly's brother was much older than them. A former U.S. Army helicopter pilot, Jason had been wounded by a grenade that had exploded near his tent one night, and had suffered traumatic brain injury. If not for Annie, who was now his wife, he might not have recovered as well as he had. Sky knew their story of tribulation, change and transformation. Jason's old personality had returned over the years. He still couldn't smell anything, and had occasional bouts of dizziness, but that was all. Sky was glad Laura and Morgan's oldest son had not only survived, but thrived, despite severe adversity. It was due to the love of his wife, and their close-knit family, Sky knew.

How he missed his own family! A dull ache centered in his chest as he opened the fridge and drew out two half-gallon containers of lemonade. After insisting on helping, Kelly had squeezed countless lemons earlier that morning. Her determination warmed his heart. She was proving to be a fighter again, which made him admire her all the more. He didn't know what to do with his chaotic feelings for her. They ranged from anger to responsibility to something else he couldn't name.

After closing the fridge with the toe of his

boot, he took the containers to the table, where Mac, Jason and Kelly were laughing and chatting. Sky ached to feel that they were his family, too. If only for a moment.

Setting the lemonade on the rough, weathered redwood table, Sky filled four plastic glasses with ice cubes from a nearby bowl, then poured the lemonade and distributed them. As he sat down near Kelly, he was surprised to see she had filled his plate with food.

"Thanks," he murmured, gesturing to it. "That was nice."

"You take care of me. Why shouldn't I try to take care of you?" she asked, lifting her lemonade in a toast.

Jason smiled. "Yeah, you two were tighter than fleas as kids. Looks like some things don't change, and that's kind of reassuring."

Sky lifted his glass and gently touched Kelly's. He looked across at Jason, who was eagerly spooning up the bacon and baked beans. "I'm glad some things don't change," he stated in a strangled voice.

"I'm the odd person out here," Mac confided, sitting on Sky's side of the table. "I learn about family every time I come to Philipsburg." He gave Sky an admiring look. "Family counts, and so do good friends. That's something I've found over the years.

Nothing else really matters."

The ache in Sky's chest deepened. "I agree," he said quietly, picking up a drumstick slathered with barbecue sauce. He figured that Mac didn't know his sordid story. And he wasn't going to broach it with him. Today, he just wanted to deal with Kelly's move to the cabin — and into his life.

Jason seemed to sense the sudden discomfort. "Sis, what are you going to do to earn your keep around here? Mom was saying you're going to help Sky with the raptors?"

Relieved that the conversation had turned to practicalities, Kelly picked at her potato salad. "I hope to. Right now, I can't do much, but maybe after I do the rehab exercises, I'll be able to."

"Your birds out back are incredibly beautiful," Jason said to Sky. "Annie and I never realized your cabin was just ten miles up the road from our place. About the only vehicles we see going up and down are timber trucks. And maybe some lost tourists looking for a trout stream." He smiled.

"I like to keep a low profile," Sky answered gruffly. He glanced up at the raptors' mews. "My birds are my life," he added. "They make me feel free. They're very healing, if you allow them to enter your world."

"How did you get into this line of work?" Mac asked, wiping his mouth with a yellow paper napkin.

"When I was twenty, I came back to Philipsburg and met Frank Edwards. He was not only a raptor rehabilitator, but a falconer of international repute. He bred gyrfalcons and sold them all over the world. I was looking for work and he needed help. I'd never seen a hawk or an eagle close up, but he took me under his wing, so to speak, and taught me. Here in Montana you have to work with a licensed rehabilitator for a year, then take a written test from the Fish and Game Department, in order to get your papers. I stayed with Frank for four years, until he died of lung cancer." Sky motioned to the cabin. "I got the shock of my life after he passed away. In his will, he left me this cabin, the land and all his birds."

Mac raised his dark eyebrows. "That was quite a gift. Did you suspect he was going to do that?"

Shaking his head, Sky said, "Didn't have a clue. But Frank had no family left. And I sort of became the son he'd lost a long time ago in an auto accident. I felt like he was a foster father to me. And we had a good working relationship."

"That's lovely," Kelly whispered, touched.

She reached over and squeezed Sky's bare forearm, and felt his muscles tense beneath her fingertips. They were solid and lean, like the rest of him. "You deserved that kind of luck, Sky. And I know you must have earned it, the hard way — by working hard, being responsible and reliable."

Jason finished off a chicken breast and reached for the platter in the center of the table. "Those three things will stand you in good stead your entire life," he agreed. Scanning the meat available, he chose a thigh. "Do you breed hawks?"

"No," Sky replied. "I was more interested in rescuing injured and sick raptors from the wild. I sold off Frank's gyrfalcon stock to someone who really wanted those breeding lines."

"Do you take care of eagles?" Mac asked, spooning more baked beans onto his plate. "I didn't see any back there in the mews."

"Eagles require a special state license," Sky told them. "They have a different personality, and I preferred working with hawks, owls and falcons instead. Frank had a golden eagle and a bald eagle. After he died, the state came in and transferred them to another rehabilitator, near Billings, who had the right type of license."

"Do you do shows?" Jason inquired. "You

know, where you put your raptors through their paces and win money or prizes?"

"There's a national and international falconers circuit, but I don't go. I'm not interested in that part of the business," Sky said. It was part lie and part truth. If he went to such competitions and events, his name would get out there, and he didn't want Talbot to track him down. Despite this, he knew the place and time would come for him to look in the bastard's eyes before he defended himself.

"Maybe it's your Navajo blood coming into play," Jason said. "My wife, Annie, is Native American, and she isn't much for showing off. She's real quiet, almost self-effacing, and doesn't get on the radar very much."

Sky let them think what they would. Most people didn't know about Talbot's threat, and it was very possible that Morgan and Laura's family didn't know the details. Truth was, Sky wanted to compete with his raptors. He had wonderful hawks and falcons, but Talbot's threat stopped him from fulfilling that desire. After that confrontation occurred, and if he survived it, he hoped to enter some competitions.

"Come to think of it," Jason added, "do you give educational seminars with your birds? You know, go into schools and give talks? I bet children would love it if you brought your raptors along. What a great way to teach them they shouldn't hunt these magnificent creatures."

Kelly saw the darkness in Sky's eyes and the tension in his very male mouth. "I think Sky is shy, so probably doesn't find it easy to get up in front of a group and talk."

"Ah," Jason said. "That's understandable." He gave Sky a searching look. "But I'd sure love to have Annie and the kids come up here some afternoon when you aren't too busy, Sky. I know our children would love to see your birds. They need to know that raptors are a necessary balance in nature, as important as any other creature."

"Sure," Sky said, picking an ear of corn from the bowl, "that would be fine. I'd like to show your family my birds. Best time of day is early afternoon, since I feed the raptors morning and evening. Drop by anytime."

Kelly turned to her brother. "Give us a couple of weeks to settle in here, Jas, and then come on up." She gave Sky a warm look. "He's saddled with me now and will have to cope with my presence twenty-four-seven."

"Gotcha, sis."

Kelly smiled and felt more of her appetite returning. Sky had made all the food the night before. From what she understood, he'd lived by himself for a long time. He had no one to cook for him, so had learned to make his way around a kitchen.

Seeing a hint of turmoil in his blue eyes, she wondered what he was thinking. His hands shook a little and that bothered her. Was he upset? Had all their questions stressed him for some reason? Kelly tried to fathom what it would be like to live alone half of one's life, but couldn't imagine it. She'd always had friends and family. Sky had neither. Did he talk to anyone? She hoped so, since human contact was important. Perhaps later, when things quieted down, she could quiz him about that. Right now, she felt a definite bubble of joy encircling her heart. Coming here was the right thing to do.

"Hey," her brother called, "do you think Mom and Dad are glad to get you out of their house?"

"Probably," Kelly said wryly.

Jason grinned broadly. "Mom wasn't happy. But Dad said you needed to get out on your own, for your own rehabilitation."

"Thanks to Sky, I have an opportunity to

do just that."

Shifting his shoulders, Sky tried to shed the nervousness he felt at her statement. If Kelly knew he was doing this out of a sense of duty, she would be devastated.

Last night, he had dreamed about her — a torrid dream that had him waking up drenched in sweat. Sky found the whole situation with her disconcerting. What the hell was happening to him?

He tried to smile at Kelly, but found his mouth twisting nervously. "I'm sure there will be adjustments and challenges, but we'll weather them like we did when we were kids." He was relieved that she would be gone long before Talbot left the penitentiary.

Talbot's mother, Lena, lived in Philipsburg. Sky kept careful tabs on her, through various means. She had suffered a mild stroke last year, but still lived at home. He always feared meeting up with the older woman, who hated him as much as her son did. Thankfully, he never had.

People at Harley's Feed and Seed had been talking about her one morning when Sky was in, getting some straw. No one cared for the pushy woman, and some whispered that the chronic fatigue and the stroke hadn't slowed her down or changed her abrasiveness. Apparently, Lena Talbot's acidic personality was just as biting as before.

Billy Jo Talbot picked up the phone. He was allowed one call a week, which was monitored by a guard. His ailing mother, Lena May Talbot, had sent him a phone card so he could talk with her.

Talbot didn't like the fact that his calls were monitored. He hated prison life with a vengeance. It was one more thing Sky McCoy was going to pay for once Talbot got out.

"Hello?"

"Mom? Hey, it's Billy Jo. How you doin'?"

"Son? Oh, it's so good to hear your voice. Are you okay?"

"Yeah, Mom, I am. Fit as a fiddle. How about you?"

"Not too good of late. My doctor said I just had a TIA, a ministroke, the other day. My right arm was pretty useless yesterday, but now the strength is comin' back. So don't worry, I'll bounce back like I always do. You can't keep a Talbot down, you know."

Grimacing, Talbot felt his heart wrench. "I'm really sorry to hear that, Ma. Is there anything the doc can do to get your arm in shape?"

"He says I can go for physical therapy. And I'm going to do that. I'm right-handed, and need the use of it. But I've got about eighty percent strength back already." She chuckled. "You know Doc Greene. He said if I'd quit smoking I wouldn't have these TIA episodes. I told him there was no way I was gonna stop smokin'." She sighed. "I wish you were home, son. You could live here and help me get along. And I do need help. It's hell getting around, some days. This growing old is for the birds."

Talbot clenched his teeth in frustration. If he was home, he could help her. His mother had always been a highly independent woman. She had a big garden, and canned and dried her own fruit and vegetables every year. After having chronic fatigue for years, she finally rebounded. Then with her stroke a year ago, she'd been housebound for a month. Out of sheer stubbornness, she had put in her garden, anyway. And with physical therapy, she'd healed.

Anger surged within him. If McCoy hadn't put him in prison, Billy Jo would be home to support her. His mother loved her house, and he could have put in the garden for her. He could get her outside in the open air, where she loved to be. There was so much upkeep on a house, whether it was painting,

158

putting on a new roof, or fixing so many other things that required a man's presence.

"Listen, Ma, if I could be home, you know I'd be there for you. It's important you be able to have control over your own life after that stroke. I dream of the day I can drive you to the store and even help you trim the roses. Wouldn't you like that?"

"That sounds good, son. My only wish is to have you home with me once more. That's all I want."

Billy Jo felt a wave of emotion at his mother's words. The stroke had crippled her to a degree, and affected her ability to remember conversation. When her voice sounded faraway like that, he knew she was checking out mentally, a result of that stroke. Where she went, he didn't have a clue.

His hand tightened on the phone. "Ma? I can't make calls from prison or I'd talk to Dr. Greene myself. Please get Mrs. Johnson, our next-door neighbor, to help you when you need it. Will you do that for me?"

"Your five minutes are up, Talbot," the guard announced, tapping him on the shoulder. "Say your goodbyes."

Fresh rage filled Billy Jo, but he masked it. "Ma, I gotta go. I'll call you next week, okay?"

"Sounds good, son. I love you. And I miss you."

"I love you, too, Ma. Bye."

Turning, Billy Jo hung up the phone and let the next man in line have his turn. The guard escorted him out of the area and back to his cell, on the third floor of the big stone building. With his gut churning, Talbot tried to think of a way to get help for his mother. There was Harve, his friend, who visited him monthly. Maybe a letter? Billy Jo was allowed to write letters. Each one was read and approved before sending, but that didn't bother him. Maybe Harve could fly over to Philipsburg and help out his mother, just this once?

The cell door slammed shut and locked with a terrible finality. Looking around his small enclosure, which held a cot, a toilet and a shelf for his books he loved to read, Talbot felt frustration simmer through him. He clenched his hands, covered in calluses from his daily workout in the gym, and shut his eyes. His mother was defenseless against the effects of that damn stroke. If McCoy hadn't caused his father to have a heart attack just outside the courtroom, during the trial, he'd be alive to help her. But Talbot's dad was gone.

"Dammit," Billy Jo whispered between

gritted teeth. He was sure McCoy had caused his mother's stroke, too. The stress of the trial had finally gotten to her. She was only fifty, far too young for such a debilitating blow to occur.

McCoy was going to feel the same way once Billy Jo got out. First, he'd make sure his mother received the help she needed. He had plans to keep her in the house where he'd been born. And he was going to do everything in his power to see that she had everything he could give her before he started tracking down McCoy.

Oh, he knew the Injun was hiding, but Billy Jo was a damn good tracker. He'd been raised in the Rocky Mountains near Philipsburg. His father had been an experienced hunter, had taught him how to handle all manner of firearms, how to fight with a knife, how to defend himself. Talbot could survive in the mountains like few others ever could, since the Rockies had been his backyard when he was growing up. And Billy Jo had a sneaking hunch McCoy was still in the Philipsburg area because he, too, had been born there.

Sitting on his cot, Talbot sighed. He needed to go to the prison library and start boning up on what having a stroke could do to a person. Maybe he could beg the warden to allow him an extra phone call to Dr. Greene, his mother's physician, to answer his questions. Whatever it took, Talbot vowed, he'd do it for his mom.

He stood and tucked in his shirt, made himself more presentable. In another fifteen minutes, it would be time for chow. After that, he'd be allowed an hour in the library. Combing his hair, which had just been cut, he went over to the sink and brushed his teeth. As he did so, he wondered what McCoy was doing. The son of a bitch had better enjoy this summer, because it was going to be his last.

CHAPTER NINE

Sky sat at the kitchen table, which was strewn with leather, scissors and several lightweight metal swivels. It was nearly 10:00 p.m. He tried to ignore the sight of Kelly sitting at his elbow. She was learning how to cut and make jesses for the raptors.

He gave her a quick glance and saw how focused she was on the swivel. Without the device, a raptor could get tangled up in the kangaroo leather and possibly break a leg. A swivel was a vital element in every jess, and meant ultimate safety for the raptor.

With great effort, Sky tried to remain immune to the way the lamp's soft glow showed off the burgundy, gold and crimson highlights in her hair. Kelly's lips were pursed, revealing the intensity she brought to whatever she did. He smiled grudgingly as he laid a new pair of jesses on the table.

"You're doing fine. Breathe. Relax. This isn't brain work. Just simple hand stuff."

Snorting, Kelly muttered, "Says you. This is like threading a needle, with different types of knots at different places. I went through Annapolis and learned to tie all kinds of knots, but this . . . !"

She glanced up at Sky. The shadows emphasized the high cheekbones in his rugged, handsome face. Gone was the little boy she'd grown up with. The person who sat at her elbow was all man — and more. Kelly wrestled with her female response to him, and sternly reminded herself that she was here as a guest. She smiled weakly. "I can't tie knots and I can't fly."

Hearing the sadness in her tone, Sky wanted to reach out and touch Kelly's hand, but he didn't dare. His fingers literally itched to slide through her hair. Would the strands be strong, like a horse's mane? Sleek like warm silk on a chilly day? "Maybe by working with the birds you'll regain a little of your flight status. I know it isn't like sitting in the seat of a helicopter again, but there's an incredible joy to be had, watching a hawk take off from your arm."

Shrugging, Kelly finally finished her first jess, and handed it to Sky for his appraisal. As soon as their fingers touched, heat pooled in her lower body. "I'm struggling with all of that, Sky. I don't like to admit it, but I am. Flying was my life, my escape. And now I'm permanently grounded."

Taking the jess, he studied it critically. "I know. And I wish I could change that for you, Kelly. I really do." He held up her creation. "This is excellent. You do good, careful work. In fact, once you're done with that second flight jess, we'll give the pair to Bella, and they'll be her new set." He saw Kelly's green eyes lighten momentarily with his encouragement. How badly Sky wanted to make it possible for her to fly once more. But everything the doctors had said suggested she'd never climb into a cockpit again. A pilot needed strong legs to move the rudders of a helicopter, and her left limb had nerve damage. She couldn't feel part of her foot, and without sensation, it would be impossible for her to monitor her pressure on the rudder. She might overcorrect the flight path and cause a critical situation. No, Sky realized Kelly wouldn't fly again, and he ached for her. It would be akin to one of his raptors striking a power line, clipping off part of its wing and being forever grounded.

She seemed to be reading his thoughts. "I'm a grounded eagle," Kelly grumbled as she worked with the second flight jess. "My physical therapist, Janice Hartwig, told me I need to strengthen my left leg, to get it back into service."

"Grounded but not dead," Sky reminded her. He chose a piece of soft, reddish kangaroo leather and with the scissors clipped out lengths for another pair of jesses. "And the sooner you get that leg healed up, the better you're going to feel."

"I suppose." Kelly sat back, clutching the supple leather between her fingers, and scanned the cozy kitchen. The log cabin was of the old style, with plaster between its logs. The kitchen counter was of white Formica, and rather bland-looking blue curtains framed the wide window that looked out on the backyard. The decor was definitely male. Maybe Sky would appreciate her adding a feminine touch, but she wasn't going to ask him now.

Kelly had to see if this arrangement would work or not. Still, she wanted to give the cabin a softer, brighter look. Why? And then the truth slammed into her: she had romantic feelings for Sky. She was attracted to him again.

The thought startled her. Romance had been the last thing on her mind recently, as she tried to escape her dreaded depression. How could puppy love suddenly flare to life again, and grow into so much more?

"As a matter of fact, tomorrow morning, after feeding, you can work with Bella," Sky said. "I want you to get comfortable attaching the regular jesses we use when she's not flying. Those long ones are used when she's perched, giving her plenty of room to run around, or even fly up in her enclosure in order to see better. Raptors always go to the highest point possible in any given area."

"They go into look-down, shoot-down mode," Kelly muttered, with sudden insight.

The creation of the second jess was going much more smoothly. After she finished assembling it, she handed it to Sky for final approval.

"Exactly," he was saying. "Military lingo fits a raptor, for sure. Good work on the flight jesses, by the way. I'll bring Bella up tomorrow, after she's fed, and you can work with her on swapping out the long jesses for the shorter flight ones."

He noticed Kelly seemed upset suddenly. He wanted to ask why, but was unsure of what to say or do.

"I hope she's patient." Kelly grinned at him. "Is that an oxymoron? A hawk being patient?"

Her comment made him smile in turn. "Raptors are much like people, Kelly. All different types of personalities and temperaments. The reason I want you to work with Bella is that she's very, very patient and forgiving. She's a wonderful teacher for someone who wants to learn falconry from the ground up."

"She won't peck me?" Kelly wanted to keep the conversation light as she scrambled to comprehend her feelings for Sky. They were real. Frightening. How could this be happening, on top of everything else?

His mouth curved. "No. Hawks don't peck. They use their beaks for tearing fur from the flesh." He bent his fingers to mimic claws. "Hawks have big, strong feet with long talons. They 'foot' a prey. When they fly in to grab it, they do so with their feet, not their beaks. They strike a rabbit, for example, by sinking their long claws into its spinal column, killing it instantly. That's what is called a clean kill. Juvenile hawks just learning how to hunt often won't strike correctly, and have to reposition their feet to get to the spinal column."

"Sounds a little gory for the poor rabbit."

Resting his hands on the table, Sky said, "It's nature, Kelly. Rabbits are the main food for a lot of hawks, but not all of them. They go after mice, gophers, rats and snakes. They help keep all these critters in check, or they'd overrun us. Having a couple of hawks around reduces the rat and mouse population. There aren't too many people who wouldn't love to have a raptor about for that reason alone. Red-tailed hawks, in particular, are snake hawks. If you live in an area with a high rattler population, you want red-tails around. They go after them big-time, grabbing them with their large claws."

"I guess I've seen enough killing, Sky, over in Afghanistan." Kelly told him briefly about her time in that country, and as she did, his blue eyes darkened with what she felt was compassion. "I still have nightmares about the crash over there," she admitted. "If you hear me screaming some night, don't get worried. It's just one of my nightmares replaying."

"I didn't know," he said, suddenly more worried than before. Without thinking, he reached out and grasped her hand. Given the agony in her eyes and the strain in her voice, he couldn't help himself. "If I hear you scream, I'll understand, okay?"

Sucking in a sharp breath, Sky realized what he'd just done. More touching. More closeness. Instantly, he released her, his fingers burning where he'd made contact with her soft, firm flesh.

Kelly looked away. "Okay . . ." How badly

she'd wanted his touch just then, and miraculously, Sky had responded. She couldn't help but remember how automatic their affection had once been. They'd been inseparable. One time, when they were running at the edge of the playground, she'd lost her footing and fell. Sky had run over and wrapped the handkerchief he always carried around her bloody, dirty knee. He'd then helped her up, put his arm around her waist and led her to the nurse's office.

Now they were adults, and to Kelly, his touch meant something different, something more than friendship. She couldn't control the hammering of her heart, or the yearning she felt for Sky.

"I guess this is confession time," he stated huskily. Sky had seen the flare of surprise in Kelly's eyes when he'd made contact. His fingers were tingling madly as he folded them on the table, to stop from touching her again. "When Talbot set fire to my parents' home, I had recurring nightmares, and still do to this day. I hear their screams, their cries for help. Even now, so many years later, I sometimes wake up yelling."

"Looks like we're both wounded by life circumstances." Kelly eyed him sadly, her heart opening even more. "I'm so sorry you lost your mom and stepdad, Sky. I know you loved them so much." Shaking her head, she whispered, "I try to think how I would feel if Talbot had torched my parents' home and burned them alive. How would I survive?" Opening her hands, she said, "I just don't know how you got through it. I don't think I could. I'd want to kill Talbot."

"I went through all those emotions afterward," Sky confessed. Rubbing his brow, he added, "I had years where I plotted revenge. And then I realized I was turning into him."

"How did you rise above it?"

"Over time, I just made a decision to live my life differently. Talbot's taken so much from me already. First in grade school and later, taking my parents' lives. I just didn't want him stealing more from me." Sky knew he wasn't being completely truthful with Kelly. He didn't want to share his plan to face Talbot after his release from jail, or the fact he knew the convict would hunt him down. Sky understood Kelly was concerned, and genuinely cared for him as a friend. But she had enough on her own plate. With all the shock and trauma she'd suffered, she didn't need his, too. Sky wanted to lighten her load, help reorient her to a new life without flying. He hoped his raptors would become the magical healing potion she needed to do that. And just as in grade school, Sky would be there like a quiet, supportive shadow for her. That was all he would do, even though he felt drawn to her so powerfully he couldn't think two thoughts clearly in her presence. He was so afraid of blurting out stuff that would give away his building desire for her as a woman, not just as a friend.

"Wow," Kelly said, sitting back in the chair, "you have a lot more strength and resilience than I do." She gave him a look of admiration. "I don't think I could move on. How did you do it?"

"I started taking karate lessons. And the more I got into it, the spiritual teachings behind the moves especially, the more it felt released. You took karate as a child, remember? Do you still practice it?"

She shook her head. "When I left for Annapolis, I dropped out. I loved basketball, and played on the women's team at the Academy. I'm glad you took karate, though. I know your stepdad and mom believed in using only peaceful means as a way of resolving problems. I always wanted you to learn how to fight back and bloody Talbot's nose. He's the type of guy who doesn't respect anything or anyone. And peaceful means wouldn't make him back off."

Gathering up the jesses, Sky pushed his

chair back and stood. "My parents weren't wrong about wanting harmony, or trying to resolve things in a peaceful manner. It's just that some situations aren't handled like that." He laid the jesses on the counter and turned to Kelly. "I practice karate every morning. You might see me out back here, doing my katas. My teacher lives in Philipsburg and I go there once a week, at night, to study with him."

"What color belt are you?"

"Black." Sky would make damn sure he was fully prepared when Talbot stepped back into his life. He was becoming a peaceful warrior, and would take on the murderer one last time.

Brows raised, Kelly said, "That's really something. You're a black belt! That took a lot of hard work and time. Black belts aren't handed out often." She gave him a once-over. "That's why you're so lean and fit. I was wondering if you got that way by flying your raptors." Her heart wouldn't settle down. Every time she met Sky's turbulent, stormy blue eyes her entire body hummed, as if reacting on every conceivable level.

Sky could feel her respect toward him and it sent tendrils of pleasure through him. Her admiring gaze heated his blood. Suddenly, he was like a hungry raptor on the edge of starvation. Maybe he'd gone too long without feminine company. Because of Talbot's threat, Sky had refused to get seriously involved with anyone. He just wouldn't put another life on the line. Still, Kelly's green eyes had a powerful effect on him. How could he possibly survive the next few months?

"I like the spiritual tenets of karate," he finally managed to answer. "They suit my personal beliefs." And if needed, he could use the art of self-defense to subdue Talbot.

"I'm sure it makes you feel stronger and far more capable of facing someone in a fight. Unlike in grade school, where you didn't have any training in fighting back. Are you more confident?"

Sky eased away from the counter. "I am." He had to break this connection, at least for now, so he glanced at his watch. "It's bedtime for me. I get up at dawn to feed the raptors."

Shifting on the chair, Kelly pulled the crutches toward her. "Right you are. I don't know that I'll be up when you get up, though." She smiled slightly and watched as Sky turned off the overhead light. A small night-light shone on the kitchen wall over the two sinks.

"Don't worry about that," he said. "You

174

have everything you need? Towels? Wash-cloth?" Just the thought that Kelly was under his roof, barely a room away from his own bedroom, made him tremble inside. It was as if he'd been offered his most cher-ished gift and couldn't accept it. No way could he ever let Kelly know how much he wanted her as a woman. He didn't dare, for so many reasons.

"Yes, I do. You go get your shower first, though. I'm a lot slower because of these . . ." She frowned at the crutches.

"Keep up the physical therapy and you'll be off them sooner than you think." Sky fol-lowed her as she made her way out of the kitchen. Though the living room held a butterscotch-colored leather couch and two lamp stands, it was large and roomy enough for Kelly to move around without difficulty. The two bedrooms were on either side of the living room. The bathroom was at Sky's end of the cabin, so at some point, they would run into each other. He thought about shifting to the guest room instead, since it might be easier on Kelly. He'd wait a few days to see how she adjusted, he decided.

"Good night, Sky," Kelly called softly, turning and looking at him as he walked toward his bedroom. "Thanks for everything. You have no idea what this means to me. I'm forever indebted to you." She swallowed hard. How badly she wanted him. Wished he would slide into her bed beside her and simply hold her. The thoughts collided wildly within her heart and she had absolutely no explanation for what was happening between them.

Sky wanted to cross the room and take Kelly into his arms. She had such a bereft look on her shadowed features. He restrained himself, but just barely.

"See you in the morning . . ." he said.

How the hell was he going to keep his hands off her and hide his feelings? She had come up here with a sense of safety, of trust, he reminded himself savagely. Not to be stalked by a sex-starved male who had been without a woman for too long. Worst of all, Sky didn't want just any woman. He wanted Kelly. Always Kelly.

Sky jerked awake, a scream on his lips. Sweat trickled down his temples. Light from a nearly full moon slanted softly through the curtains above his bed. Breathing heavily, he sat up and then yanked the sheet and coverlet off his perspiring body. Having his bare feet on the cool cedar floor soothed away some of his terror.

He ran his fingers through his damp hair and stared sightlessly at the closed door to his room. His breathing was heavy, like that of a wild bull on the loose. Flashes of the nightmare continued even with his eyes open, and he was gripped with restlessness. He had to get up and out of the room. He had to escape! Naked in the milky moonlight, he pulled the door open and headed to the kitchen to get a drink of water.

The clock on the counter read 3:00 a.m. Trembling inwardly, Sky stood at the sink and drank in large gulps. The cool water washed away some of his fear, but not all. Setting the glass on the counter, he moved soundlessly to the back door and slipped out into the night. As he stood on the sidewalk, Sky saw the deeply shadowed mews straight ahead of him. He oriented to the present by listening. All the birds were quiet except for Luna, who was hooting. She was an owl, after all, and nighttime was when she was most active.

Sky wiped away the sweat from his brow and planted his feet on the earth. The towering firs were sighing in the breeze as he passed, heading toward the training area. Moonlight lit the way, but he knew the route by heart. The night air caressed his hot, sweaty body and it cooled him down.

In the distance, Sky heard the familiar hooting of a great horned owl that lived in the area. It was responding to Luna's call.

As he walked out to the flight oval, some of his shakiness dissolved. Sky felt better just being outside. If only he could control the nightmares. Tonight's had been different. More devastating. What he'd seen was far scarier than the normal dreams he had, about once a week. In them, he was always confronting Talbot and fighting him to the death.

Sky walked around the oval, avoiding the tall metal perches, as his mind kept replaying the dream. He had gone to sleep quickly, being exhausted from the day's activities — Kelly's move and all the company. As an introvert, Sky didn't do well in crowds, which seemed to drain his emotional batteries.

He looked up at the fat moon moving toward the western horizon, above the spires of Douglas firs.

Kelly . . . he'd dreamed of Kelly being with him in the cabin when Talbot had found them. And instead of attacking Sky, Talbot had captured her. Sky had seen Kelly fight with all her strength, but in the end, Talbot had bloodied her face and savagely subdued her. And then he'd raped her —

repeatedly — as Sky had watched, tied to a chair. He'd sat bound and helpless, the ropes cutting into his wrists. He'd felt the warm blood purling down his fingers from the wrist wounds he'd created, trying to get free. . . .

But he hadn't saved her. Virulent hatred welled up in Sky as the great horned owl flew past the moon, on the hunt for something to eat. How badly he wanted to hunt and kill Talbot, especially as he remembered the last part, where the demon had taken out a long hunting knife, grinned, and pulled Kelly's head up by her beautiful red hair to finish her off. . . .

CHAPTER TEN

"Are you ready?" Sky asked Kelly as they stood at one end of the flight oval. Bella sat relaxed on her gauntlet, flight jesses attached. The Harris hawk ruffled her feathers, as if enjoying the bright afternoon sunshine and pleasant eighty-degree temperature. The day was without a breeze, a good time to teach Kelly how to fly a hawk.

Excited, she supported her left leg with a cane. Where had the month of June gone? Just like a peregrine falcon, the fastest bird in the world, four weeks had flown by. Now, the July heat was upon them, and she reveled in finally being free of her crutches.

"I'm more than ready," she said breathlessly, giving Bella a smile. The hawk made rumbling noises in response, which meant she wanted some meat. Kelly had food in her bag, but Bella would have to earn those choice morsels.

Sky came to her side, looking attractive as

always in his tan cowboy hat, white cotton shirt and formfitting jeans. Every cell in her body tingled as he drew close. The past month had been heaven on earth for Kelly, but her ongoing yearning for Sky made her restless. Kelly had managed to keep things light and friendly, but her heart cried out for much more — a touch, a smile. She ached for those things from Sky, yet knew she had to keep her longing a secret. Sky did not communicate that kind of interest. She'd have to deal with her unreciprocated feelings all by herself.

"Okay, today is the day," he said in a low tone. "I've shown you how to get Bella from perch to perch with the clicker, and by use of hand signals." Her excitement made him smile. He'd seen such a difference in her health in the past month. Sky's heart swelled with pride and another emotion he didn't dare touch. She was regaining weight and was now curvy like a woman should be. Her beautiful eyes sparkled like emeralds, and more often than not, Sky saw gold in their depths. She was happy. So was he.

"I'm ready," Kelly told him. "Nervous, but ready." Secretly, she absorbed his nearness like a starving raptor looking for food. Only she didn't want food from Sky. She wanted to be held by him, kissed. . . . If he only knew the torrid dreams she had of his mouth crushing hers. Swallowing convulsively, Kelly made herself focus on the hawk.

"You've done this so many times, it will be automatic. Go ahead, release Bella." Sky forced himself to ignore Kelly's closeness. His fingers literally itched to reach out and touch her, but he didn't dare. Duty first. And then protecting Kelly against his coming confrontation with Talbot. . . .

Kelly lifted her gloved hand after unsnapping the leash from one of Bella's legs. The signal wasn't lost on the hawk. Her dark brown wings unfurled and she launched herself off Kelly's glove. Flying directly to the perch at the other end of the oval, she turned around and waited.

"Very good," Kelly said. She picked out some meat from her hawking bag. Stretching upward, she placed it on the perch above her, then snapped the clicker.

Instantly, Bella was airborne again. Kelly's hair, which was growing longer, was mussed by the hawk landing just above her head. Bella gobbled down the meat treat and then stood waiting for Kelly's next signal.

"Great. You're doing great," Sky told her. Since that terrible nightmare, he'd reined in his desire to pat her shoulder or touch her hand. The past month had been hell on him in some ways, and a miracle in others. He saw the soft smile on Kelly's lips as she moved to the eastern perch. Every day, with physical therapy and morning exercises, her leg was getting stronger.

Today she wore a blue sleeveless tee, body-hugging jeans that showcased her long legs, and one shoe of leather, the other of softer material for her injured foot. His gaze automatically settled on her mouth, and he took a moment to simply watch how her lips moved, and imagine how they would feel against his. To kiss Kelly, well, his whole body trembled at that thought. But she was off-limits. She had to be.

Kelly used a hand signal, tapping her fingers on the perch, to ask Bella to fly to her.

Instantly, the Harris hawk took off, flapping over to the east perch. Sky watched with pleasure as Kelly pulled some meat from her bag and placed it on the perch for Bella, who pounced on it eagerly.

Sky knew it was important for Kelly to continue to gain confidence in her growing falconer skills. Bella got her exercise this way, too. He didn't allow his raptors to sit for days on end in their mews, sluggish and depressed. They loved flying as much as Sky loved watching them fly.

As he stood there, arms crossed on his chest, watching Kelly lure Bella to the north perch with a snap of the clicker, he smiled to himself. The hawk clearly loved being with Kelly. Just as he did. More and more, this woman was becoming a part of his home, his life. He couldn't let this happen. He had to push away his growing feelings for Kelly. Having her under his roof was a twenty-four-hour-a-day test for him. When he awoke every morning at 5:00 a.m., Kelly was already in the kitchen, frying bacon and eggs for them. She made a helluva good pot of coffee, too. How could any man not be happy with that? He'd never lived with a woman before, so this was a completely new experience for him. Sky found himself liking it all too much.

Scuffing the toe of his boot into the loose, fine grit of the training oval, he divided his attention among Kelly, Bella and his own dark inner world. The nightmare of Talbot raping Kelly and slitting her throat came at least once a week now. He never gave voice to that terrible dream. Would never share it with her.

Sky's need to protect Kelly had grown fierce over the past month. He wondered daily if he'd done the right thing in allowing her to stay here. When he looked at her sparkling eyes, saw her ready smile, and watched as she regained her lost weight, he knew the answer. Her parents were thrilled with her progress. Sky could see the relief and hope in their eyes.

Pulling his hat a little lower, he watched as Bella suddenly flew off the west perch and headed to a fir tree far above the oval. The hawk grabbed hold of a branch and flopped awkwardly. She lost her grip, tumbling earthward, then caught herself and flew to an inner limb on the same fir. Hawks usually didn't like getting entangled in leaves and branches, instinctively knowing they could break a wing or leg in the process. Today, Bella was feeling her oats, acting more aggressive than usual by tackling the hundred-foot tree.

Kelly looked up at Bella, perched about fifty feet above her. She put meat on the crossbar and tapped it with her fingers. Bella teetered on the thick branch, partially hidden from view. Kelly knew the hawk liked to fly into trees and had often done so in other training sessions, so she wasn't concerned. The Harris hawk was clearly having fun, jumping from one limb to another now, her wings half-open.

"She seems to like doing this," Kelly called to Sky.

"Yeah. It's okay. She's just feeling frisky. Hawks have ups and downs just like we do." He forced a smile for Kelly's sake, because he could hear a note of worry in her tone. "Just let her be. Bella will come down for the meat in a minute. She's like a kid playing hooky. She needs a break from routine just like we do."

Nodding, Kelly smiled in return. But something was off. Sky seemed far away suddenly, his black brows drawn downward. She didn't want to pry, so kept her attention on Bella, who was climbing through the thick green branches above. One couldn't lose focus when a hawk was flying free. Sky had attached a small radio receiver to one of her tail quills so in case she did fly off on a whim, they could track her.

But what was wrong with Sky? This morning, his eyes were bloodshot, with shadows beneath them. Was he sick? Or unhappy with her being here? Kelly was unsure. She tried to be a good guest by doing her share of chores around the cabin and mews. With so many raptors, Kelly had come to appreciate how much time was involved in caring for them. But clearly, Sky loved what he was doing, and the raptors loved him.

Grateful that he'd allowed her into his amazing world, Kelly tried to ignore her worry over him. He was such a quiet, withdrawn person. He never divulged his feelings, even though Kelly wanted exactly that — deeper communication with him. But it wasn't something she could demand.

They were becoming friends once more, not lovers — although, she often felt waves of longing for him. Serious longing. Yet he never touched her. Never gave the slightest hint that he wanted something more meaningful with her.

Tapping the perch, Kelly watched with delight as Bella exploded like a shot out of the fir, heading to the perch where she stood. She was clearly happy, and Kelly found it exhilarating to feel the hawk's radiant energy. Bella had bad days just like Kelly, sometimes seeming irritated or even snappish.

Kelly's frustrations stemmed from her impatience about her leg. Healing took time. That was what her doctor and physical therapist said, and she didn't want to hear it. Kelly longed to go to the meadows with Sky when he was training a young raptor to hunt. But until she could get off the crutches for good and get rid of the cane, she had to stay put.

Bella suddenly flew off the perch to Sky. Kelly laughed, especially when she saw Sky rouse himself from his introspection and reward Bella with a piece of meat.

"I guess she wanted to fly over and say hello," Kelly called, grinning.

"Yeah. Bella's like that. Like a big kid who wants everyone to play with her." Sky saw the joy in the hawk's dark eyes. Birds were always happiest when flying free and doing what nature intended. Bella then gave several grumbling croaks and flew back to the perch near Kelly. He watched her reward the hawk with a treat.

"I like her attitude," Kelly exclaimed. She grinned up at the raptor, admiring the way the sunlight highlighted her cinnamon shoulders and darker brown flight feathers.

"Keep her moving," Sky instructed. "Let's give her a good workout today, because she's clearly ready for it."

Nodding, Kelly moved to the north perch. Her leg was tired and her left heel hurt, but she ignored that. Pain was something she lived with all the time. She refused to take painkillers because they clouded her thinking. There was so much to remember about falconry and the handling of raptors, and she didn't want to forget any of it. Nor did she want to disappoint Sky.

"Hey," she called to him as she set meat

on the perch and tapped it, "do hawks fly at night?"

Sky sauntered over to her. "Usually not, but they will if they have to. They're diurnal raptors, not nocturnal. But sometimes, under duress, or the threat of a bobcat or cougar trying to climb up to get to them, they'll take off from the tree they're roosting in. They can see at night, just not as well as they can in daylight." Sky enjoyed watching Bella flying toward them. The whoosh of her wings as she landed lifted strands of Kelly's hair, and he saw the awe and appreciation in her face as she rewarded the hawk.

"So they aren't blind at night?"

"No, not at all. When your leg improves, I'll take you out with me. There have been many times when I've flown hawks after sunset, and they see just fine. They can fly from half a mile away to your glove and land without a problem. Out in the wild, if there's a forest fire, or a predator stalking them, they'll do whatever they need to to survive."

"That's good to know," Kelly murmured. She walked to the next perch and Sky followed, checking his stride to stay near. "I was wondering about that the other day and forgot to ask you. Luna is an owl, and you fly her during the day. But she's a nocturnal raptor and normally hunts at night. I was just wondering if the reverse was true, for daylight raptors."

"It is," Sky assured her. He was keeping six feet between himself and Kelly. He wanted to slide his arm around her waist and pull her close, but resisted. Tucking his disappointment deep within him, he watched as Bella followed them, landing on the perch and emitting several rumbling sounds.

Sky had to be satisfied that their old friendship was blossoming. It was as if they were picking up as adults where they had left off as teens. Rubbing his chest, he didn't try to probe those memories. As a teen, he'd fallen deeply in love with Kelly — at least he'd thought it was love. Maybe it was a mix of sexual desire and need. He'd never acted on his feelings, and now found himself wondering what it would be like to love Kelly. Fully.

Laughing softly, Kelly delivered a reward to Bella, then looked at Sky. "Are you okay?"

"Uh, I'm fine." He shifted uncomfortably. He wasn't used to having someone gauging his mood. Above all, he must remember his duty, understand that the Trayherns were expecting him to follow through. He took a step away from Kelly. She was just too close.

"You seem preoccupied. Are you worried about something?" she asked.

"No, I just didn't get a lot of sleep last night." That wasn't a lie, but it wasn't the complete truth, either. Sky hated being dishonest with Kelly. Care and concern were evident in her gaze. How beautiful she was! Sky liked the freckles that spilled across her cheeks and nose, the plumpness of those lips he so desperately wanted to taste. Even at this distance, he could smell her feminine scent. Kelly loved bathing with a favorite soap, Herbaria orange and oatmeal. Throughout the day, he'd often catch delicious whiffs of it, combined with her own womanly fragrance. It was like an aphrodisiac for him.

"Are you sure that's all it is, Sky?"

Her prodding bothered him, and he wrapped his arms across his chest, a defensive gesture. "I . . . well." He cast about for an excuse. "I'm fine," he said flatly.

"Is it me, Sky? Am I too much of a burden on you?"

Her words, like a soft breeze, found their way into his aching heart. It contracted instantly with pain and denial. Lifting his head, he blurted, "No. Absolutely not!" Seeing her look of anxiety, he softened his tone.

"I want to help you get you back on your feet." Despite himself, he reached out and squeezed her shoulder. "I've just got a lot on my mind, is all."

He realized his mistake and instantly released her. Oh, to touch her! To run his fingertips up her firm, suntanned arm . . . He swore every night as he went to bed never to touch her, never to let her know how much she meant to him, and now his gut crumpled with fear. There was no way to undo what he'd just done. If he let himself, one touch would lead to another, and another.

Kelly saw frustration banked in Sky's blue eyes. Was he upset with her? His words and touch belied what she heard in his voice. Confused, she stammered, "Look, we c-can undo this three-month gig anytime you want, Sky. I don't want to be a pain in the ass to you. I know how much you have to do, and you're used to living alone. I can't imagine what it's like to suddenly have a cripple underfoot. I wouldn't blame you and I wouldn't be angry if you needed me to leave." Reaching over, she gripped his hand. "More than anything, I want to be your friend, like we were when we were kids. I never want to lose that connection with you again. And if my presence here is creating

192

an unbearable strain on you, I'll go."

Groaning, Sky lifted his free hand and slid it along her sun-warmed cheek. "Listen to me, will you? You're not a pain to me. I just have some issues that I'm trying to sort out inside." He withdrew his hand, inwardly berating himself for his lack of discipline. When her lips parted, he clenched his teeth, then backed far enough away that he couldn't touch her again. Above all, he must fulfill his duty to Kelly's family, and she must never know about it. Sky refused to hurt her by revealing the real reason she was with him right now. He would protect her from that truth at all costs.

"Oh . . . all right," Kelly whispered unsteadily. Her skin tingled in the wake of his unexpected caress. What she'd seen in his eyes — the heat of a man wanting to mate with his woman — startled her. Maybe her feelings weren't so one-sided. Kelly had kept her sweet dreams of Sky to herself. At night, those dreams were starting to replace many of her PTSD nightmares. Since coming to his cabin, her bad dreams had been dramatically reduced. She wasn't so afraid to go to sleep.

Touching her cheek where his callused fingers had just been, she smiled. "I just don't want to be a burden to you, Sky. Not ever."

"You'll never be a burden to me," he replied, taking in a ragged breath. He wanted to run as far away from Kelly as he could, because if he didn't, he was going to step forward, sweep her into his arms and kiss her senseless. There was no disguising the look in Kelly's half-closed eyes, those thick lashes a frame to highlight the dappled gold depths. She liked him touching her. In fact, she *wanted* him to touch her. And judging from the pouty look of her lips, she wanted more. Sky groaned internally.

More gruffly than he intended, he said, "Keep flying Bella for another ten minutes, then bring her in and put her in her mew. I — I need to handle some paperwork." Turning on his heel, he stalked away, feeling like a raptor that had been denied dinner. He was hungry, anxious and frustrated.

Kelly obviously didn't understand that her nearness drove him crazy. How badly Sky wanted to make hot, wild love with her.

As he reached the cabin door, he removed his hat and escaped inside. Going to the office, he drew the chair to the desk and sat down, glowering at the stacks of paper that really did need tending, though his mind and heart wouldn't focus on the work.

Kelly's eyes, so luminous and gold, haunted him.

Planting his elbows on the desk, Sky covered his face with his hands and took several deep breaths to try to get her out of his system. The phone rang.

"Hello?"

"Mr. McCoy?"

"Speaking."

"This is Wilma Winslow from the Washington State Penitentiary."

Sky's stomach dropped. His hand tightened around the phone. "Yes?"

"This is a courtesy call to remind you that Billy Jo Talbot will be released from here in June of next year. The date isn't set yet, but we'll keep you apprised of it as we get closer. He has exhibited model behavior for a prisoner. So there should be no denying him release at that point."

"I see. Thank you. I appreciate your keeping me up-to-date. Tell me, is there any way he can get my address or phone number?"

"Absolutely not, Mr. McCoy. The only place that information is available is here, in my office. And no prisoner is ever allowed access to this area. You don't need to worry."

Nodding, Sky said, "Okay, that sounds good. Thanks."

"You're welcome. Goodbye."

There was a dial tone and Sky put the phone back into the cradle. He stared at it for a long minute, his gut tied into painful knots. Gone was his yearning for Kelly. All of it. In its place were thoughts of his nemesis, Billy Jo Talbot. Every six months, prison officials called to give him updates. And they always promised to phone him several weeks in advance of Talbot's actual release date. Getting the phone calls was never easy. Talbot's freedom was becoming an inevitable reality.

Sky sat back in the chair and closed his eyes. It was impossible to get rid of the rabid fear that ate away at him. Before Kelly came back into his life, he'd had no one to worry about except himself in the coming confrontation with Talbot. He knew he could die. And he'd accepted that possibility. But now he didn't want to. He wanted to live. Live to court Kelly. Did he dare dream of a life beyond Talbot? With Kelly? Suddenly, Sky's plan crumbled into dust as his heart beat wildly. For the past decade, he'd prepared to give up this life. But now he had someone to live for. He could live to love Kelly fully and without threat of Talbot destroying them. His love made the battle with Talbot even more important than before. He would have to fight for his love.

CHAPTER ELEVEN

"Sky, I have a great idea," Kelly said as they ate a lunch of grilled cheese sandwiches and sweet pickles. The August sunlight was strong, though area thunderstorms threatened. She sat at his elbow, as she always did at the kitchen table. The windows were open to allow the wonderful scent of pine to waft through the cabin.

"Uh-oh," Sky muttered, enjoying the sharp cheddar cheese on the toasted, whole wheat bread, "here we go again." In truth, the second month with Kelly under his roof had gone more smoothly than he had anticipated. Since he'd touched her cheek in July, he'd been ironclad in keeping his distance from her, his yearning suppressed. Instead, Sky treated her as the friend he'd had in childhood. Kelly had responded. In the second month, she was blossoming. Her weight was back even more, and she walked for hours a day without the cane. Her leg was healing quickly, according to her physical therapist. Sky wanted her whole. Her depression was dissolving as a result of being here with him and his raptors.

Raising her hand, Kelly grinned and said, "I've been thinking. You're so good with the raptors and know so much about them, I wonder if you've thought of giving a program to people in Philipsburg? It would be a wonderful way to educate them on why they shouldn't shoot these beautiful birds. So many people in the West, particularly, think of hawks as 'vermin' and kill them. We know they're vital to a stable environment, that they're the top predators controlling mice, rats, gophers, squirrels and snakes. If only people knew that. Your expertise would help them understand."

Sky felt a twinge of dread as he considered her enthusiastic plan. The problem was if he surfaced, if his name got around, Talbot might find him first. Compressing his lips, Sky set his sandwich back on the plate. "I don't know, Kelly."

"Come on, Sky!" she exclaimed. "People would be enthralled with them and your incredible information. I thought you got into this line of work to save the raptors. What better way to do so than speak about them? I know how I felt when you walked up to me with a hawk on your gauntlet. It was awe-inspiring. And what a way to get people's attention!"

"Whoa," he growled. "It would take a lot of time I don't have, Kelly. You see how busy we are here. Even with your help, there're still loose ends. Things that need to be done. I really don't want to take more time out of my schedule to drive down to Philipsburg and give presentations. Besides, I don't want to stress my birds. Some travel well and others don't."

"But you said falconers always transport birds in travel cases and it doesn't bother them at all if it's done right. Falconers drive across states for meetings or to fly their birds in competitions. Philipsburg is only twenty-five miles away. That's a short trip, compared to other stories you've told me." She gave Sky a pleading look. His usually clear blue eyes were dark and hooded. She could tell he was shutting down, but she couldn't put her finger on why. Why would he want to keep himself so isolated?

"I don't know . . ." he hedged, not wanting to discuss it any further. Having lost his appetite, he pushed his chair back and stood up, resting his hands on the Formica counter as he looked out the window. "I just don't have time, Kelly."

"Well, okay," she said defiantly. "How about if I do it? You've taught me enough that I can easily transport Bella in a travel case, give a basic talk on raptors to a club or group."

His conscience pricked him. How badly Sky wished he could give in to Kelly's request. He wanted to please her, to make her happy. He rested his hip against the counter and folded his arms across his chest. If Kelly gave such a talk, his name might not factor into it. "I don't mind if you do it. I don't like talking in front of groups. It's just not my thing. You're more outgoing than I am." Hesitating, he added, "But if you do this, Kelly, you have to promise me you won't ever mention my name. Okay?" As he drilled her with a dark look, he saw her eyes widen in surprise.

"But . . . why? They're your birds. You're my teacher. How can I not mention your name, Sky?"

He shook his head. "Listen, Kelly, if you want to do this, I'll let you. But if you can't keep my name out of it, I'll squash the whole plan."

Kelly frowned. "Well, okay, sure. I can promise not to mention your name. But what if people want to know how I got my knowledge? Where the birds live? What can

I tell them? I won't lie."

"My business is called Rocky Mountain Raptors, Incorporated. You can use that name. You can say, in general, that it's located in western Montana. That should do it. Just don't drag my name or where I live into it. You can't."

There was a hard finality to his tone that Kelly had never heard before. He meant every word. Because she had never seen this side of him, she was stunned. The firm set of his mouth, the determination in his copper-colored features all affected her and she didn't quite know how to respond. But she couldn't let the matter go. "Don't you think you're carrying your introversion a little too far?" she challenged. "It's one thing to keep a low profile because you don't like crowds and you're uncomfortable in them. It's quite another to literally hide, Sky. I mean, that isn't normal."

Stung, he dropped his arms, walked over and jerked his hat off the hook near the door. "Dammit, Kelly, you either do as I say or you don't do it at all."

The screen door slammed shut as he departed as if to emphasize his angrily spoken words.

"Ouch," Kelly muttered, watching him through the screen as he stalked off toward the mews. She returned to her sandwich and tried to understand his reaction. This wasn't the Sky she knew. He was always willing to work with her, and made compromises when necessary. Oh, he had his moments, for sure, but this was different. And upsetting. They'd never had a fight before.

"And over something so stupid," Kelly said out loud. Getting up, she walked with a limp to the counter and poured herself a second cup of coffee. Sky had disappeared among the raptor enclosures, she noted, before limping back to the table and sitting down.

Well, to heck with him and his precious isolation. Opening the Philipsburg paper, she turned to the local section that listed all the clubs and organizations. With or without his help, she was going to carry through on her plan. People needed to know that shooting one of these beautiful raptors was wrong. And if he didn't have the guts to get out there, working for a higher, better cause, then she would!

Taking a pen, she circled the two retirement homes, three assisted-living facilities and four social clubs in the Philipsburg area. She could at least talk to the administrators and see if there was a positive response to her giving a raptor program.

School was out for the summer or she would arrange to talk to students as well. For right now, this was a good training-wheels exercise. Besides, Bella was such a show-off. Kelly knew the Harris hawk would eat up the added attention.

Excitement thrummed through her. Instinctually, Kelly knew her small program would be a hit with seniors as well as service club members. And if all went well, she'd contact the schools in late August to see if she couldn't speak to classes. Reaching teens and young children was crucial. If they saw Bella, none of them would ever lift a gun or throw out poisoned meat to kill her or her kind again. Kelly just knew it.

Setting the pen down, she grinned. She liked her plan. She knew it was a good one, even if Sky was being a sourpuss. Maybe once he saw her success, he'd crawl out of his hole and join her. He knew so much more about the raptors than she did.

Well, time to get to work! She took the paper and walked over to the wall phone. Dialing the first number, she drew a deep breath and hoped for the best.

Billy Jo Talbot phoned his mother as he always did when he had his five-minute weekly call from the prison. Only this time, because of his model behavior, the warden had gifted him with an extra five minutes. Best of all, he got to use the prison cell phone, which wasn't monitored. Now he could really talk without eavesdroppers listening in. All he had to do was keep his voice low so the guard near the door couldn't overhear the conversation.

"Hello?"

Billy Jo heard his mother's thin, reedy voice at the other end. "Ma? It's me. How are you feeling?" He would never tell her that he was anxious about losing her. He'd been so close to his father, and when Alfred had suffered that fatal heart attack in the courtroom at his second trial, Billy Jo had hardly been able to assimilate the news. He blamed Sky McCoy. And when his mother suffered a minor stroke that had slowed her down, he blamed McCoy for that, too.

The doctor had told him that fifty was early for a stroke, and that stress had probably triggered it. As he gripped the phone more firmly, Billy Jo's thick lips puckered. He knew the "stress" was due to him being put in prison for twelve years. Lena had always doted on him, and he loved her in return. To lose a second parent would be beyond his comprehension. The one thing Billy Jo was looking forward to when he got released was going home to care for his mother. She deserved that. He didn't admit he felt guilty that his own actions may have caused all the catastrophe in his family; he refused to accept the responsibility. Instead, he projected his rage onto McCoy. Billy Jo wanted to give his mother the life she deserved, to make her happy once more. If she was happy, he'd be happy.

"Son, it's so good to hear from you."

Surprised at the enthusiasm and strength in her voice, he said, "Mom, you sound really good." Her tone conveyed happiness, something he rarely experienced from her. His own spirits rose. What had made her so upbeat?

"Son, we just had a wonderful program at the garden club I belong to. You won't believe it. A woman came with a Harris hawk named Bella, which sat on her glove. She gave an hour-long talk about how raptors are good for our environment." Snickering, Lena added dramatically, "And you'll never guess who it was."

"Tell me, Ma. I'm all ears."

"The woman was none other than Kelly Trayhern. You know, the Trayherns who paid for Sky McCoy's defense at both your trials."

Shaken, he barked, "You've got to be kidding me! She's one of the Trayhern twins. The one that got me into all this trouble."

"That's right," Lena said primly, practically oozing with excitement. "And you know how you've been looking for McCoy? And Harve has never found him?"

"Yes," he said impatiently, wondering where all this was going.

"Well," Lena exclaimed triumphantly, "I know where McCoy is! The Trayhern bitch is living with him! She accidentally slipped and said that the bird belonged to him. He runs a place called Rocky Mountain Raptors, Inc. I don't think she meant to give out his name, though. It sort of popped out by accident, because she was so enthused over the hawk and how McCoy had trained the raptor. One of the other members asked who her teacher was, and out came his name." Lena crowed with delight. "Can you imagine, son? You've wanted to hunt him down and finish off the job once you get released. Now you can! This Trayhern girl gave us all kinds of information about raptor rehabilitation. McCoy is licensed by the state of Montana, so I'm already busy looking for his address."

Stunned, Billy Jo blinked a couple of times. "Ma . . ."

"I couldn't believe my eyes and ears, baby

boy. You know, Kelly Trayhern didn't attend your trial. The Trayherns didn't allow their children to show up. But Kelly was the one who beat you up, remember? You'd defended yourself against McCoy's attack, and she came running up with all her karate moves and knocked you down? Knocked the knife you were defending yourself with out of your hand?"

Billy Jo had lied to his parents and told them that McCoy had threatened him with a knife on the playground. And that he'd drawn his own knife in self-defense against the Injun. His parents had bought his lie, as had their lawyer, who vigorously defended him in court. In the end, the jury had believed McCoy. No other knife had been found on the playground except Billy Jo's, and they'd convicted him. His parents, however, believed his made-up story. And his mother remained angry and wanted to extract revenge on McCoy. Even after suffering a stroke, she'd tried to find out where the bastard was hiding.

"That's good, Ma. Real good. This is the break we've needed," he said, his voice rising in sudden excitement. "So that Trayhern girl is living with McCoy?"

"Well, she said they were friends. She asked us to forget that she'd mentioned Mc-

Coy's name, that he was very shy and didn't want to take credit for what he did." Snorting, Lena said, "I bet the son of a bitch didn't want his name mentioned because he was in hiding, trying to avoid you."

Billy Jo frowned thoughtfully. "I'll bet if he's licensed by the state of Montana, that's on public record, Ma," he said in a whisper. "You could go online with that computer you have, then let me know. Maybe I can send Harve out to quietly investigate and confirm McCoy's whereabouts. Then I'll set my plans into motion." When he had McCoy in his sights, he'd take him out, but only after destroying everything he loved first. McCoy was going to suffer as Billy Jo had. As his parents had.

"Leave it to me, son. It will give me plenty to do. I'm pretty good at using a computer. I'll get all the information."

"Can you get me a map of the area where he lives? Send it to me? That would be handy. Even though all my mail is checked by the guards, they won't have a clue as to what a map means. But I will."

"Of course. I can do that real easy."

Joy soared through Talbot. He felt a wave of relief, and of anger. Finding McCoy was the key. And Kelly Trayhern had just handed over the one thing he wanted in his life besides care for his mother: Sky McCoy, his nemesis. "That's great, Ma. You've done good. You sure made my week, month and year," he exclaimed, laughing euphorically.

"Let me get all the details, son, and I'll send you a care package."

Talbot knew his mother wanted revenge. Before they'd sent him off to prison, he'd promised her he was going to kill McCoy, who'd been the cause of his dad's death. Lena was in agreement. They were descended from Tennessee hill people, where an eye for an eye was a way of life.

But this time, Billy Jo would make damn sure that he wouldn't be pinned with another murder. No, he was older, smarter, more patient. He'd make sure his tracks were covered, and no one in law enforcement could ever accuse him of killing Sky McCoy. Not this time . . .

Chapter Twelve

"I only made one mistake," Kelly assured Sky as she sliced tomatoes for their salad. "Midway through my presentation, someone asked who my teacher was and your name slipped out." She glanced over her shoulder to where he was setting plates on the table.

"Where exactly did you mention my name?" he demanded, his voice tight with tension. Kelly didn't realize the implications. She hadn't heard Talbot's threat in court. And her parents had obviously kept it from her, wanting her focus on schooling and going to the Academy. Sky fought to keep his alarm to himself. He'd known that this might happen. No one was perfect, least of all him. Sooner or later, Talbot would find him.

Sky had wanted to keep the convict at bay for as long as possible, so that he had the element of surprise and not the other way around. Billy Jo was an excellent hunter. But so was Sky. He'd have to be more alert than ever after the release date in June.

"It was at the gardening club. There were twelve women present." She saw anger in his eyes as he straightened, disappointment etched in his face. "Don't worry," she added hastily, putting slices of tomato on each salad. "I really don't think your name remained on their radar very long. They were too excited over Bella."

Sky went to the stove, slipped on oven mitts and drew out the tuna-and-noodle casserole he'd made earlier. Usually the sharp cheddar cheese and salty Fritos on top would make his mouth water. But right now, his stomach was churning. "It doesn't matter, Kelly. I asked you not to divulge my name or where I live. Did you tell them that, too?" He shot her a penetrating glance.

"No. Someone asked, but I didn't say. I told them I was living with you for three months while my leg healed." Kelly handed him the salads and opened the drawer to get a spatula. "I'm really sorry. It won't happen again, I promise."

"Don't promise what you can't deliver, Kelly." Sky walked to the fridge and picked out the salad dressing.

Kelly smarted at his sharp tone, but

wanted to reassure him. "If you saw how those gardeners responded to Bella, how their eyes lit up, Sky, I think you could trust that your good name is safe. They were enthralled and enthusiastic about her, and I doubt they remember little else. Bella would flap her wings, roll her feathers, delighting them all. They begged us to come back with another raptor."

Mollified, Sky pulled out the chair for Kelly to sit down. It wasn't the end of the world, he told himself. Talbot would find him anyway. There were so many avenues available on the Internet to track a person. The fact that his raptor incorporation had to reveal his home address was proof of that. Sky just wanted to keep the confrontation off his property. For now, he made an effort to hide his unease. "It sounds like they really enjoyed your presentation."

"They did. That's a dozen people who will pass on their experience with Bella to their families and friends. That's not a large number, but I have plans to spread the word. The president, Susan Perkins, said she'd like me to give talks to other gardening clubs in western Montana. I'd love to do that if you're okay with it."

After spooning some of the casserole onto her plate, Sky handed it to her. He'd come to value their dinners together. It was a moment of intimacy and a chance to relax. They didn't have to rush off after eating as at breakfast and lunch. With the extra money coming in from the Trayherns for Kelly's stay, he took a three-month hiatus from his night job. It was nice to sleep at night once more. "Why not? If you like being an educator, go for it," he said, making an effort to sound upbeat.

Kelly's face glowed, her clear green eyes sparkling with such life that Sky couldn't be angry with her. "Would you have a problem with me taking Bella to other towns to give talks?" she asked eagerly. "I know you said falconers travel all the time with their birds, and the raptors arrive fresh and rested."

"I don't mind. Part of our job is to educate, but I'm just not outfitted to do it. If you want to, go ahead. Luna would be good to take to talks, too. Many people think owls are vermin. When they realize hawks go after daytime rodents and owls take over at night, they might consider their neighborhood owl a real feathered friend."

Kelly grinned and attacked her food. The day had gone well and her talk had been successful. Even more important, Bella had traveled well, and Kelly had handled the Harris hawk with ease. They were a good team. "I know. I'd love to take Luna with me. But she's partial to men because she imprinted on you when she was a chick. Do you think she'll be okay with me?"

Nodding, Sky absorbed her warmth and eagerness. "She'll be fine, don't worry." It hurt him deeply not to be able to forge a more intimate connection with Kelly. But if he really loved her, he'd protect her from Talbot's coming release.

His fork halted midway to his mouth. *Love?* Scowling, he popped the salad into his mouth and started chewing. Did he love Kelly? Sky would need time alone to feel his way through that question.

Kelly sighed happily. "It's hard to believe I'll be gone at the end of August. I'll sure miss you and this place. I love getting up in the morning, helping to feed the raptors, watching the sun rise and having a cup of coffee with you."

The salad jammed in his throat. Sky refused to look at her. Oh, he heard the nostalgia, the longing, in Kelly's husky words, but he didn't dare comment. Under no circumstance could he urge her to stay. Instead, he said, "I'm happy it's been of help. But I'll be glad to get back to my usual routine."

Hurt riffled through Kelly and she dipped

her head so Sky wouldn't see how his gruff words affected her. Eating without tasting, she swallowed hard. "I'm sure you'll be happier when you're back to normal. I appreciate how much my being here has interrupted that."

"You need to find a condo in Philipsburg. Have you started looking?" Sky chastised himself for his brusqueness, but concentrated on eating. His gut hurt, his heart ached. He disliked himself for doing this to Kelly. He knew how happy she was here. She'd blossomed. Her leg was improving every week. She'd graduated from crutches to using the cane and was taking mile-long walks every night. Sky wanted to tell her how proud he was of her, but he couldn't. Anything that suggested her staying on was off-limits. He would not put her in the crosshairs of Talbot's rifle. His life was on hold until the confrontation came and he managed to survive it. Until then, he couldn't think of a future.

Did he want one with Kelly? Hell, yes. But why let her know he might die in June? Was it right to hurt someone like that? Sky had had too much ripped away from him in his life to do that to Kelly.

"Uh . . . y-yes," Kelly stammered. Sky had suddenly grown cold and distant. His jaw was set, his mouth flexed downward as he ate. "I've got a condo rented from my parents. I'm all set to move out of here at the end of the month." Trying to stave off her feelings of loss and hurt, she asked timidly, "Does this mean you never want me to come back up here, except to take the raptors to groups and do the talks? I know you need help with them. I could still do small things to help you out, Sky."

"Maybe," he muttered. "I don't mind you coming up here to take a raptor to a club, or travel with them to do talks. Let me think about the rest, Kelly."

Drawing a deep, serrating breath, Kelly let the shock roll through her. It hadn't occurred to her that her three months here might have put a terrific strain on Sky. How could she have misunderstood him? So often, when she caught him off guard, he was looking at her with warmth and longing. How could she have misinterpreted those glances? Confused, Kelly said, "Of course, I understand."

Sky hated himself for hurting Kelly like this. But it had to be done. He couldn't have her just popping back into his life unannounced. What would happen if she came up to his cabin after Talbot was released? What if Billy Jo found her here? Sky couldn't erase the nightmares he'd had since she'd come to stay. They occurred with sickening regularity. He understood it was his subconscious fearing for Kelly's life. He loved her . . . and he refused to see her put at risk.

Love? There was that word again. Sky dropped his fork on his plate with a clatter. Excusing himself, he set his dishes on the counter and strode out the back door, hat in hand. He had to think. And he couldn't do it with Kelly present. She didn't realize how much her womanly scent, her lovely red hair framing her freckled face, called to him. His heart thrashed wildly in his chest as he headed through the dusk toward the flight oval.

Standing there in the middle of the clearing, hands planted on his hips, Sky looked up at the purple sky. *Love.* He loved Kelly. When had that happened? How had he not seen it coming?

He'd felt a lot for her in his youth, but thought it was just a phase, puppy love. Rubbing his face, he uttered a curse, something he didn't do often. Then he stalked off down one of the many hiking trails. The path would lead to meadows where he trained his raptors how to hunt in the wild once he released them.

As he walked through the darkened forest, Sky felt the full extent of his suffering. His emotions rolled through him like an avalanche. Tears flooded his eyes, and anger toward Talbot flared. Sky was a prisoner until he could confront the man, after his release. Worse, he had to deny and hide his love for Kelly. The sense of deprivation, of being tortured and hurt all over again by Billy Jo, washed through him. The hunter and the hunted. Talbot was the predator, and Sky the target. But this time, Sky was going to turn the tables on him.

The hurt in his heart and the knowledge he'd wounded Kelly tonight pulverized him. She was the last person he ever wanted to hurt. And yet, to protect her, he had to. He loved her enough to shield her from the truth.

Gradually, the night sounds of the forest began to intrude upon his agonized thoughts. He looked up at the stars, just coming out above him. The wind blew softly, carrying the piney scent of the evergreens surrounding him, as if to ease his grief and rage. Somewhere off in the murky shadows, he heard the hooting of a great horned owl. The predator was getting ready to hunt. The queen of the night, as the Cherokee referred to the largest owl in

North America, was nearby, and the deep sound soothed his raw state.

Sky kept walking, toward one of the high mountain meadows where he trained his hawks with lures. The moon was full, its radiance filtering through the firs enough to light the trail. Right now, he couldn't return to the cabin. Not in his current ravaged state.

What was he going to do? Life was such a twisted path for him. He could never tell Kelly he loved her. More than anything, Sky wanted to go back, apologize to her, hold her, kiss her and let her know how deeply he cared for her — and always would.

Time and distance had not dimmed his love for Kelly. It was a helluva fix to be in.

Kelly awoke screaming. The nightmare had returned with a vengeance. Sitting up in bed, she clasped both hands to her mouth to stop her shrieks. The darkness was muted by moonlight, seeping through the curtains at the window. Sobbing for breath, Kelly climbed out of bed, covered with sweat, then hobbled out the door toward the bathroom. Splashing cold water on her face always helped bring her back to the here and now.

In the living room, she gripped the edge

of the couch as she passed. The coolness of the cedar floor beneath her bare feet helped reorient her, but she had to keep pressing her fist against her mouth to stop the sobbing. She didn't want to wake Sky. He'd made it very clear last night at dinner that she was no longer welcome. Her breathing ragged, and with hot tears running down her cheeks, she made it to the bathroom.

She had to be quiet! Turning on the faucet with a shaking hand, Kelly leaned over and splashed the cold, soothing water across her eyes and cheeks. Doing so slowed the mental images flashing through her head of the helicopter falling to the ground, the forest fire blazing around her like hell itself.

"Kelly?"

Sky's voice, thick with sleep, intruded.

She jerked upward. Sky stood in front of her, wearing only light blue pajama bottoms, his broad chest gleaming in the moonlight. His hair was tousled, his eyes sleepy, his voice husky with concern.

"I, uh, I had a bad dream," she stammered, grabbing a towel and pressing it to her face. "I'm sorry. I didn't mean to wake you. I tried to be quiet." And suddenly, despite herself, Kelly began to cry again. How embarrassing that she couldn't control the terrible sounds tearing out of her mouth.

Sky had never seen her like this. Since she'd moved to the cabin, her nightmares had become much less frequent, and Kelly was forever grateful.

Sky reached out to her. "Come here," he rasped, his hands moving to her shaking shoulders and pulling her toward him. He did so automatically, without thinking. His heart was screaming at him to help her. He couldn't stand to see Kelly suffering.

At first she tensed. And then she tried to pull away.

"Don't fight me," he growled, and gripped her even more firmly.

"But you don't want me here!" Kelly cried, dropping the towel from her face. "Let me go, Sky! Just let me go!"

Her hoarse voice shattered his reserve. He saw the anguish in her red-rimmed, watery eyes, saw the pain he'd caused her. Digging his fingers into her shoulders, he shook his head.

"I do want you here." He held her tighter.

Kelly sobbed. It was useless to fight her feelings for Sky. The burning look in his eyes, the way his mouth set, the strength of his grip on her shoulders all persuaded her to stop fighting him. If only for a few minutes, she could sink into Sky's arms and feel safe. He was a warrior, a protector, and had always made her feel secure in an uncertain world.

She nestled her head against his neck and wrapped her arms around his waist. His own arms, strong and comforting, pressed her shaking, trembling body to his own solid form, and she reveled in the contact.

Sky stood there, legs apart, supporting Kelly. He closed his eyes, and pressed his head against hers. They both needed this release, for different reasons, he guessed. Heart pounding erratically, he lifted one hand and gently smoothed his fingers through her red hair. How soft it was, more silky than he could ever have imagined. He was touching her, and couldn't stop himself even if he tried.

Sky was so tired emotionally, tired of repressing his love for Kelly, that in this instant he could only follow the dictates of his heart. After sliding his fingers through her hair again, he moved his hand downward, grazing her neck and shoulder, which were damp with perspiration. He understood all too well the virulence of her nightmare, and he wanted to soothe her. Tenderly he stroked his palm down her long, lean spine, hoping to ease her anxiety. Kelly clung to him, her arms clasped so tight around his waist that he was surprised by her strength. Nothing had ever felt so good, so right to him.

"It's going to be all right," he promised thickly. "Just let it out, Kelly. I'm here. I'll hold you. I'll help you . . ."

The roughly spoken words touched Kelly deeply and set off a new wave of sobbing. Sky released her and carefully led her to the couch. Limping at his side, she relished the strength of his arm around her shoulders, the care radiating from him like the sun itself. He was so strong, sure and confident, and Kelly knew she could lean on him in this terrible moment of weakness, brought on by her awful nightmare of the crash.

"Come on, sit down and lean against me," he coaxed. As she sank onto the couch, Sky fitted her against him. She buried her face against his shoulder, sliding her arms around his neck. Her womanly form settled against his harder angles like water flowing around rocks, and he sat back, closed his eyes and simply held her.

Over time, Kelly's trembling abated. With each stroke of his palm against her shoulder and back, she relaxed more. Silence blanketed them.

She seemed perfectly content to lie curled up against him. Sky savored the moment because he knew it would never happen again. It couldn't. But like the thief he'd become, he greedily absorbed the feel of her breath against his skin, her slim arms around his neck, her breasts pressed against his chest, her hip melded against his. Strands of her hair tickled his jaw. His body was on fire wherever they touched.

The quietness of the early morning was complete. The windows were open; the fragrance of pines surrounded them; the moonlight was luminous. Sky had the woman he loved in his arms. He lifted his head and pressed a kiss to Kelly's tousled hair. His body ached for her. How badly he wanted her, wanted to make slow, healing love to her and let her know that her life didn't have to be held captive by the nightmares from her past. That his love for her would help orient her back to him and into the present. There was so much he wanted to do, but he was imprisoned by his own past and an inevitable moment in the future. Until then, his life was on hold — as was his love for Kelly.

If not for Talbot, Sky would be free to pursue a relationship with Kelly. Clearly, she liked him. He was all too aware of her longing looks, the light in her eyes when they were together. All the signs were there, and yet he couldn't take advantage of them.

Kelly couldn't have an inkling of how he really felt. There would be no shared dreams with her.

Hurting badly, Sky pressed his face against her hair and closed his eyes. All he wanted was this stolen moment, this one time together.

"I — I'm sorry I woke you." Kelly hiccupped, then shifted slightly. She didn't want to, but she had to stop holding Sky. While she understood he was consoling her as a friend, she felt other feelings burning in her body — feelings that could never be acted upon. Pulling away, she looked up through her wet lashes into his shadowy face. The moonlight emphasized his high cheekbones, the strength of his masculine jaw.

When she saw the glittering look in his half-closed eyes, she was startled. It was the look of a man wanting his woman. How could that be? Confused as a mass of conflicting emotions roared through her, she hiccupped again. "When I cry, I hiccup," she apologized.

Sky's hard features grew tender. A slight smile curved that very male mouth she so desperately wanted to kiss. What would it be like to kiss Sky?

Threading his fingers through her hair

once more, he whispered unsteadily, "It's okay, Kelly. It really is. You needed to cry, to release the poison from that crash."

She looked down, unable to witness the warmth burning in his eyes. "Yeah, but after last night's conversation at dinner, I know you need me to leave. And I will. Soon. I — I just didn't expect this . . . this nightmare to come back." She brushed the tears from her cheeks.

Sky hadn't released her. His arms enfolded her like a warm, comforting blanket. Kelly knew he wanted to help her, but he didn't love her as she loved him. She stiffened for a moment as she considered the ramifications of that thought. And then it all fell into place. Of course she loved Sky. When had she not loved this man? She'd grown up with him, shared so much good and so much unhappiness. Kelly had spent more time with him than with any other man in her entire life. What was there not to love about Sky?

"Our talk last night probably brought it back," he agreed tiredly. "It was upsetting for both of us. I just meant that it was time for you to leave, in order to continue your healing process, Kelly. I didn't say I never wanted to see you again, because that's not true."

Hiccupping once more, Kelly lay in his arms and considered her predicament. As his fingers stroked her hair, her scalp tingled delightfully. The need for him, the need to kiss him, nearly drove her to do just that. Yet Kelly was old enough to know that would be folly. Sky had made it clear he wanted her out of there by the end of August. She'd given her word and she'd keep it.

Not wanting to, but knowing she must, she eased away from him. Dropping her feet to the floor, she sat up and wiped her face once more. "I overreacted," she said brokenly. "I should just go to bed. I'll be okay now, Sky. Thanks for giving me a few moments reprieve." Kelly hoped he knew how grateful she was. As she stood, she saw him raise his hand, as if to reach out and touch her. Kelly limped out of range, when what she wanted to do was slip into his bed, lie beside him, love him and sleep with him. She instinctively knew if she did that, her nightmares would end; such was the sense of protection Sky gave her.

Sky swallowed hard as he watched Kelly limp across the living room on her bare feet. Her bedroom door quietly closed. Frowning, he sat up, propping his elbows on his spread thighs. What the hell did he expect?

For Kelly to ask him to take her to bed? A bad taste coated the inside of his mouth.

He hated himself. But he hated Talbot more. Billy Jo had again put his life on hold and denied him the woman he loved.

This dance would end shortly. Sooner or later, the issue would be resolved. One of them would die.

But Sky wasn't sure which of them it would be.

CHAPTER THIRTEEN

It was the last day Kelly would be living under Sky's roof. Sadness blanketed her, as did a sense of loss. Since their talk in early August, when he had made it clear she was a hindrance, she had become a shadow of her former self. He'd been unreachable since then, retreating deep inside himself.

Thunderclouds hung around the mountain today. Kelly could hear the far-off rumble that meant impending rain. A good thing, because western Montana had suffered drought conditions and the whole forest needed a drink.

Moving slowly, but with much less of a limp than before, and without her cane, she watched Jason and Annie pack the last of her belongings in their Toyota Tundra truck. Warmth for her older brother and his hardworking wife filled her. Their two kids were at their grandparents' home while Jason and Annie helped her move into her condo.

The cabin had been a soothing place of healing for her, but how would she say goodbye to Sky? He'd been conspicuously absent during the moving process and she had to find him. Kelly walked through the kitchen and pushed open the screen door. She spotted him with Luna, out at the training oval. He was teaching the huge owl to fly from one perch to another. Luna had grown a lot and was now six pounds. No wonder˙the people of Europe called this mighty owl an eagle.

The chronic pain in Kelly's leg had diminished considerably and she wanted to push her rehab once she moved down to Philipsburg. Her physical therapist had suggested she begin jogging — albeit slowly at first — and Kelly could hardly wait. She'd rather be jogging up here on the logging road, but Sky wanted her gone. *Out of his life.*

Sky brought Luna from the perch to his glove. The owl ruffled her gold-and-brown feathers and made little growling noises. Smiling at the huge bird, he gave her a piece of meat. Luna quickly grabbed it in her curved yellow beak and gulped it down. And then he noticed Kelly walking toward him.

Swallowing hard, he tried to steel himself against her leaving, but found it impossible. He was guilty as hell for his abysmal treatment of her, ignoring her and discouraging further contact. If only he could tell her why! But he couldn't. Better that Kelly move on with her life and find some guy who would love her freely. . . .

His heart was heavy, and he rubbed his chest as she stopped before him.

"Hey, we're done moving my stuff out. I just wanted to say goodbye, Sky. To thank you for all you've done for me." She gave the owl a fond look. "This place, you, the birds, all helped me heal." Her gaze met his shadowed one. "I just want you to know you gave me a reason to live again."

Kelly's voice dropped to a quaver. "I know you don't think you've done much, but you have, Sky. When you walked in with Bella on your glove that day, I didn't realize that you would help me heal." She gave him an appreciative smile and patted her left thigh. The removable cast had come off a week ago, the doctor pronouncing her leg well on its way to recovery. "I went from being a cripple to almost whole in the three months I spent here with you."

"I'm really glad you're getting better," he murmured. A look of love shone clearly in Kelly's eyes. Sky didn't try to fool himself; he loved her, too. But those words couldn't be spoken. At least not now. Maybe never.

Grief rolled through him, with such force he felt momentarily suffocated. His voice dropped to a rasp. "Thank you so much for all you did. You're incredible with the birds. They love you." *I love you.* Gulping, he added, "I'd still like you to come up once a week to help me. I think the educational programs, if you want to continue them, are a good idea. I don't like having raptors shot up by stupid hunters who think they're vermin. Your talks will make a difference, and I'd like you to continue doing them if you want."

"I'd love to continue the raptor talks. I'll come back in a week," she promised. Stepping forward, Kelly reached out and gripped his right hand. "You've always been a dear, dear friend to me. I want to reciprocate."

When he pulled his hand from hers, Kelly realized he didn't want the contact. Pain flooded her heart. She wanted so badly to touch Sky. To love him. But he wasn't interested.

"If you come next Saturday, that would be fine," he said, his voice low. "I gotta go, Kelly. Luna needs to be put away. I'll see you around." He stepped away from her and headed toward the mews.

Frowning, Kelly stood there for a moment, reeling from the shock of his abrupt departure. Well, what did she expect? Sky was being honest with her. He always had been. He didn't want her around much, nor did he want her touch. Rubbing her palms against her jeans, she turned and headed back to the cabin to get her purse and then drive down the mountain with Jason and Annie.

As Kelly left the cabin and walked out to the Tundra, where the others awaited her, a bolt of lightning shot across the sky above them, instantly followed by a booming, thunderous roar. The ground shook. The very air seemed to vibrate with the power of the approaching storm. Wiping her eyes clear of tears, she gave Annie a wobbly smile and opened the passenger door.

What was that lightning bolt about? Kelly wondered. A synchronistic symbol of their shattered relationship? As she shut the door, she looked longingly back at the cabin. Sky was not there to send her off. Why should he be? She swallowed her disappointment and put on the seat belt.

Annie gripped her hand. "You okay, Kelly?"

Sniffling, she shook her head. Annie passed her a tissue as Jason eased the truck onto the rutted road heading toward Philipsburg.

Giving her a sad look, Annie said, "We know you love Sky. We think he loves you, but he's afraid, Kelly."

Blowing her nose, Kelly was unable to speak.

"Hang on . . ." Jason warned, gripping the wheel more firmly, "we've got a timber truck on our tail. I'm going to get over as much as I can, because he's highballin' it."

Kelly was used to seeing the massive, heavily loaded logging trucks barreling down the mountain road. The grade was steep near Sky's cabin, which was always a dangerous situation. Many times in the past three months, Kelly had been pushed off the rutted dirt road onto the soft shoulder by loggers.

Jason whispered a curse as he hauled the Tundra over to one side. A few feet away from them was a solid wall of trees. If they ever made impact, neither the pickup nor its occupants would likely survive the crash.

The timber truck blared its horn and sped by, kicking up thick, yellow clouds of dust.

"Wow, that guy is going way too fast!" Annie said, frowning. She turned to her husband. "You okay, Jas? That was close. Too close."

"I'm okay. That driver should be fined for reckless driving and speeding. If I hadn't seen him coming in my rearview mirror, he'd have hit us. This section of road is a lot narrower than elsewhere and there's hardly any room to pass." Easing his foot off the brake, he gave a quick glance back to ensure that Kelly's bags and gear were still tied down and in place. Then he pressed the accelerator. "We'll take our time here. I don't want all that dust on Kelly's stuff even though we've got it covered with a tarp."

Shaking her head, Annie glared at the timber truck, which was already nearly out of sight below. "Stupid idiot. He'll get someone killed on this road sooner or later."

Kelly blotted her eyes. "I can't tell you how many times they've raced past Sky's place, nearly out of control. The timber they carry is so heavy it pushes the truck to high speeds, even with the brakes being applied."

"Well," Jas muttered angrily, "I'm reporting that guy when we get home. The sheriff needs to know about this. What about the tourists who come up here?" He gestured toward the road. "They'd never expect to have these timber trucks hurtling out of the blue at them. They'd panic and probably hit the brakes in the middle of the road, and then the truck would plow into them. Nothing can withstand being hit by a timber truck. They're just too big and heavy. Did either of you see his license plate?"

"No," Annie said, "there was too much dust."

"I got three numbers — 520," Kelly said. "The rest was impossible to make out."

"That's enough," Jas said, scowling. "I wish cell phones worked up here. I wish they'd get a cell tower up there on that peak above us. I know there's an accident going to happen on this road. I can feel it."

Her older brother had damn good intuition, Kelly knew. And sometimes he could foretell future events. "I hope you're wrong, Jas, because if there's ever an accident, there'd be no way to call for help. This mountainous region is a dead zone for all cellular service."

Annie patted Kelly's hand. "Let it go. You have a brand-new life starting as of right now. I love the condo your parents gave you, with its three bedrooms and so much space. You and I need to look at decoration details. Aren't you excited?"

Kelly tried to be. Annie was a wonderful sister-in-law and she'd always felt close to her. Kelly saw her as an older, wiser sister who was strongly family oriented. "I need the help, Annie. Dad used that condo for mercenary teams to stay over and rest. It's so masculine and dark-looking at the moment."

Annie rubbed her hands and grinned. "On Monday morning, I'll be over at nine. We'll go to the hardware store and you can pick out some brighter, prettier colors of paint for the rooms. I'll help you. Laura is going to take care of the kids while we get that condo spruced up for you."

Jas chuckled. "Me? I get to go to work with Dad at Perseus."

"Are you feeling left out?" Annie teased, placing her arm around her husband's broad shoulders and giving him a quick hug. "You want to paint instead of learn your dad's business? You know, someday he's going to retire, and then it will be in your hands, Jas. You're learning fast, but there's so much more you need to know."

Grinning, he said, "No, I'm just jealous, I guess. Some days I wish I could go paint a room instead of dealing with the complexities of those wild, chaotic missions."

Kelly gave her brother a warm glance. "You can always come over for lunch, Jas. I'll make you something good to eat and you can check our progress. Fair enough?"

She saw Jas glow. He loved home-cooked food. "You got a deal," he answered.

As the three of them chatted together,

trundling along on the bumpy, winding road, Kelly tried to feel happy. She was grateful for her family's support. Annie was perceptive and knew there was more than just friendship between her and Sky. Yet Kelly couldn't do anything about that, because he didn't want her as anything but a friend.

Kelly forced herself not to cry. She'd cried so much the past few weeks, in the privacy of her room. She would miss Sky terribly, but enough tears had been shed.

Sky felt like a crazy man. Since Kelly left, he'd been unable to sleep. Sitting at the kitchen table over coffee, a newspaper he'd picked up in town in front of him, Sky couldn't read a sentence. He was completely distracted. Five days without Kelly. Great Spirit knew, he'd never been so lonely.

Even his raptors were flighty and nervous. It was as if they sensed his deep dissatisfaction with life since she had moved out. With a heavy sigh, Sky put the paper down. He'd made himself scrambled eggs, bacon and toast, but his breakfast had gotten cold. He began to understand how depression worked its evil upon a person. Oh, he'd suffered depression when his parents had been burned alive by Talbot, no question. Now, that dark hopelessness had returned.

But it was laced with an acidic loneliness he couldn't combat. Working with his raptors, an activity he'd thrown himself into this past week, like a madman chased by a ghost, had not alleviated the feeling. Nothing helped. Nothing worked.

Sky rubbed his bleary eyes. How badly he wanted to drive down the mountain, drop in for an impromptu visit to see how she was getting along at her new condo. He grabbed his coffee, took a sip and burned his tongue.

Uttering an uncharacteristic curse, he scraped his chair back and stood, then looked at his watch. It was 10:00 a.m. Time to go about his normal business in town. Running his fingers distractedly through his short hair, he got his checkbook, grabbed his cowboy hat and headed out the door.

The morning was warm, the sun bright and the sky turbulent with the threat of more thunderstorms. It had rained last night, making the road in front of the cabin a quagmire of yellow clay. It would be slow going down the mountain today and a little more precarious than usual, with the clay making for slippery conditions.

Sky climbed into his beat-up old Ford pickup and set down his checkbook and list.

The rain started, along with booming thunder. As he began to back out of his driveway and turn onto the road, Kelly's face flashed in his mind. How much he missed her! His heart felt like a black hole. Would he ever experience joy again, the way he had when she was with him? He hated that his situation with Talbot could hold such power. Mouth flattening, Sky shifted gears and headed down the mountain at a conservative pace. As the rain grew heavier, its pounding on the cab nearly drowned out the country music on his radio.

For nearly twenty minutes, Sky drove through a boiling, raging thunderstorm. Navajo people feared them, believing that lightning represented angry spirits. If a person got struck by a bolt, they were sometimes kicked out of the family, in the hopes that the bad luck wouldn't affect everyone else.

Gripping the wheel, Sky felt the truck's tires start to slide. The worst part of the road was coming up, a long curve with hundred-foot-tall pines lining both sides, creating a corridor. This was no place to lose control.

The windshield wipers were working overtime. Wind slammed into the pickup, and the tires skidded again from the power of the gust. Quickly correcting the truck, Sky slowed down even more, careful not to overcorrect. A less skilled driver would have caused the vehicle to go out of control.

Another bolt of lightning sizzled in front of him. Light blasted into the cabin of the truck. Momentarily blinded, Sky automatically put on the brakes. The lightning was so close that the resulting thunder occurred almost simultaneously. Blinded by the discharge, he put up his hand in reaction. When he did, the truck lost traction. And then began to spin out of control.

Rain pounded down around him. Half-blinded, Sky gasped, and grabbed the wheel as he started sliding sideways. And as the Ford spun more, facing the wrong direction, his eyes bulged. A logging truck was careening out of the storm, coming straight at him.

With a cry, Sky slammed on the brakes, to try to avoid the heavily loaded truck. Then everything went into slow motion. Through the heavy rain Sky saw the driver's features, how surprised he looked. The horror in the redhead's face, his mouth open in a scream Sky couldn't hear. The timber truck suddenly jackknifed, trying to avoid hitting Sky's truck. The load of timber, tons of it, came swinging past the cab and directly at the Ford.

Sky felt his entire world collapsing in on him. And then everything went black.

CHAPTER FOURTEEN

The phone rang in Kelly's condo. Annie was helping her put the finishing touches on painting the living room a delicate light pink.

"Word from the outside world," Kelly called out, wiping her hands on a rag. Her heart sped up in the hopes that Sky had finally called. All week long, she'd ached to hear his voice, find out how he was and how his beloved birds were doing.

Briskly rubbing her hands, she limped over to the phone, which was resting on top of the couch.

"Maybe it's Sky," Annie called, from atop the ladder where she was painting the ceiling.

"I wish . . ." Kelly tried not to sound so glum.

"It could be him," Annie said.

How badly she wanted to talk to Sky. Hearing his voice did funny, wonderful, uplifting things for her spirits. "Maybe he wants me to drop by before the weekend." Sky had made it clear that on Saturday she could come out for a couple of hours and help him with the raptors. It couldn't be soon enough. She missed him so much that her sleep was broken and the nightmares had come back full force.

"Hello?"

"Kelly Trayhern?"

"Yes, speaking."

"This is Dr. Perkins from the Anaconda Hospital calling."

Kelly frowned. "Yes?" Her mother routinely went up to Anaconda to visit any of the Perseus mercenaries who had been wounded in action, or to visit the veterans who gave so much for their country. But her mom wasn't there today. A feeling of dread came over Kelly. "Is there something wrong?"

"Ms. Trayhern, Sky McCoy was airlifted up here an hour ago. He was in an accident on a back road that involved a timber truck. I'm sorry, but he's in critical condition and in surgery right now. My nurse just went through his billfold and we found your name and phone number, so I assumed you are a relative."

Kelly nearly dropped the phone. For a

moment, she was speechless. "Oh, my God. Sky . . . is he . . . is he going to live?"

"I don't know. *Are* you related?"

Without thinking, Kelly blurted, "I'm his fiancée." She knew the hospital staff would allow her to see him under those circumstances. If she said she was a friend, they'd bar her from visiting him. Her stomach twisted into a tight knot and she shut her eyes.

"He's going to be in surgery for a while," the doctor was saying. "Can you get up here? Your phone exchange is for western Montana, but I don't know where exactly."

"Philipsburg," Kelly managed to say in a strangled tone. She opened her eyes and gazed at Annie, who was watching her from the ladder. "I'll get up there as soon as I can. Please, is there anything else you can tell me? What are his chances?"

"Ms. Trayhern, I really don't know. The admitting nurse can tell you more when you arrive. If I were you, I'd come as soon as possible."

Numbly, Kelly hung up. "My God, Annie, Sky's been in an accident. They've airlifted him to Anaconda." Her voice broke and she pressed her hands over her mouth to stop a sob.

Annie quickly climbed down the ladder.

"Let me fly you up there. The chopper's at the airport. I know your dad would approve the flight. Come on," she told her grimly, "get your stuff together. We can make it in about forty-five minutes. Did they say how it happened? How he is?"

Kelly told her everything as she quickly grabbed her purse, coat and keys. She didn't care that she was in old, paint-splattered clothes. "Drive me to the airport, Annie. I'm still not supposed to drive." In another week, her doctor was going to approve her driving a car once again because her leg was healing so quickly.

"Roger that," Annie said, opening the door. She drew out her cell phone. "I'll call your father, and then you might want to talk to your mom."

"Yes," Kelly said, tears burning in her eyes as they walked quickly toward the elevator in the hall. "Let's hurry . . ."

"He's still in surgery," the admitting nurse, Angela Kincaid, told Kelly and Annie. The woman peered intently at her computer screen. "Mr. McCoy was driving on a logging road this morning. There was a thunderstorm. Apparently his truck slid around a corner and an oncoming timber truck slammed into him." She grimaced and pushed her bifocals up on her nose. "No one discovered them for over an hour, Ms. Trayhern. I guess that's a remote area. Some tourists driving up there found the wreck. They went back down to Philipsburg and called the volunteer fire department. The rescue team had to use the jaws of life to extricate Mr. McCoy from his truck. The other driver was found unconscious. Both are here and in surgery right now. I'm sorry," she added, giving Kelly a sad look.

Gripping her purse, Kelly whispered, "Thank you, Angela."

"You should go to the visitors' room on the fifth floor. That's near the surgery center, and the doctor can find you there. The elevator is right behind you. The cafeteria is in the basement if you get hungry. Mr. McCoy is critical, according to the E.R. doctor," she added soberly.

"Is . . . is there any way to find out how long Sky will be in surgery?" Kelly stammered, battling back a fresh round of tears. She felt Annie's comforting arm around her waist.

"I'm sorry. I don't know the extent of his injuries. The nurses' station at ICU might, though. Go up there and ask. Be sure to tell him that you're his fiancée, and they'll give you what they knew about his condition at admittance."

The world tilted and spun. Kelly rasped out a thank-you and stumbled toward the elevator. She was glad for Annie's steadying grip on her arm. "My God, Annie. My God . . ."

"Take it easy, Kelly. There's a lot to find out yet. Don't think the worst." Her sister-in-law pressed the elevator button. "What about Sky's raptors? Who is going to feed them?"

Kelly groaned. "I completely forgot about that!" She turned and looked toward the doors. "I can't stay here. I have to get back to take care of them."

"One thing at a time," Annie urged. She looked at her watch. "It's 1:00 p.m. Let's go find out what's happening. Then I can fly you to Sky's cabin. I know there's a meadow near his place. Hopefully, the chopper won't scare the hell out of his birds. You can stay there and care for them."

Kelly was torn. She wanted to stay at the hospital, to be near Sky, but knew that without daily feeding the raptors would starve. "You're right. Okay," she whispered, dragging in a breath, "it's a good plan."

Annie patted her shoulder. "Once I drop you off at Sky's place, I can pick up your mom and fly her up here. She'll be glad to stay with Sky. Don't the birds have to be fed around dusk?"

Nodding, Kelly stepped into the elevator. "They do. You have a global positioning phone on you, don't you?"

She nodded in turn. "It's here in my backpack."

"Give it to me. I want to make sure that I can get through to the hospital after I leave, in case Sky's landline is down from the storm. You can get another one at the office."

Annie set her backpack on the shining tile floor and dug out the GPS phone. "Great idea!" She handed over the device.

Kelly thanked her numbly, feeling another wave of dread crashing over her. Sky could die! The man she'd loved so fiercely all her life might not survive surgery due to a stupid timber truck accident. Anger waged a war with fear and grief.

In no time, the elevator had whisked them to the surgery floor, and the doors opened. At the desk, Kelly introduced herself to the nurse on duty. She went through the motions of asking questions and getting information, while her thoughts raged out of control. What if Sky was paralyzed, or had suffered brain damage? Jason, her oldest brother, had suffered traumatic brain injury in an attack at his air base in Afghanistan. Kelly recalled the trials and tribulations her family had gone through in helping Jason get back his memories. Would she go through the same thing with Sky?

Nurse Linda Franks gave Kelly a reassuring smile as she opened Sky's file. "He's in surgery with Dr. Stanton, our best neurologist."

"Don't tell me. Brain injury?" Annie sighed.

"Mr. McCoy had to be extricated from his vehicle by the fire department and paramedics on the scene," the nurse said. "He was conscious at the time, but couldn't move his legs. When he was admitted here, Dr. Stanton was called. From what I could find out before they sent him to surgery, I believe there was spinal cord damage. How severe and what type, I don't know."

"Paralyzed?" Kelly managed to ask.

"Yes. From the waist down. But Dr. Stanton is world-renowned, Ms. Trayhern. If my memory serves me, he was one of the attending physicians on your brother's case a number of years ago. Jason Trayhern?"

"That's right," Annie said. "Sky really *is* in good hands with Dr. Stanton. He performed a number of surgeries on Jason over the years, after the initial brain damage.

He's wonderful, Kelly. The man is magic. If there's anyone who can help Sky, it's him." Annie gave the nurse a nod of thanks. "Come on, let's go to the helo. I'll get you to Sky's cabin."

The approaching dusk was frightening to Kelly. She stood forlornly inside Sky's empty cabin, and found the silence deafening. She'd been busy feeding raptors for an hour after Annie dropped her at the cabin by helicopter. But she was done now, and soon darkness would blanket her world.

Rubbing her face, she looked at the GPS phone again and wished it would ring. She knew her mother and Annie were at the hospital in Anaconda, waiting for Sky's long surgery to end. Would he live? Would he die?

Kelly pressed her hand to her heart, because it felt like it was breaking. She had to eat. No matter how upset she was, she had to keep going. Sky would worry about his birds once he became conscious. He'd want to know they were being looked after. That would take stress off him.

Why wouldn't the phone ring? He'd been in the operation theater almost eight solid hours. How much had gone wrong in the accident? Mind spinning, Kelly forced herself to go to the refrigerator. When she opened it, she saw it was nearly empty. Just some frozen dinners. . . .When she had lived there, the fridge had been stocked with lots of homemade items. Not now.

Staring into the fridge, Kelly began to realize how differently Sky had lived when she'd been with him. She pulled out a frozen dinner and unwrapped it.

The GPS phone rang.

Dropping the container on the counter, she jogged to the living room, her heart pounding with fear. It had to be her mother. Was Sky all right? What would she do if he died? With a groan, Kelly grabbed the phone and pressed the button. "Hello?"

"Honey, it's me," Laura Trayhern said.

Her mother sounded very tired and grim. Holding the phone tightly, Kelly whispered, "Mom? How is Sky? Is he out of surgery?"

"Yes, he is, honey. They just brought him out and he's in ICU, in critical condition. I just talked to Dr. Stanton, bless him. He saw me and I told him that you were Sky's fiancée, so we had a very good, private talk because of Jason, and seeing me all those times after his surgeries."

Barely breathing, Kelly asked, "Will he live, Mom?"

"Dr. Stanton said the first twenty-four hours will tell. Honey, he was a mess. Sky has four fractured vertebrae in the middle of his back. Dr. Stanton said the spinal cord wasn't cut, which is good, but was severely smashed, for lack of a better word. He said the surgery took so long because he had to put steel pins in the vertebrae to stabilize them, and attach them to healthy vertebrae above and below. He said the spinal column is swollen and that's what is causing Sky's paralysis."

Kelly moaned.

"That isn't all, honey," Laura said in a strained tone. "Sky has four broken ribs on his left side. His pickup was crushed beneath the overturned logging truck. It was awful, from what Dr. Stanton said. Sky's ribs were shattered, so they had a lot of repair there, too. His head, thank God, escaped injury, except for a cut and bruise on his left temple. Dr. Stanton doesn't think there's brain damage, judging from the CAT scan, but they won't know until he regains consciousness, which won't be until the early morning hours."

Knees weak, Kelly sank onto the couch, her fist balled up in her lap. "But he's going to live, Mom?"

"I think so, honey," she said tiredly. "But no promises. We'll know a lot more in twenty-four hours. Annie is flying me home

253

now. What we'd like to do is drive up to Sky's cabin, pick you up and bring you down to the local airport. Then we'll fly you to the hospital. You'll be allowed to see Sky in ICU. And Annie will fly you back in time to feed his birds tomorrow evening. How does that sound?"

"Wonderful," Kelly quavered. Hot tears blinded her. "Oh, Mom . . . I love Sky so, and I never told him that. I — I just didn't think something awful like this would ever happen. He's been through so much . . . Why is this happening to him? Isn't it enough that his parents were murdered?"

"I know, I know," Laura soothed gently. "I don't know why, Kelly. All we can do is pick up the pieces. Sky is going to need a lot of help, whether he wants it or not. I know he didn't want you at his cabin anymore, but are you going to be there to help him?"

"Of course I am, Mom. I love him. He may not know that, but it doesn't matter. I want to help him."

"Are you prepared to deal with him being in a wheelchair?"

The possibility sounded like a terrible prison to Kelly. Sky, who loved the outdoors so much, who ran through the meadows with his raptors, teaching them to fly, would no longer be able to do that. Her heart broke for him, for what had been unfairly taken from him. Scrubbing her eyes, she rasped, "Whatever it takes, Mom, I'll be there for him. I love him no matter if he has no legs, one leg or two."

"That's what I thought. Okay, we're here for you, in turn. Annie will be your helicopter taxi driver." Her mother tried to sound upbeat. "And don't worry about the costs of hospitalization. I told Dr. Stanton to put it on our tab for Perseus. Your father will ensure that Sky doesn't have any bills, on top of everything else. We'll work out things so you can be here with him daily, by having Annie fly you back and forth."

"Thanks, Mom. You have no idea how much this means to me . . . and to Sky." Kelly shut her eyes.

"We love you, honey. You've gone through your fair share of awful things, too. Your father and I are grieving so much for Sky — and for you — right now. We'll move heaven and earth to see that he gets the best of care and that you can be there for him."

CHAPTER FIFTEEN

A warm, soft sensation moved across Sky's cheek. Next came the sound of a female voice. With his eyelids feeling like weights, he struggled to come out of the darkness. Another voice, that of a man, intruded. The touch of those warm fingers trailing across his hair and cheek helped him focus. A slight ripple of pain drifted up his back. What was going on? Why was he feeling like this? His brain wouldn't work. He had no memory.

Tension sizzled through Kelly as she leaned over and pressed a kiss to Sky's pale, wrinkled brow. She'd just arrived, and Dr. Stanton had authorized her entry into Sky's room in the ICU. He was breathing on his own, and the doctor said that was a good sign. But clearly, the physician was concerned. Sky was supposed to have eased out of the anesthesia in the middle of the night, but it had been a long operation. Now, with her at his side, caressing his cheek and holding his cool, motionless hand, he was finally responding.

"Sky? It's Kelly. I'm here. You're coming out of an operation. Can you hear me?" She tried to keep her voice soft as she leaned over near his right ear. Nausea assailed her but she willed the sensation away. Sky's coppery skin was leached and pale. She'd never seen him so sick-looking. The doctor said he'd be paralyzed from the waist down — or higher. If Sky couldn't squeeze her hand, that was a very bad sign.

Dr. Stanton moved closer. He lifted one of Sky's lids and flashed a light in his eye. "Good, his pupil is responsive. Let's see if the other one is . . ." He flashed the beam in Sky's left eye.

Kelly glanced up at the doctor. "Well?"

"Both respond. That's good. I believe he's finally coming out of the coma."

"But . . . you said he was under anesthesia," Kelly said, alarmed.

"Ms. Trayhern, he should have come out of the anesthesia around three this morning. When he didn't, we realized he had slipped into a coma." Stanton grimaced. "Not what we want. But sometimes, after a spinal surgery of this magnitude, it's a normal reaction." He continued to watch

Sky's brow wrinkle and unwrinkle. "I believe he's going to become conscious. All the signs are there."

Kelly looked at the bandage on Sky's left temple. He'd suffered a long, deep cut in that area and his skull was clearly swollen. The doctor had given him steroids to reduce the pressure on his brain. As she touched Sky's stubbled chin, Kelly battled tears of anxiety. "He has to come out of it," she mumbled. "He just has to!"

Stanton patted her hunched shoulder. "We all want that," he said gently.

And then she felt Sky's hand weakly squeeze her fingers. Excitedly, she told the doctor. Stanton grinned hugely.

"Good sign!"

Sky's eyes barely opened. They seemed unfocused, but Kelly stared down at him, feeling a thrill coursing through her. "Sky? Sky, can you hear me? It's Kelly. I'm here. You're going to live. You're in a hospital and you've just had surgery."

Sky closed his eyes. It was such an effort to keep them open. He heard a woman's husky, excited voice, and when he forced his eyes open a second time, her blurred face became clearer.

"Sky? It's Kelly. Do you hear me?" She gave him a trembling smile as she watched his blue eyes focus on her. His lips, which were cracked and dry, parted.

"Who?"

Frowning, Kelly turned and looked at Stanton. The surgeon scowled.

"Could be minor amnesia caused by the drugs," he told her.

"Wouldn't he know me, though?" Her voice rose a notch, in terror that she tried to conceal.

Stanton moved to the bedside. "I don't know. Keep talking to him. Let's see what he comprehends. It is good he's coming out of the coma, though. Don't panic. The brain is pretty jumbled after anesthesia, being on painkillers of a morphine derivative, plus that injury to his skull. Give him time."

Trying to quiet her panic, Kelly bit down on her lower lip. How could life turn from bad to worse? Leaning over, she gave him a soft smile, looking deep into his murky eyes. "Sky? Do you remember me? Kelly Trayhern?" Her heart pounded erratically.

Blinking slowly, Sky assimilated her question. Where was he? Her words were partly jumbled, though some of them he could make out. The woman looked familiar. . . . Opening his mouth, he rasped, "Thirsty . . ."

Stanton crowed. "That's what I want to hear!" He fiddled with the IV to allow more fluid to drip into Sky's vein. "You can pour him some water there and put a straw in it."

Kelly nodded and did so. When Sky started sucking strongly on the straw, she smiled for the first time. "Drink all you want, Sky. Welcome back . . ." Her voice cracked.

The water tasted heavenly. Sky discovered a lot of raw pain in his throat as he gulped down the precious, life-giving fluid. He clung to Kelly's dancing green eyes and her beautiful face. Her red hair glinted like a halo beneath the bright fluorescent lights. From what she'd told him, he realized he was in a hospital. His mind refused to work well, however. As he finished the water, he noticed Kelly's smile.

"More, Sky? Are you still thirsty?"

He was and nodded his head. As he watched her graceful movements as she filled the glass, Sky found himself mesmerized. But his mind was sluggish. *Kelly.* Kelly was her name. His gaze drifted to the doctor in the white coat, who was staring at him critically.

"Where — where am I?" Sky croaked.

Kelly turned with the glass in her hand, telling him again, in more detail. Then she placed the straw between his lips, and he eagerly drank a second glassful.

Stanton walked around to the other side of the bed. "Mr. McCoy, I'm Dr. Stanton, one of your surgeons. You were in an auto accident two days ago. We've repaired your injuries. When I pick up your hand, I want you to squeeze it as hard as you can."

Sky did as he was instructed. The doctor's face blossomed into a smile. "Squeeze Kelly's hand?"

He did so, and she smiled, too. He liked holding her hand. The physician went to the foot of his bed and drew the covers off his lower legs. Sky saw him pull out a long needlelike instrument, which he placed against Sky's left foot, moving it across the sole.

"Do you feel that, Mr. McCoy?"

"N-no. What are you doing?"

Stanton said nothing and performed the same movement on the sole of his right foot. "Did you feel that?"

"No." Sky gazed up at Kelly, who looked upset. "What was that? What's happened to me?"

Stanton pricked Sky's left calf and then his right. Sky felt none of those jabs. The doctor seemed worried. He came up and placed his hand on Sky's shoulder. "Mr. McCoy, in the accident, you broke four

261

vertebrae in the middle of your back. We've put steel pins in them and anchored them to other vertebrae in order to stabilize them.

"There was a lot of pressure on your spinal cord in the area of the fractures. It appears, at least for now, that you are paralyzed from the waist down. I just jabbed you with this instrument and you didn't feel any sensation." He patted Sky's shoulder. "The spinal cord was not cut or broken, so that's good news. But it's been squashed and inflamed, to put it into civilian lingo.

"That means that you may have paralysis for a time. I don't know how long. I believe that over the next weeks and months, as the spinal cord swelling goes down, you'll feel the gradual return of sensation and be able to walk again. But I don't want to promise that. Sometimes, people remain paralyzed for the rest of their lives. And frankly, we don't know what your body will do or what will happen. All we can do is hope and pray that you'll have full function at some point in the future."

The doctor's words jarred Sky. He tried to move his legs, but they lay still. Frustrated, he tried again. Nothing happened. He felt Kelly squeeze his hand, as if she wanted to comfort him. Gasping for air, Sky felt weak from all his efforts and looked at Stanton. "I don't recognize the name you're calling me. I don't know who I am." He glanced over at Kelly, regret in his tone. "And I'm sorry, I don't remember you, either."

"Will this amnesia last, Dr. Stanton?" Kelly asked, as she stood with him and Annie outside Sky's room in the ICU.

Shrugging, he said, "I hope not, Ms. Trayhern. I believe it is acute, due to the high amount of morphine in his system to manage pain. It isn't unusual that people on high doses get very confused."

Swallowing hard, Kelly murmured, "Then . . . you think he'll remember me? Remember his own name? Who he is?" She forced out the words from between thinned lips, trying to stop the tears, which wouldn't help the situation.

"There's a second possibility," he told her. "If his memory loss isn't due to the morphine, then it could be a result of the trauma he's suffered from that blow to his head."

"Traumatic brain injury?" Annie asked, her voice filled with terror.

Kelly looked at her sister-in-law and saw the fear in her cinnamon-colored eyes. Taking in a ragged breath, she turned back to the neurologist. "Is that possible, Doctor?"

"Certainly, it is. We just don't know at this point. But I can't reduce his pain medication right now. His injured back is going to be quite uncomfortable for the first week, so he may not know anyone in that time frame. After that, I can start reducing it, and his mind will begin to clear. Then we'll see what he recalls." Reaching out, Stanton patted Kelly's shoulder. "Don't give up," he urged. "Mr. McCoy has been through a lot. His body is strong and young, and I've got a feeling he'll get his memory back."

Heartened, Kelly thanked the doctor. As he left, she turned to Annie. "What do you think? You went through this with Jason, when they brought him here for all those operations. Does Sky look like Jas did?" Kelly feared the answer as she gazed into her sister-in-law's shadowed eyes.

"Not really," Annie admitted. "To me, Sky looks drugged up to his eyeballs. I know what morphine does, and he seems completely confused from being on the med."

"He didn't know me," Kelly repeated helplessly.

"Jas didn't know me, either, when he awoke, Kelly." Reaching over, Annie slipped her arm around her waist and gave her a hug. "Don't go there, okay? I can see the worry in your face and eyes. Come on, we need to get you to Sky's cabin. I'll fly you in, and then, tomorrow morning after you've fed his raptors, we'll fly back up here. I'm sure Sky will be better tomorrow."

"But he'll still be on that high dose of medication."

Annie led her toward the elevator. "Yes, but it takes twenty-four to seventy-two hours after a massive operation like that for any patient to regain mental clarity," she told Kelly. "And if Sky is going to recognize anyone, it will be you. So hang in there . . ."

"It's been two weeks and Sky still has amnesia," Kelly told Annie wearily. She carried a raptor travel case holding Bella, the Harris hawk, as the two women walked down the immaculate hall on the second floor of the hospital. Dr. Stanton had released Sky from the ICU, and he was now in a private room, continuing to recover. The physician had also approved them bringing in one of Sky's hawks, in hopes of jump-starting his memory. Kelly figured that even if he couldn't remember her, he would certainly recall his hawks, which he loved more than life. She gripped the carrying case handle until her fingers ached. She

265

wanted so badly for Sky to remember something — anything — about his life. *Oh, please, God, let it happen,* she prayed as they reached his door.

Kelly knocked and then stepped into Sky's room. It was a pale lilac color and didn't look much like a hospital room at all. She immediately saw Sky sitting up in bed, watching television. Best of all, the color was back in his face.

"Hey, how are you?" she called, smiling gamely. Annie followed her in and said hello.

Sky turned to Kelly and managed a slight smile. "I feel a lot better. Dr. Stanton finally got me off that pain medication and switched me to something else last night. I woke up this morning feeling halfway human."

Sky liked the way the red T-shirt fit Kelly's long-limbed body. She was curvy in all the right areas, her legs beautifully sculpted beneath the white linen trousers she wore. He glanced down at the green cardboard box she was carrying.

"Hey," he said, pointing to it. "That looks familiar to me."

Her hopes rising, Kelly set it on the movable tray beside his bed. "That's wonderful. Maybe an old memory is coming back."

Annie clapped her hands with delight and

moved to the other side of Sky's bed. "What good news. Maybe Dr. Stanton was right, after all, Kelly. That it was the morphine clogging Sky's memory."

"I hope so," she muttered. Taking a leather glove out of her purse, she held it up to him. "What about this?"

Staring at it, Sky blinked. "Why . . . that's a gauntlet."

"Wonderful," Kelly whispered, her voice off-key. "What can you tell me about it?" Her heart pounded as Sky wrestled with that question, his gaze moving from the travel case to the glove and back again.

"I — I . . . It's there, I just can't quite reach it," he said, frustrated. "I know that glove. It has something to do with . . . something I know. I can't place it, but it looks familiar." Hope rose in Sky's chest. He hated not recalling anything, especially the red-haired woman who was so devoted to him, coming every day for several hours to be with him. Sky realized she liked him a lot. But she mostly kept him focused on a few photos of his family, of his mother and father, whom he didn't recognize, either. She would tell him stories of growing up with him, of them going to the same schools together. Sky wanted to remember, but his mind stubbornly refused to cooperate.

Kelly opened the traveling case out of Sky's view and put on the gauntlet. "Well, maybe this will jog your memory," she said, giving him a quick, hopeful glance. When she placed her hand in the box, Bella quickly stepped onto her glove. Kelly carefully lifted out the Harris, then turned around and showed Sky. "Do you remember this?"

The room grew quiet. Explosive. Kelly held her breath. At first, Sky seemed perplexed. And then, when Bella started her grumbling growls, begging for meat, and began fluffing her feathers, he gasped.

"Bella! That's Bella!" He stared at the hawk, tears forming in his eyes. "I remember her. I do . . ."

Relief, sweet and comforting, rolled through Kelly. "Yes, this is Bella, your Harris hawk. Look at her, Sky. What else do you recall?"

For the next fifteen minutes, Sky felt his brain thawing as memories cascaded, one after another, about the hawk and his raptor rehabilitation center. Both women grinned widely, their eyes shining with joy because finally he remembered something about his past.

Kelly had brought another glove along. She handed it to him and then transferred the grumbling hawk to his hand. There was such happiness in Sky's face, and his glacier-blue eyes were finally clear as he stared with love at Bella. Kelly's heart shuddered with an upsurge of hope. Would Sky remember her now? She also wondered when his paralysis would lift, and tried to steel herself inwardly for that moment. Sky had not wanted her at the cabin. Would he remember that, too? Selfishly, she hoped he'd never recall that. He would need help daily with his hawks, being incapacitated with his back fractures. He'd be in a body cast of sorts for six to eight weeks. Only after that would Dr. Stanton authorize physical therapy and a motorized, battery-operated chair for him so he could begin to get around.

All of it was heartbreaking to Kelly, though she shared none of her anguish with anyone. She would love Sky unequivocally, whether he had use of his legs or not. But would he allow her into his life to help him, once he got his memories back?

CHAPTER SIXTEEN

The November winds whipped off the Rockies and shook the cabin. As she sat at the kitchen table, working on some new flight jesses, Kelly relished the change of weather. She heard the shower running and knew that Sky was up and moving around.

She concentrated on cutting the kangaroo hide just so with the scissors. Where had the time flown? Sky's memory was spotty at best now. He still couldn't recall Kelly, though he did remember all his raptor experience and knowledge. The worst bit was that he had no memory of his life before he'd started learning about raptors from his mentor. His childhood and adolescence remained a blank slate. Shaking her head, Kelly felt a twinge of heartache, as she often did in quiet moments.

Sky had grudgingly accepted that his paralysis was permanent. He never had regained the use of his legs after the horrific accident, though his back had healed and he was whole again, as much as he could be. A physical therapist, the same one who had helped Kelly with her own leg injury, came three times a week to the cabin to put Sky's thin limbs through the motions, so that the loss of muscle mass wouldn't continue.

Still, Kelly felt happy, or something akin to it. She and Sky had become friends once more, and that was better than his seeing her as a stranger. She'd rearranged his cabin furniture so he could get around in his battery-operated chair. Her father and Jason had built strong ramps at the front and back so Sky could easily enter and exit the cabin.

A feeling of contentment stole over Kelly as she heard Sky turn off the shower. The bathroom had had to be rebuilt to accommodate someone in a wheelchair. In fact, half the cabin had undergone renovations to deal with his paralysis. They'd installed a lift that would move him from bed to chair and back. It was a metal monster, but it worked.

Setting the flight jesses aside, Kelly got up. Time to make Sky breakfast. It was one her favorite parts of the day. He usually liked bacon, eggs and toast. Moving to the fridge, she got out the supplies and put them on the counter.

"Hey, Kelly," Sky called from the doorway. She turned. He was dressed in his jeans and a white T-shirt, his black hair beaded with water drops. To her, he looked incredibly handsome. "Yes?"

"Come see!" He pointed to his bare feet, on the footrests of his chair. "Something is going on."

She set the skillet on the stove and walked over to him. Worriedly, she asked, "Are you okay?" His cheeks were ruddy, his blue eyes clear. He looked fine.

"Do me a favor? Pick up my right foot and run your fingernail over the sole."

Kneeling down, she eased her hand beneath his heel and ankle. Just to touch Sky gave her a secret pleasure. When she did as he'd asked, he gasped.

"Again?"

She looked up hopefully. "You felt something, didn't you?"

"I think so. Do it again?"

Kelly complied, and saw a smile blooming on his face.

"I felt it! I felt you do it both times, Kelly!"

A cry of joy erupted from her lips.

"Try the other one."

Quickly, she followed suit, and with a

relieved sigh, Sky said in an emotional tone, "I think I'm getting feeling back in both feet, Kelly."

She placed his foot gently back on the platform and stood. "Can you lift them, Sky? Why don't you try it."

With a grimace, he attempted to do so. They didn't budge. But then he wiggled his toes.

"They moved! Oh, my God, Sky, your toes *moved!*" Excitedly, Kelly leaned over and hugged him. She could smell his damp hair, his earthy male scent, and she closed her eyes, drawing it deep within herself.

As he wrapped his arms around her, Sky laughed nervously. "Hey, good sign, huh? I'm going to call Dr. Stanton. I think he'll be happy, too." Reluctantly, Sky released her. How beautiful she was. Kelly was letting her red hair grow and now it touched her proud, strong shoulders.

Straightening, Kelly laughed. "I'm sure he'll want to see you right away. I think Annie's home today, and the helicopter is at the airport in Philipsburg. She could fly us up there."

"Son, there's no question," Dr. Stanton told Sky. "Feeling is returning to your legs." They sat in his office as he delivered the good news to his patient and Kelly Trayhern. "Your body has healed sufficiently that it appears the spinal cord's swelling is finally beginning to diminish. And as it continues to go online, so to speak, you'll get more and more feeling, sensation and movement." He held up his hands. "Now, I don't know how long this will take, but at least the process is in motion."

Sky gripped Kelly's hand and smiled at her. "That's great, Dr. Stanton. What now? How do I help this along?"

"I'd suggest that you get bars installed somewhere in your cabin so that you can haul yourself up to your feet and stand. The physical therapist should work with you five days a week now. We want to send signals to your spinal column and brain for your legs to move and support you. The fact that you can flex your toes tells me that it should be possible for you to get your entire lower body back with time, hard work and a lot of sweat."

Kelly giggled and eyed Sky warmly. "Hey, what else do you have to do with the rest of your life, right?"

Sky wanted to continue holding her hand, but they were just friends. In the past month, he'd begun to see Kelly differently, and his dreams about her were becoming torrid. Sky no longer saw her as just a companion and loyal friend. He wanted to love her fully. "Right," he confided huskily, giving her hand one last squeeze and then releasing it.

"This is the best kind of news," the neurosurgeon said, smiling with them.

"Doctor, what about Sky's memory? We know now that he suffered some brain damage, that part of his memory still hasn't returned. He recalls back to the time he started working with the raptors, but nothing before. It's blank," Kelly said with concern.

Stanton shrugged. "The brain, spinal column and central nervous system are all part and parcel of one another, Kelly. We don't know if Sky's brain tissue will ever regrow, or if he'll ever reconnect with those memories. It's a wait-and-see situation. The fact that his legs are now sensitive to feeling tells me his body is healing itself. Maybe his brain will, too, but I can't promise anything."

Feeling sad, Kelly nodded. "Okay, thanks." She looked at Sky, whose face was flushed with joy. Just seeing the hope burning in his blue eyes sent her heart pounding with longing and happiness. "We should celebrate what has happened, not what hasn't happened," she agreed.

"Well, young man," Stanton said, "it's off to a lot of exercise and perspiration, to get those legs of yours to work for you once more. That and building up your muscles."

"Sir, nothing would give me greater pleasure." Sky glanced at Kelly. The golden light in her forest-green eyes sent a keen ache through him. She'd been an incredible friend to him, helping him daily and in every way. Reaching out, he gripped her hand. "I couldn't have gotten this far without you, Kelly. Thank you."

Startled by the emotion in Sky's husky tone, she squeezed his fingers. "Hey, I wouldn't have it any other way." Then she released him and patted her leg. "I'm so glad you're on the road to recovery. Being able to walk is such a blessing."

"Well," Sky muttered, "you're a blessing to me . . ."

Kelly stood at the far end of the cabin, watching Sky walk toward her between the newly installed wooden rails. The February snow was thick and heavy outside the windows, the cabin warm and filled with a quiet joy. Since January, Sky had been working to get his legs back. And today, on Valentine's Day, he was showing visible progress. As he made his way toward her, a determined look on his face, he wasn't gripping the bars. He was walking on his own.

Clapping her hands to her mouth, Kelly watched his uneven progress. Sky was still learning not to tilt to the left or right. His muscles had to be rebuilt so that he could remain upright.

His legs, once emaciated, now looked healthy and flushed from being worked daily. Below the hem of the shorts he wore, she saw his muscles bunching and moving.

"You're doing it!" she whispered, gaze riveted on his legs. "Keep coming toward me, Sky. This is wonderful! First time, no rails!"

Laughing nervously, Sky kept his hands about six inches above the smooth wooden bars. "Look, Ma, no hands." He chuckled. Being able to walk without help was a delight. He noted how Kelly's green eyes were glistening with tears. Tears of joy — for him. Swallowing hard, he forced his legs to keep moving. He had on tennis shoes and socks because he had to relearn how to walk in them. No more bare feet. That was fine by him!

As he neared the end of the rails, Kelly dropped her hands from her mouth and backed away.

"Keep coming toward me, Sky," she encouraged. "Force your legs to step beyond the rails. I'm here. I'll catch you if you lose your balance." She raised her arms and urged him on. "Come on, I know you can do it. You're more than ready . . ."

The conviction in her voice spurred Sky on as nothing else could. Leaving the rails, he walked toward her with an unsteady gait, his arms held out at his sides to aid his balance.

"Good, good," Kelly whispered, excitement in her tone. She backed around the couch. "Keep coming. If you can do this, you can walk around more and build more muscle."

She was right. But it took a hell of an effort. Perspiration dotted his face, and his mouth flexed with grim determination. "This is a good challenge," he panted.

"Incredible," Kelly exclaimed. "You can do more than you thought, Sky. Use the back of the couch if you feel like you're going to fall."

"Right. Keep backing away. I'm coming for you."

Smiling, Kelly moved to the front of the couch. "I *want* you to come to me."

Buoyed by her coaxing, Sky pushed himself onward. Kelly remained just out of reach, her hands stretched toward him in case he got dizzy. The brain damage, they'd discovered, created some imbalance. Little by little, however, that was going away.

"If you can make it completely around the couch, I'll give you a Valentine's Day surprise I have for you," she said with a teasing smile.

Sky's face brightened, and with fierce concentration he doggedly placed one foot in front of the other. "Oh, now you're bribing me. I like that." He chuckled.

Laughing with him, Kelly watched him make a complete circuit of the couch without any help at all. It was a phenomenal step forward, literally and figuratively.

With a triumphant shout, Sky made it back to the handrails. He stood there with sweat running off his face, holding Kelly's gaze. Her sweet smile, that trembling lower lip, beckoned to him. Holding out his hand, he rasped, "Come here . . ."

Without thinking, Kelly flew to his side and felt his arm, strong and steadying, wrap around her waist. As she slid her own arms around his neck to hug him, he released the rail with his other hand. His fingers slid commandingly across her jaw as he tilted her head and lowered his mouth over hers.

A jolting shock coupled with heat roared

through Kelly. She'd abandoned any thought of kissing Sky long ago. These days, she didn't entertain the slightest hope that there would ever be anything intimate between them. Not with his memory gone.

His mouth was strong, cherishing, his breathing ragged. With a moan of surprise and then utter pleasure, she melted against his firm, warm body, hardly able to grasp the fact that Sky was standing alone, on his own two feet, embracing her.

A tingling, heated sensation skittered through her like lightning on a hot, sultry night before a thunderstorm. His lips were coaxing. As his mouth slid against hers, her lips opened and she felt the tentative touch of his tongue. Another moan of pleasure rose in her throat. She felt his hands frame her face as he absorbed her hungrily into himself, felt the pounding of his heart. How strong and capable Sky was! His fingers slid from her face to tangle in her hair. Her scalp prickling with delight, Kelly responded to his cajoling mouth, relishing the feel of his chest rising and falling, the perspiration of his skin, the tickle of his stubble against her face.

Before his accident, Kelly had fantasized about kissing him. Now, it was happening. As she nipped at his lower lip, he tensed and released a low growl. The sound moved through her, making her nipples pucker as they pressed against his chest. His hands moved restlessly, as if mapping her body an inch at a time, from her neck, across her shoulders and then down her spine. Heat leaped wherever he caressed her. The ache in her lower body exploded with want and need. Without thinking, Kelly ground her hips against his. When she felt his maleness pressing against her abdomen, she realized that not only was Sky regaining control over his legs, but the rest of his body as well. Joy swept through her as his fingers splayed across her buttocks and he hauled her tightly against him. Their mouths, wet and greedy, clung together.

And then he lost his balance. He quickly reached out and gripped the rail, and in doing so, dragged their mouths apart.

Kelly touched her throbbing lips and stepped away so he could right himself. Breathing hard, she stared at Sky in the gathering silence. His eyes were dark, stormy and hooded. Narrowed upon her, like a predator hunting its prey. Every cell in her body reacted to that smoldering look. How badly she wanted Sky as he leaned against the rail, gasping for breath and holding her gaze.

Kelly's mind couldn't seem to function logically, but she could see and feel how much he wanted her. Should she go further? Was that what Sky wanted? She did, certainly. But then, she noticed his legs trembling. He'd pushed himself to the point of exhaustion by kissing her like that, standing without any support. Kelly quickly recovered.

"Hey," she whispered unsteadily, holding her hand out to him, "time to get into your chair. Come on . . ."

Sky gripped Kelly's outstretched hand as she guided his motorized chair over to him. "Thanks," he muttered apologetically, and thunked down onto the padded seat. "I guess I did too much."

Not enough, she thought, but remained silent. Sky's reaction to her was clearly etched on his face. She saw the bulge in his shorts, too, and smiled tentatively. "I think you did just fine, McCoy. In fact —" she touched her lips "— I liked the reward for you walking around that couch without assistance. That was an unexpected and wonderful Valentine's Day gift." It really was.

Sky sat there, yearning to have Kelly in his arms, and in his bed. Understanding that he was still physically weak from his accident, he wondered if he could even make love with her. Was that what she wanted? He searched her flushed features, saw the golden lights in her luminous eyes and sensed she'd enjoyed the kiss as much as he had. "I'm not sorry I kissed you, Kelly. I've been wanting to do that for a long time. Happy Valentine's Day."

Joy vibrated through her body. Just being wanted by Sky was a surprise. He'd been so moody before, so closed and unapproachable, but now, since the accident, all of that was gone. Now the man who sat before her, smoldering with sensuality and raw masculine energy, was forthright and responsive. "Funny thing," Kelly said, grinning unsteadily, "I've been wanting that, too. Happy Valentine's Day to both of us, Sky." Reaching to a lamp stand next to the couch, she lifted a wrapped box of candy and gave it to him. "I promised you a gift."

He studied her in the silence as he opened it. Chocolate was one of his favorites. Giving her a warm look, he said, "Thank you." Her red hair was deliciously mussed, her parted lips looked well kissed. "I'd like to see where this is going to go between us. But there's no hurry, Kelly. We have all the time in the world."

Nodding, she walked over and settled her

hand on his shoulder. The T-shirt he wore was damp from all his exertions, but she didn't care. She tried to rein in her emotional response, but her voice wobbled. "I'd like nothing better, Sky. We can take our time. You need to keep getting stronger. I can wait. I . . ." She hesitated. Kelly wanted to say, *I love you,* but then tucked the thought away in her heart. "I have patience. One day, when you're ready, you let me know, okay?"

Drowning in her gaze, Sky felt the last of his depression lift. He raised his right hand and placed it over hers on his shoulder. "You've got a deal, sweet woman. This is a Valentine's Day I'll never forget."

CHAPTER SEVENTEEN

"Son, why haven't you called? You never miss phoning me once a week." Lena Talbot's voice crackled with emotion.

"Hi, Ma," Billy Jo said, trying to sound upbeat. For the past three weeks, he had been sick, and unable to call until today. He was still in the prison hospital. "I'm awful sorry. I got really sick for a while." He tried to steel himself to deliver more bad news.

"You did?" She began to cry.

Blinking back the sudden tears that surged into his own eyes, Billy Jo sat up in bed. He felt terribly weak. Wiping his perspiring brow, he said in a low, pleading tone, "Ma, I need to tell you something. I need you to sit down and listen closely to me, okay?"

"Well, sure, son."

"Are you sittin'?"

"I am."

Billy Jo took a ragged breath. "Ma, I got diagnosed with AIDS in January."

"What?"

"I had a scuffle with Terrapin, one of the leaders here in the prison. He promised to get even with me. I figure they got one of the food servers who has AIDS to spit into my tray of food. I ate it and the virus without knowing. I got diagnosed three weeks ago because I wasn't feeling good."

"Ohh," Lena wailed. "That's not right! Oh, no, son."

He held the phone away from his ear. It broke his heart to tell his mother the bad news. She had such dreams for them when he was released. There was a huge plot in the backyard to rototill. Early June was perfect for putting in the yearly garden. Now, with the disease eating up his life, Billy Jo wasn't sure of anything.

"Ma, Ma . . . listen to me, will you? I'm pretty weak right now. I've had a bad fever the past three weeks. I keep sweatin' and I've lost forty pounds since January. The doctors are keeping me here in the hospital unit for another week just for observation."

Sniffling, Lena asked, "Are they getting you the medicine you need, son?"

"Yeah, they are, Ma." Closing his eyes, Billy Jo rested his hand against his sweaty brow. "Ma, the meds aren't working well. And there's nothing else they can do. The doctors say I have a nasty type of virus that is drug resistant. When I get out in June, I might not be able to do much. I'll have to get on state welfare for help. It just kills me that I have to come home like this. I'm sorry. So sorry."

Lena bridled. "Damn that Sky McCoy! He's taken my husband, and now he's taking you! I hate him!" She broke down, sobbing.

Billy Jo felt the fever returning. Every time it did, it happened fast, and he went into hallucinations. The fever would spike, then recede, over and over. All he could do was lie there, attached to an IV, and drift off into a hot hell of heavy sweat that would soak his prison pajamas, the sheets and protective rubber mattress cover beneath him.

"Ma, I gotta go. I'll write you a letter in a few days and detail all the stuff you need to know. I love you. And I'm sorry . . ."

"I had a dream early this morning," Sky confided to Kelly over breakfast. The March wind was swaying the mighty firs, and rain mixed with sleet was falling.

Kelly looked up. "Oh?" She was eating granola mixed with strawberry yogurt. How she looked forward to each morning with

Sky. He was clean-shaven today, his face once more filling out, his short black hair clean and shiny. Best of all, he was walking again. Each day, he regained more of his old strength.

What didn't return were his lost memories, and Kelly silently grieved over that. There were few photos of his parents, but she'd told him of his childhood, the knife cut by Billy Jo Talbot in grade school, and then the loss of his parents. Sky remembered none of it. Maybe it was just as well, Kelly conceded. Leave the terrible memories and trauma buried. The old Sky she knew was no more. The new one was upbeat, positive, sharing and quite the opposite of his introverted self. Dr. Stanton had said with TBI the personality often changed. Well, his had. For the better, as far as Kelly was concerned.

"Tell me about it," she said, picking up her cup of coffee.

Raising his black brows, Sky muttered, "Not much to tell. I saw a woman's face. An older woman who had lived a hard life. I saw snakes instead of hair on her head. She was screaming at me, as if she hated me. But I couldn't make out what she was saying. She was holding up an ax and threatening me with it."

"Do you know this woman?"

Sky shook his head. "No, and I sure wouldn't want to see her in real life." He gave Kelly a teasing look. "A good thing, though, happened after the dream ended. I woke up and went to the bathroom. When I got back into bed, a bunch of childhood memories came flooding into my head."

"What?" Kelly gaped at Sky, who was smiling at her. "Memories? When? What age?" Stanton had said groups of memories might come back, or even everything at once. She held her breath, happiness flowing through her.

"Real early," Sky said. "I remember when I was three. I can picture my parents now." He sighed. "I'm so glad to have those back, Kelly. So glad . . ." He relaxed in the chair, enjoying the look of joy written across her freckled features. "I have memories of us at school until about the fifth grade, I think."

"That was a year before Talbot cut you. Maybe your brain doesn't want you to remember that traumatic time just yet . . ."

"Possibly. Dr. Stanton said the brain will withhold harmful memories." Smiling, Sky said, "I remember you. I remember our friendship and how we spent so much time together. It was a good thing, Kelly." He reached across the table and gripped her fingers. "I liked what we had. I like what we have now."

Just his strong, warm hand around hers sent a frisson of longing through Kelly. The look in his blue eyes sent an ache through her core. "I do, too, Sky."

As she glanced away, he heard the pelting of sleet against the window. His gaze settled back on Kelly, at the lovely red locks flowing over her shoulders. She had left her hair loose today and he recalled when he'd kissed her, and slid his fingers through that thick, vibrant mass. It had been their only kiss. Sky wanted to be sure he was on the mend. He didn't want to saddle Kelly with half a man. Now, a couple of weeks later, he was sure he was headed for wholeness. Time wasn't on his side this morning, however. With a look of regret, he said, "We need to get going. We've got that talk to give at the grade school in an hour."

"I know." Kelly nodded, not wanting the intimate moment to draw to a close. Their lives in the past month had become hectic, but positive. She had approached Sky about giving talks with his raptors to schools and other organizations. This time, he'd been enthused about it. The insurance company had paid to give him a vehicle to replace the one that had been totaled. Now they had two or three talks scheduled every week. He believed in getting the word out not to shoot raptors. And he'd dived into her project with enthusiasm.

"We're taking Luna and Bella this morning," he told her. Rising, he picked up his dirty dishes and set them in the sink for washing later.

"Right," Kelly said, hurriedly spooning up the last of her granola. "I'll get the travel boxes and bring them out to the mews." She glanced outside, at the nasty weather. "That road is going to be slick. We'll have to set off early because conditions will slow us down." The timber trucks didn't haul any logs until spring. That meant in May they'd once more be meeting the heavy metal monsters on this road. In the back of her mind, she worried about encountering another hurtling timber truck. The last one had nearly killed Sky. And Kelly lived in trepidation every time it rained or snowed.

"Come on," he said, gesturing for her to get up from the table, "we have lots to do before we go." He smiled warmly.

Automatically, Kelly's lips tingled. She hurried to the sink, where she set her bowl and coffee cup. How badly she wanted to kiss Sky again! Sky was wrestling with becoming whole again, understandably fearful about regaining his strength, health and memory. He still tired sooner than he liked, but at least he no longer needed a chair or a cane when he walked. And so Kelly sternly told herself to stop wishing for another kiss. It would come when he felt ready. And then maybe she could tell him of her love and the fact that she wanted to spend the rest of her life with him.

Sky fingered the small diamond engagement ring. A spring breeze, slightly chilly, drifted in the window of his bedroom. Yesterday, he'd gone down to Philipsburg and purchased the stone. Marriage. Yes, he wanted to marry Kelly. Just one kiss had sealed his heart and fate, and he smiled softly as he touched the gold ring. Easing the lid shut, he placed the red velvet box in the drawer of his bedstand.

June was the time for brides, and he wanted to wait until the first of that month to propose to her. Sky knew without a doubt that Kelly loved him. The kisses they shared, more and more often, were heating up. His loins ached with his greedy need of her. And yet Sky wanted to wait until after they were married to love Kelly completely. Wholly.

Morgan Trayhern, her father, was very conservative. Sky wanted his blessing, not his ire. Although Kelly lived with Sky, she had made it clear to her parents they weren't shacking up together, and that was the truth. Sky wanted her parents to respect their commitment as much as they did.

Rubbing his temple, where he'd suffered that deep gash and subsequent brain damage, he felt a dull ache. That wasn't unusual. Maybe once every three to six weeks he'd get the pain. The last event had yielded memories of his childhood. Maybe this one would herald more memories? Sky hoped so. He glanced at his watch. Just enough time for a shower, a quick bite to eat and then they were off to the meadow to fly a new gyrfalcon, Isis, that had just been given to him. The big white raptor had been raised from birth at a bird breeding facility in Oregon, which meant she could never be released into the wild.

Kelly had gifted him with the young, immature Arctic falcon. They were considered the Cadillac of the falconry world, and she'd surprised him recently with the mind-blowing gift. Sky's heart swelled with love. Now he would enjoy showing Kelly how to teach a young raptor to fly for a lure.

Just as he rose, Sky suffered a sharp, stabbing pain in his temple. Uttering a gasp, he sat down before he fell down. He gripped the side of the bed, his eyes tightly shut. What was happening? Fear rose in him.

Within a minute, the pain was gone. Taking a couple of deep breaths to steady himself, he scanned his quiet room. The raucous cry of a nearby blue jay drifted in through the open window. Shaking his head, Sky sat there for a moment more. He would call Dr. Stanton this afternoon, after they returned from the meadow and training Isis.

As Sky eased to his feet, the world around him suddenly changed, and he received a tidal wave of memories. Reaching out, he pressed his hand against the door to steady himself. For a full minute, the images came flooding in with a vengeance. Sky stood there, mouth parted, his breathing rate increasing with everything new he was seeing. Fear zigzagged through him. He dug his fingers dug into the wood and uttered a small cry.

In a few moments, his joyful existence was shattered as he remembered Billy Jo Talbot. And how his childhood nemesis had promised to kill him once he got out of prison in June.

CHAPTER EIGHTEEN

It was midmorning and Kelly was just putting Luna away after working with her in the training oval. Luna was full of energy as she hopped from Kelly's gauntlet to the perch in her mew.

Sky waited. The clouds promised to deliver a thick blanket of snow. It was the week before spring equinox. Heart wringing with grief, he saw Kelly flash him a smile as she shut and locked the mew.

"Hey, I was just coming in. Luna is doing wonderfully, Sky. All I have to do is tap my gauntlet or the perch and she'll sit there for a moment and then fly to me."

"She's getting the hang of it," Sky agreed abruptly. Normally, he'd place his arm around her jacketed shoulder to celebrate, but not now. Not after what he'd seen and come to understand. "Let's go inside," he ordered in a gruff tone. "I've made some hot chocolate."

"Ooh, you make the best!" Kelly said, walking beside him toward the cabin. "What's the occasion? Usually, I only get that on Sunday mornings." She noticed his grim expression. What news had he heard? Had Dr. Stanton called? And why was Sky so standoffish? Tamping down her curiosity, she followed him into the warm cabin.

"No, I just thought since it's so cold, you could use a cup," he offered curtly. More curtly than he'd intended. He waited as she hung her nylon jacket on a hook next to the door, brow furrowed in confusion, then left her wet, muddy boots on the rubber mat.

He poured the steaming chocolate, and after washing her hands at the kitchen sink, Kelly took the mug he handed her. Sky had thoughtfully put miniature marshmallows in it, her favorite. "Thanks." And then she searched his face. "Sky? Are you all right? You seem upset."

Sky joined her at the table. He sat opposite her, hands wrapped around his mug, and stared down at the table. How to tell Kelly? He groaned silently, uncertain where to start. Then he lifted his head and met her gaze. There was such love mirrored there. . . .

Twisting his mouth, Sky forced the words out. "I got another download of memories about an hour ago, Kelly."

Her brows rose. "You did?" Her joy was short-lived because Sky's face remained tight and rigid, his blue eyes moody. The way he kept opening and closing his hands around the thick white mug told her he wasn't happy. Sipping her chocolate, Kelly said carefully, "You remembered what Talbot did?"

Kelly knew just how traumatic that had been for Sky. She would never forget his panicked expression after Talbot had savagely stabbed him.

"Yeah, something like that." Drawing a ragged breath, Sky told her everything, including the vow Talbot had made in court to come hunting him down when he got out of prison in June.

Gasping, Kelly whispered, "No one told me about that threat, Sky. I was away at the Naval Academy when you went to court. My parents probably didn't want to upset me, because I was starting my first year there. They likely wanted me focused on surviving plebe year. I'm so sorry . . ."

"You didn't know. I asked them to protect you from the gory details of the trial as much as possible." His voice dropped to a growl. "I'm glad they did. You were starting a whole new life and I didn't want this dragging you down." Rubbing his brow, Sky felt as if his gut held a writhing bunch of angry snakes. "What you need to realize, Kelly, is that Talbot is good at his word. When he was sent to juvenile hall, he made the same threat against me and my parents. He said when was released, he'd kill all of us."

"That threat I remember. I thought at the time that he was bluffing, Sky. I didn't really believe he'd do it, but he did."

"He burned my parents alive. That wasn't a bluff."

Kelly sat back, digesting the information. "Wait a minute . . ." She held up her hand. "Before your accident and your memory loss, Sky, you were hell-bent on getting me out of your cabin. I knew you'd agreed to let me stay here because I was so depressed I'd basically given up. I figured you were doing it as a favor to my parents, because of them paying for your court cases. They didn't want you to get some overworked lawyer who wouldn't care for your case like they did."

"That's right," Sky said roughly, emotions building in his chest. He felt as if his heart would explode as Kelly started to put it all together: why he'd chased her out of his life last year when her three months were up. "I was falling for you, Kelly. And I couldn't let you stay on with me past the three months we'd agreed on. I didn't want you to be here, because I know Talbot will find me no matter how well I've tried to hide. That's why I kept such a low profile. I don't want him to know I'm around. I want to pick and choose where *I'll* confront *him*. I don't want it to be here at my home." Sky knew it was too late for that part of his plan to succeed, because he'd been out at so many schools and clubs giving talks on the raptors. Billy Jo was bound to hear his name, now that Sky had broken his cardinal rule of staying hidden.

"I see," Kelly said, frowning down at her hot chocolate. Sky had never told her he loved her, but it was obvious in everyday things he shared with her. "So that's why you were so detached from me those three months I was here?"

"I didn't want you to like me, Kelly. I wanted to protect you by making you think you were only here for rehab. Then I wanted you far away. Safe from anything to do with Talbot."

"Sky, why didn't you tell me then? I left feeling awful! Like you didn't want me around."

Sky barked, "I did it on purpose, Kelly. I'm not sorry I did. I couldn't put you in the line of fire when Talbot got released from prison. How could I?" He opened his hands in supplication.

"This sucks," Kelly muttered. She pushed back the chair, took her mug and paced around the kitchen, deep in thought. The silence was filled with crackling tension. "Your plan backfired on you because, in the accident, you suffered amnesia. You lost those memories, forgot the threat by Talbot."

"Right," Sky snapped, anger fueling his frustration. "I let you back into my life without those memories in place, and didn't protect you the way I wanted. Having you around was not part of the plan. And it won't be until this thing with Talbot is over, one way or another."

She heard the bitterness and stubbornness in his tone, but that wouldn't silence her. "We love one another, Sky," she exclaimed, her voice cracking. "We always have. And after your loss of memory, you changed. You weren't so dark, so unavailable emotionally to me. You've been warm, open, and you welcomed me into your arms."

"Because I had no memory of Talbot and his promise, dammit." Giving her a sad look, he whispered, "Kelly, this isn't your

300

fault. My heart is yours."

"Even now?"

"What I feel for you will never change."

Kelly could sense Sky wrestling with his love for her. "So what are we going to do about this?"

She'd said "we" and not "you." Sky held her narrowed gaze. Kelly's mouth was set. Yes, they were a team; they always had been. "I can't put you in the line of fire, Kelly. I just can't." His voice broke and he settled back in his chair. "I want you to move out. As soon as possible. I want to deal with Talbot, when he comes, one-on-one. On my terms. On the turf I choose. It's him or me . . .

"I don't want you here. I don't want you hurt. I — I love you too much to let that happen."

His words came softly, fervently. Kelly gripped the mug so tightly she wondered if it would break. Sky loved her. It was a helluva time to find that out. Not romantic at all, but forced out of him because his memories had returned.

"There's no way I'm leaving, Sky," she told him.

Fear rose, along with anger. He snarled, "You have to leave, Kelly. This is my decision, not yours to make."

"No." Giving him a sober look, she placed the mug on the counter, the sound sharp and heavy. "If you think for a second I'm leaving you here by yourself to face that son of a bitch, you're mistaken." Nostrils flaring, she dropped her hands on her hips and stared at him with defiance. "I was in the Marine Corps. I know how to handle a gun. I can protect myself. And you."

Sky saw the stubborn set of her luscious mouth. Now he was getting a taste of the military side of the Trayhern Dynasty. Kelly's eyes were not soft and velvety as they had been a moment before. Her expression reminded him sharply of a red-tailed hawk focused on swooping down upon its prey.

"Kelly, I don't want you here. I will not put your life in jeopardy. I'm hoping to meet Talbot away from the cabin, and confront him one last time. I've planned this for a long, long time. And I'm not going to let anything get in the way of my facing off with him."

Cursing softly, Kelly strode back to the table and sat down. She glared at Sky. "You aren't thinking clearly about this. You've never been in the military and you don't realize there's strategy involved, Sky. I'm your best bet, not to mention that I think we should go to the police and get protection

302

for you just in case Talbot does try something after he's released." She jabbed her finger toward the mews. "This place is just too big for one person to guard. You have a dozen raptors out there. What if Talbot finds you and discovers them? Poisons them? Shoots them? Or sets fire to the cabin here? What would you do, Sky? How would you protect them and yourself?"

Her questions were ones he'd asked himself a thousand times before. "I've got a plan in place," he growled. "And it doesn't include this land, the raptors or anything else around here. I'm not going to let him set foot on this property. I'm calling the shots this time."

"Good luck!" Kelly snorted. "You need me, Sky! You need a second person here. We have to get this place set up with motion sensor lights. What if your plan to confront him first fails? Did you consider that possibility? If Talbot thinks he's going to sneak around at night, we can stop that before it starts. Lights will force him to skulk around in the daylight hours, when it's easier to spot him."

Sky held up his hands. "You're right, I don't have a plan B if I can't take Talbot on my time and terms. Kelly, this guy is a tracker. His father taught him at a very young age to track bighorn in the Rockies. That's a tough assignment. It takes days, weeks and a lot of patience. Talbot is a stalker of the first order. He's no ordinary deer hunter. He could map out our place and wait days or weeks until the right opportunity came up, and then . . ."

"Damn," Kelly rasped, running her fingers through her hair. "This really sucks, Sky." She felt his tension, saw the rage and desire for closure with Talbot in his blue eyes. Above all, she knew he wanted to shield her.

"I know your heart is in the right place, wanting to protect me, Sky. But you're facing major problems if plan A fails. This property is so huge, the layout so open. The forest surrounding us will offer a hundred hiding places if Talbot wants to stalk you."

Grimly, Sky said, "You can count on it. He wants me dead. He already got to my parents. I'm next on his list."

"I need to talk to my dad," she muttered thoughtfully. "He's in the security business. He can surely come up with a plan to protect you and me both." She gave Sky a look that brooked no argument.

Sky's black brows fell, and he stared hard at the table for a moment, his mouth working to hold in a lot of unexpressed feelings. Reaching out, Kelly gripped his hand.

"You can't send me away, Sky. I won't go this time. Before, I didn't know why you were acting that way. But now I do." She squeezed his hand, and his fist opened and his fingers closed around hers. "I love you, Sky. I'm in this fight all the way. You can't send me away. Not a second time."

Kelly gazed straight into his eyes. "We love one another. We're in this all the way. I want to be here with you, Sky. I've faced death so many times and in so many ways . . ." She gave a strained laugh. "Hell, having PTSD ought to be a plus in a situation like this. I'm jumpy and skittish anyway. I can serve as extra eyes and ears, to spot Talbot coming before he can strike."

"You've been getting over those symptoms since being here, Kelly. Why would I want you to trigger them again? This is not your fight. It's mine."

"Because it might save our lives, Sky. And you're wrong. This is my fight, too."

He shook his head. "This isn't fair. The authorities know Talbot threatened me in open court. Why can't they keep him in prison based on that threat? He made good on the last one. But I checked with several lawyers and they said nothing could be done."

Sighing, Kelly said, "Let me talk to Dad.

He's got lawyers and people in high places. Maybe he can find out more."

Holding her hand, her warm, strong fingers, Sky felt his heart rush open with love for Kelly. He had a wedding band and engagement ring hidden away in his bedroom, but now, he couldn't ask her to marry him. If his time and terms for the confrontation with Talbot failed, there was real fear of losing her to the man who had already taken his parents. Sky couldn't begin to calculate how losing Kelly would traumatize him. He'd rather be killed than have her taken by Talbot. Or burned alive, like his parents. He avoided thinking about the nightmares he'd had. "There are no easy answers on this, Kelly."

"No, there aren't. But one thing you need to get clear on, Sky." She squeezed his fingers firmly. "I'm staying. We'll fight Talbot together. I'm not leaving you or running away. It's not my nature." Kelly forced an uneven smile. "Our love has to sustain us."

Sky didn't want to agree, but he knew this time she wouldn't go. "I wish I hadn't lost my memory," he growled unhappily. "The time I was going to spend putting my plan into action is nearly gone."

"And look what happened because you

did lose your memory," Kelly said gently. "Sky, you can't allow Talbot that kind of power over you. We need to live. We need to get on with our lives. Together, if you want."

Nodding, he sighed harshly. The soft green was back in Kelly's eyes. Sky ached to love her. "You have guts," he told her quietly.

"So do you, Sky. You've never been a coward. Ever. I understand why you're wanting me out of here. You're scared for me, not yourself. You're willing to make a stand here if your first plan fails. I know that." She tilted her head. "But this time, it's different. You have me, and I love you. Our love will help us through everything that will happen in our lives, the good and the bad. It's got to."

Unwilling to put her life on the line, Sky said, "I just wish there was another way." He was going to ensure his plan worked, so this would never happen and Kelly would be safe here.

"Maybe there is. Dad will have some ideas. His company is dedicated to freeing people caught in terrible situations."

Though he felt little hope, Sky nodded. "Okay, give it a try."

"It's March. We've got three months before Talbot gets out. That's plenty of time to make this place as safe as it can be."

Flexing his fist, Sky rasped, "Yes, and time for me to set up where I want to confront him. I'm going to meet the son of a bitch at his own home, on the other side of Philipsburg, and see how he likes it."

CHAPTER NINETEEN

Lena Talbot could barely contain her excitement over her son being released early from prison. Because of the aggressive form of AIDS he'd acquired, she'd lobbied hard to get Billy Jo out before June. Moving with unusual vigor, she knocked on the door to his room.

"Billy Jo? You up?" she called.

"Yeah, Ma, I'm awake. Come on in."

Opening the door, she saw him sitting on the side of the bed dressed in white T-shirt and threadbare jeans. His face was ashen, his eyes dark and his shoulders slumped.

"How long you been up?" She went over and opened the venetian blinds to allow the early April sunlight to filter in. He'd arrived home just two days ago.

"Maybe fifteen minutes." Billy Jo wiped his perspiring brow. "Sure feels nice to wake up in my own bed, Ma."

Coming over, she slid her arm around his

shoulders and gave him a fierce hug. "I'm so glad to have you back in the house!" Straightening, she said, "Feel like walking out to get your breakfast? You got a whole bunch of new pills to take. I'm so glad you signed up for that experimental drug that's been touted to stop the aggressive AIDS."

Groaning, Billy Jo nodded. "Yeah, I'll come, Ma. I just started those a week ago. I don't feel any different."

Hearing the gloom in his tone, Lena said, "I think they'll work. Remember, Dr. Horner said it would take a week or two before the medicine kicked into gear. Matter of fact, I have to take you over to his clinic this afternoon, at one-thirty."

Getting to his feet, Billy Jo shuffled after his mother, down the narrow hall. "I hope you're right." During his stay at the prison hospital, Billy Jo planned different scenarios to find McCoy and take him out. But at the moment he didn't feel up to doing much of anything.

The phone rang. Lena hurried to the kitchen to get it. Billy Jo saw that his mother had already put scrambled eggs, bacon, orange juice and toast on the table for him. He was happy to be home even if he felt lousy.

"Billy Jo? It's that private eye I hired,

Tommy Parker. He wants to talk to you." She held out the phone in his direction.

Scowling, Billy Jo took the receiver. "Hello?"

"Mr. Talbot? This is Tommy Parker, P.I. I've managed to locate where Sky McCoy is living."

His heart rate skyrocketed. "Yeah? You did? Where's he at?"

"I'll come over this morning with the information. You can pay me and then I'll hand the file over to you."

"Fine. The sooner, the better."

"I'll be there in an hour. Goodbye."

Disbelievingly, Billy Jo hung up the phone and gave his mother a gleeful look. He told her the good news.

Lena grinned. "See? I told you it was worth hiring a private eye. They can cut through the crap and find someone." She gestured for him to sit down. "Come on, son, eat before all this good food gets cold. This is a day to celebrate!"

"Everything that can be done to make your place as safe as possible has been," Morgan told Kelly and Sky as they sat in his home office. Scowling, he added, "But it's not foolproof. You have motion sensors installed everywhere around the property. Lights will go on if any movement on the ground or air is detected. A buzzer will sound inside your bedroom, kitchen and office simultaneously if any one of them is triggered. Of course, if an owl flies past, you'll be awakened as well." He sent a thin smile in Sky's direction.

"Yes, sir, I know that. But it's worth the inconvenience." Sky glanced at Kelly, who sat beside him. "It's April, and we have two months to fine-tune everything. I don't anticipate Talbot coming to the cabin. I intend to confront him at his home shortly after his release from jail." Sky knew that allowing the sensors to be installed would lessen Kelly's worry.

Nodding, Morgan took a sip from his coffee cup. "While your plan to meet him on his turf is good, you always have to have plan B. Something could go wrong. You want those sensors in place just in case he finds you first."

"The prison will notify you when he's been released," Kelly told Sky. "That's good news."

"It is." Sky felt jumpy for no discernible reason. "I still wish you'd reconsider, Kelly. Stay at your condo here in Philipsburg, drive out during daylight hours to work with me and then head home before dark. I worry about you." Sky glanced at her father for support.

"It would be best, Kelly," Morgan agreed.

"No to both of you." She gave Sky a pleading look. "I'm not leaving you alone up there. If something happens you're not anticipating, you're going to need help. I'm your backup."

"I believe it was a good move to notify the police, Sky," Morgan interjected. "They're just a small enforcement unit here in Philipsburg, so they can't spare an officer to sit out in front of your house and guard you. But I know that when they can they'll keep an eye on Talbot when he gets back to town." Opening his hands, he said, "But come June, when you get that call from the prison, Sky, I'll put a two-person mercenary team from my company up there to keep watch. You'll never see them, but they'll be around. Both are sniper trained, and we'll keep them on duty around the clock. When Talbot shows up here in Philipsburg, I'm putting a permanent tail on him, to know his movements twenty-four-seven. We're doing everything we can to protect both of you."

Sky nodded. "I'm deeply indebted to you, sir. I know this has to be costing you a lot of money."

Morgan smiled. "Just take care of my baby girl. That's payment enough. Okay?"

Sky met the man's gray eyes. Morgan always wore a suit, looking corporate in demeanor, his black hair peppered at the temples with gray and cut military short. Sky knew Kelly's dad had strong morals and valued serving his community and country, and helping others. "I promise that I will protect her at all costs, with my life."

Hearing the deep note in Sky's tone, Kelly reached over and slid her hand into his. "All this drama. Stop it, both of you. Dad, I think if you have a permanent tail on Talbot, things will be equalized. Sky can meet him and try to settle this peacefully, once and for all."

"We'll see," Morgan growled. "We've installed a state-of-the-art burglar alarm system in your cabin. If he so much as tries to get in a window or jimmy open a door, he's in for a helluva surprise. You're as safe as we can make it."

Getting up, Kelly walked around the desk and gave her tall, broad-shouldered father a fierce hug. "I love you so much. Thank you for all you're doing." She placed a quick kiss on his brow. "And I know Mom will stop worrying, too."

Morgan slid his arm around his daughter

and squeezed her gently. "Your mother is very upset, Kelly. I wish you'd reconsider. I think she'd sleep better at night and stop having those nightmares if you'd consider living at your condo and go to Sky's cabin during the day."

Kelly went over to Sky and rested her hands on his capable shoulders. Because he was coming to visit her father, he'd worn his best clothes — a pair of tan Dockers, a white shirt and a tie. He'd taken great pains to shave and ensure his hair was neat. Her heart swelled with love for Sky. Smoothing her palms across his shirt, she told them, "I refuse to live my life in fear of Talbot. If I go home at night, that's admitting defeat, Dad, and you know it. I'm sorry Mom is having such a hard time with this."

"Well, maybe we're just edgy," Morgan murmured gently. "When June rolls around and we get the tail on Talbot, we'll all breathe easier and start sleeping better at night. At least, that's my hope."

Sky looked up at Kelly. She gave him a smile, but he saw the glint of a warrior in her eyes. It was a Trayhern trait, for sure. She was wearing a dark blue sweater with a cowl neck, which complemented the color of her hair. Her jeans did nothing but accentuate her womanly form. Her leg was healed and working almost normally, despite the fact she'd had irreparable nerve damage, losing feeling in three toes and her heel. With aggressive rehabilitation, Kelly had gotten rid of her crutches and cane. Anyone looking at her walk would never suspect she had broken her leg.

"Time to go," she told Sky, peeking at her watch. "I have a raptor presentation this afternoon at the local elementary school. I have to get Luna, Bella and Isis ready for it."

Since Sky had gotten his memory back, he'd refused to do any more talks with his raptors, and Kelly understood. But he was fine with her carrying on the program.

Smiling, Sky nodded. "You're right. Let's go." He felt her palms slip from his shoulders, and his skin prickled with need of more of her caresses. He stood and shook Morgan's hand, thanking him. Then he picked up his black felt cowboy hat, settling it on his head as he followed Kelly from the room.

As Sky walked down the beautiful cedar hallway with Kelly, he felt a frisson of terror go through him. Why? It was April fifth, not June first. Maybe he was just frazzled by all the activity at the cabin as workmen installed the different warning systems. Sky admitted that all he wanted was peace and quiet to prepare for Talbot. When he faced the convict, he wanted to be in the right frame of mind, with his emotions under control.

The trucks, the men, the activity reminded him of a busy beehive. It had worn him out and left him irritable the past two weeks. Today, the work had been completed. Peace could once more descend, so he could make final preparations without all this undue distraction.

"We have two months," Kelly told him as she shrugged into her red nylon jacket and put on her scarf and gloves. "I really think we'll be okay, Sky. My dad is a stickler for stuff like this. We've got the best eyes and ears in the business on it. Don't you feel better?" She looked up at him as he donned his well-worn sheepskin coat.

Opening the door, Sky said, "Yes, I do," though he really didn't. He was lying to Kelly because he didn't want to stress her out any more than she already was. Her nightmares had increased in frequency since January. She was getting them more and more often, and Sky now knew it was due to her fear of Talbot.

Sunlight lanced down through the firs that surrounded the Trayherns' large home. The asphalt in the parking area gleamed from a recent snow shower. The two of them walked to his pickup, and Sky opened the door for Kelly. She hopped in, removed her gloves and put on her seat belt.

The day was crisp and barely above freezing. Around the Trayhern home he could see yellow, white and purple crocuses coming up. They were usually the first flowers of spring up here in high mountain country. Only patches of snow remained up at the cabin. April was turning out to be warmer than usual.

Unable to shake the dread that hovered over him like a cloud, Sky climbed into his truck. What was he picking up on, energy-wise? Of course, when he thought about Talbot, he always got a sense of nearby danger. Was his current paranoia based on all the activity up at his cabin? It had to be. Talbot wasn't getting out for two more months, so Sky figured it was a false alarm. He explained it away as unease over the workmen being on his property.

Billy Jo listened raptly to the private investigator's report. His mother had written out a five-hundred-dollar check, and then Tommy Parker had started presenting his findings. Hardly able to squelch his delight over the information, Billy Jo felt a hell of a lot better. He wasn't sure if it was due to the experimental drugs kicking in or the good news that he'd located his nemesis, Sky McCoy.

Lena sat there smoking her cigarette, drinking coffee and trading glances with her son and the P.I. After the presentation was complete, she said, "And all this stuff is on the Internet?"

"Yes, ma'am," Tommy said, folding up the file and sliding it across to her son. "But you have to know where to look. I'm registered as a P.I., so I can get to deeper layers of information that are not available to the public. Once I had his social security number, everything else began turning up. Mr. McCoy pays taxes, so I was able to run some info through the IRS for starters." The thin young man, in his late twenties, smiled. "A good day's work, for sure, but I believe you have what you want — his address. He has no listed phone number for a landline or cell. He does have an unlisted number, but I can't get to it. Obviously, he was trying to hide, for whatever reason." Tommy glanced at Lena. "The fact that you heard his name mentioned at your garden club meeting was a pure stroke of luck, Mrs. Talbot. Even though the speaker wouldn't give you his address, it was a step forward to know he lived in the Philipsburg area."

Lena smiled, pleased. She had not told the P.I. why they wanted McCoy's address. Nor did the P.I. know Billy Jo was an ex-con. Lena figured the man wouldn't take the time to nose around and find out about them. He was only interested in making the money they'd agreed on. And what they'd asked for wouldn't really raise many suspicions. The less said, the better.

"Well," she drawled, flicking ashes into the ashtray in front of her, "it was lucky, that's for sure."

Patting the file, Billy Jo said, "You've done good, Mr. Parker. Thank you."

Rising, the P.I. shook both their hands. "Glad to be of help. I'll be seeing you folks." He laid his business card on the table. "And should you need anything else, you just give me a call or e-mail me."

Billy Jo nodded and Lena walked the P.I. to the door. Once she came back to the table, he said, "Good work, Ma. It was worth diggin' into your savings to get this info."

Snuffing out her cigarette, Lena groused, "It was the last of my money, son. We gotta figure out a way to survive. I'm on disability from the state, and we've applied for you to get the same, but it ain't a lot."

"When I was in prison, there was a lot of talk about eBay. I think I'll look into that. Maybe start up a little side business."

Lena looked at the file resting beneath her son's large, pale hand. "What you gonna do next? This time around, you can't be fingered once you kill McCoy."

"Don't worry, Ma, I've learned my lesson. I'm gonna go to the library and use their computers. I need to read up on what a raptor rehabilitator is. I intend to do a lot of background research. I'm not gonna get caught this time. Prison may have been hell, but I learned the business of not gettin' nabbed. I'm a hunter and stalker with the best of them. I learned about things like wearing gloves so they can't find my fingerprints and trace it back to me. And to have two pairs of shoes, one to kill him in, and another that have a different tread mark, for when I leave the area. I'll burn the first pair so no one can find them and point the finger at me." He gestured to his thick, short hair. "And I'll wear a knit cap to make sure none of my hair falls off, so the forensics guys won't find a strand and link my DNA to the crime scene." He grinned, pleased with his knowledge. "This time around, they're gonna find McCoy and whoever he's with dead. And no leads. We'll just continue to live a quiet life here at home."

"You know the police will come after you," Lena warned, "whether there's proof or not."

"Yeah, I know that. But I took a lot of law classes while I was in prison. I know my rights. I'll say nothing, make my one phone call to an attorney here in town and that will be that. I'll also make sure I have a foolproof alibi in place beforehand."

Nodding, Lena said, "Then all that's left is for you to get better so you can plan."

Sighing, Billy Jo looked around the cheery, sun-filled kitchen. His mother had painted the room a pale pink, the cabinets white and gleaming. She kept a neat house. And he loved her for being such a support to him through thick and thin. Harve Gunnison had chickened out and refused to help him any longer. All his friends had deserted him since his release.

"I dunno, Ma, I feel pretty good right now." He flexed his fist. "Why, I even have some strength in my hand this morning. Maybe those pills are helping, after all."

"Absolutely. I can see your face is flushed. You got life in your eyes again, son, and that does my ticker good." Lena reached out and patted his hand, still resting on the file. "I'll drive you over to the library later if you want."

Talbot had no driver's license yet; that was on his to-do list. "Good plan, Ma. How about after lunch?"

"I'm making you your favorite today as part of our celebration," Lena declared with a wide smile. "Potato salad, hamburgers and French fries."

That actually sounded good to him, for the first time since he'd contracted AIDS. Rubbing his stomach, Billy Jo laughed shortly. "By gosh, I am hungry, Ma. I'm sure these pills are working!"

Lena picked up her coffee cup, walked over to the drain board and set it down. "I can see they are. But you've got to take it easy. You go lie down and rest now. I'll call you for lunch. And if you nap, dream of how you're going to kill McCoy for us."

CHAPTER TWENTY

"Do you feel safer, Sky?" Kelly handed him a cup of coffee, then sat beside him in the wooden porch swing. As always, she looked forward to dusk, when they could review the day's events together.

Taking the cup, he thanked her. "Yes and no." While he ached to love her, he reminded himself that come June, he could be dead. He loved Kelly enough not to consummate their relationship until the confrontation with Talbot was over.

The blazing oranges and reds of the sunset were enhanced by scudding cumulus clouds drifting above the firs. For Kelly, it was an incredible scene. The warmth of the evening was very welcome, too. One day it would sleet or snow; the next would tease them with a promise of summer weather.

Sipping her coffee, she glanced at Sky, studying his profile and especially his wonderful mouth. His brow was furrowed in thought as he contemplated her question.

"Everything's in place. Now we wait," she said, relishing the Camano Island coffee they were drinking. Sky was very "green" in his lifestyle, including the coffee he drank. This particular company gave farmers in South America fair wages for their coffee harvest.

"I don't like the wait. But there's nothing I can do about it." Tipping his head, Sky looked over at her in the dusky light. Kelly's red hair was now short for the summer season to come. She was beautiful no matter if her hair was long or short. He tried not to stare at her soft, full lips. His body responded, anyway. "And I wish you would move out at the end of May. I don't want you around here. It won't be safe, Kelly."

"This is *our* fight," she reminded him, sliding her hand down his bare arm. Sky wore a short-sleeved, blue plaid cowboy shirt and jeans. His short hair was flattened from wearing his hat all day. "Trayherns don't cut and run," she said. "Ever. We're a military family and we've served our country. I don't see this situation any differently. I know you intend to intercept Talbot, but if that fails, then he's our enemy. We'll handle that together, Sky, if the time comes."

Growling in frustration, Sky took a drink

of his coffee. The woods were growing darker by the minute as the sun set. "I feel jumpy, Kelly. I can't explain it. I shouldn't, but I do."

"Nerves," she whispered, squeezing his forearm and then releasing it. Kelly wanted to touch Sky all over. He had gained back all his lost weight, and the head trauma was seemingly healed, much to everyone's delight. His bones were knitted and he was fully recovered, according to Dr. Stanton.

"I worry about your safety," he confided huskily, and gave her a worried glance. "I don't want Talbot knowing you and I are together. If he finds out, then he'll go after you."

Lifting her head, Kelly looked out across the dirt road to the trees on the other side. "I'll be okay," she assured him, even though the skin on the back of her neck prickled, signaling that danger was near. She'd often got that same sizzling sensation when she was over in Afghanistan. As a warning for the times the Taliban got too close to their base, the hairs on the back of her neck would tingle. And sure enough, their enemy would soon be launching grenades or mortars into the compound.

Rubbing her neck now, she didn't say anything to Sky. Kelly didn't want to aggravate his worry. But she narrowed her eyes, trying to pierce the gray shadows of the forest across the road from their cabin. What was out there? What danger lay in wait?

Billy Jo Talbot sat without moving about a hundred feet back from the logging road. With his binoculars, he watched Sky McCoy sitting on the porch swing with his girlfriend, Kelly Trayhern. Talbot's mouth curved faintly. Lucky for him the prison had had a recent meltdown of their computer system. Talbot counted on the chance that the office staff may have lost or misplaced the contact information, and McCoy had no idea Talbot was on the loose now. His prison buddies informed him the system still wasn't functioning correctly.

Talbot chuckled. The couple behaved as if they hadn't a clue he was here. That made him feel a thrill of triumph. This was the tenth day in a row that he had felt well enough to stalk them. McCoy and Trayhern never varied their routine. That was good for him and bad for them.

Wiping the sweat from his brow, Billy Jo noted the longing looks they shared. He remembered little Kelly Trayhern in grade school, a redheaded, arrogant hellion, a rich bitch from the west side of Philipsburg. She'd always protected McCoy and vice versa.

Billy Jo's smile deepened as he watched the night fall and their shapes grew into silhouettes. He couldn't afford state-of-the-art equipment like night-vision goggles; there wasn't enough money for such an expensive purchase. But he had his 30.06 rifle, and stealth was all he needed. That and a little daylight. And lots of detail work beforehand, to make the project successful.

Billy Jo had counted on the prison not calling McCoy. Maybe he'd get lucky and nail him before they straightened out the mess in the computer. Let the bastard be overconfident about his ability to hide; it would just bring the inevitable sooner, long before June.

Sliding the binoculars back into the case, Talbot thought about angles, shots and the best place for a sniper to set up near McCoy's cabin. Oh, he saw the motion sensors and had even tested them out several nights to see how McCoy and his girlfriend would react to such an intrusion. The lights flashed on and he could hear an alarm sounding somewhere in the cabin. Always, McCoy came out in his pajama bottoms, a pistol in one hand and a flashlight in another, looking around. Talbot would sit beyond the lights, hidden in the brush, and watch. They were predictable in their reaction, and that was what Billy Jo counted on.

Moving with extreme slowness and dressed in camouflage trousers and a green T-shirt, his face smeared with a mixture of green, yellow and black paint, Talbot made sure to cover his tracks by quietly sweeping a broken tree limb back and forth as he retreated. The brown pine needles that carpeted the forest floor were perfect for hiding boot marks. This time, he wasn't going to get caught by the law. His life was shortened by AIDS anyway, and Talbot was hell-bent on enjoying whatever was left of it in the pure air of his beloved Rocky Mountains. He wasn't going to prison ever again.

"Here's the plan, Ma," Billy Jo said after eating a late dinner she'd fixed for him. Laying out the maps he'd drawn of McCoy's property, he pointed to the motion sensors. "I've created four firing zones in different places, at different angles, to kill McCoy."

His mother, who was a consummate hunter like her husband had been, hunkered over the papers and studied them intently. Cigarette smoke wafted between them as she analyzed his work.

"You've done a fine job, son," she said finally, lifting her head and drawing in a deep drag. Blowing out the smoke, she smiled at him proudly. "You've got the angles. Who you taking out first?"

He shrugged. "I don't know. I'd like to get them together. Two head shots. Both dead. Someone will find them days later, where they fell."

"But it's rare that they'd be together. One of them goes out and feeds those birds twice daily, at specific times."

Unhappily, Billy Jo said, "I know, Ma. The only thing I can do is shoot one of them and then wait for the other to come out and discover the body, then take that one out. I can't get into the cabin because that would set off the alarm. I'll have to wait for the second person to show up."

"That could be an hour, maybe more." Lena puffed several times on her cigarette, deep in thought. "I have another plan. Listen to this . . ."

Kelly was in the kitchen, writing out a list of groceries they'd need for the weekend, when a knock came at the front door. The early morning sunlight had long since moved around from the east window. Sky had gone into town to pick up a shipment of frozen food for his raptors. Glancing at her watch, Kelly saw it was 10:00 a.m. Who could be calling so early? She knew her mother was coming up today, bringing some new curtains for the front room. But she had said noon, not ten o'clock.

Kelly pushed away from the table as the soft, hesitant knock came once more. Hurrying through the quiet living room, she opened the door. A woman with gray hair and watery blue eyes, dressed in a dark red blouse and black slacks, stood before her.

"Hello," she said. "I'm sorry to bother you, but I'm lost."

Seeing the pleading look in her eyes, Kelly smiled. The woman was barely five feet tall, and carried a large, brightly colored canvas purse on her small, bent shoulder. Kelly could smell cigarette smoke on her clothes, and automatically wanted to take a step back, though she didn't. "Oh, that's okay," she reassured her. "We get a lot of tourists up here that became confused with the roads. Can you tell me where you want to go?"

The woman smiled and pulled a map from the gaudy canvas bag she carried. "Yes, I can." She started to open it up. "Can I set this on something? So you can show me the way?"

"Of course," Kelly said. "Come in. We can go to the kitchen and spread your map on the table." She stepped aside to allow the frail-looking woman to enter. Kelly figured she was in her fifties, judging by the hard lines etched in her face. "Let's go in there." She gestured to the kitchen, shutting the cabin door after the woman walked inside.

"I'm just confused as all git-out," the stranger confided with an embarrassed laugh. "I thought I was going up the right road, but by golly, I wasn't. You were the last house I saw, so I decided to stop and get some help." She smiled up at Kelly, who walked at her side to the kitchen. "This is very kind of you." She held out her hand. "My name's Debby Thomas."

"Kelly. Nice to meet you, Debby. Let's open that up." It was a large Montana road map, and Kelly busied herself moving everything to one side of the kitchen table. Her back was to the woman as she spread out the map.

"Okay," she said, shifting to one side to allow her access, "show me where you want to go."

Lena Talbot watched the redhead's eyes widen into huge pools of disbelief as she pointed the Glock pistol at her, holding it. "Now, dearie, you just sit down over there

332

in that chair next to the table and we'll get along fine. If you think for a heartbeat you're gonna take this pistol away from this little ole lady, I'll blow your damn head off right here. Now go sit down."

Shock bolted through Kelly as she stared down the muzzle of the semiautomatic weapon. The kindly older woman was gone; this one's gaze was fixed, her voice icy. And her hands, both of them gripping the pistol, did not waver. She meant business.

"What — Who —"

"Shut up! Sit yore ass down!"

Kelly quickly complied, her gaze never leaving the woman. Her heart pounded violently in her chest, underscoring the danger she felt. Who was this person? What did she want?

Lena dropped the large, bulky purse on the table. Keeping her gun trained on Kelly, she riffled through the bag. Finding the gloves, duct tape, the scissors, she brought them out and set them beside the purse. "Now, put both your hands together and hold them out in front of you."

Should she try to take the pistol away from her? Kelly considered the possibilities. But then, as if reading her mind, the woman clicked back the trigger.

"Don't even think about it."

"What are you doing? Who are you? What do you want?" Kelly gulped.

"You'll find out in a minute." Lifting her head, she yelled, "Come on in, son!"

Kelly heard the cabin door open and then close. She twisted around. A large man dressed in camo fatigues and an olive-green T-shirt entered, and she gasped. "Talbot!"

"Get the duct tape on her, son."

Grinning, Billy Jo, who was wearing gloves, quickly grabbed the tape, cut off several pieces with the scissors and wrapped them tightly around Kelly Trayhern's wrists, binding them together. "You're a genius, Ma," he said, pride in his voice. "And I was right — they don't have the alarm system on during the day. They just put it on at night. Anyone could walk up to their cabin and waltz right in, like you just did. Your plan was genius." Throwing the tape back into the bag, he laughed triumphantly.

"Don't go crowin' too soon, son. Get her up. Get her to our car." Lena put on her gloves.

Kelly's mind spun in shock. Fear arced through her. This was Talbot's mother, she realized belatedly. She vaguely remembered hearing her name when she was a kid. Kelly had never seen her at the trial. The day Kelly testified against Billy Jo, Lena Talbot had been sick and unable to attend. But this woman with the murderous blue eyes, the Glock gripped in her hands, wasn't to be trifled with. Talbot wrote a note and left it on the table. As he jerked her to her feet and shoved her toward the door, Kelly realized where he had gotten his criminal bent: from his deadly mother.

"Where are you taking me?" Kelly demanded, stopping in her tracks.

"Shut up or I'll put duct tape over your mouth," Talbot snarled. He gripped her shoulder and jerked open the door to the cabin.

Kelly saw an old blue Ford sedan parked in front of the gate. Why hadn't she looked at it more closely? Why had she trusted the woman in the first place? And how had Talbot been released early from prison? Why hadn't the federal officials called Sky to let him know that? None of this made sense to Kelly.

Talbot's fingers dug deeply into her shoulder, and she groaned from the pain radiating from his talonlike grip. Billy Jo was a big man and greatly outweighed her. Within moments, Kelly was in the backseat of the car, with Talbot sitting next to her. Lena handed him the pistol and got in to drive.

Kelly looked around wildly. They were

both smiling, as if congratulating themselves. She stared at her old classmate. "You
weren't supposed to get out of prison until
June first."

Chuckling, Talbot said, "You didn't know
I was out?" The car lurched forward. Lena
turned it around and they headed back
down the timber road toward Philipsburg.
"What a pity," he declared. "The prison officials didn't call you? They were supposed
to."

"No," Kelly muttered, "they didn't."

Lena laughed gaily. "Oh, that's rich! Son,
tell her how the prison computer crashed
and was screwed up just before they gave
you an early release. And they're still trying
to fix the damn thing. They'll probably call
McCoy on June first." Lena cackled indul-
gently. "Yep, that's just great! McCoy
doesn't know you're out."

Talbot wiped his sweaty brow. His heart
was pumping with both fear and exhilara-
tion as Lena drove carefully down the rutted road. McCoy had appeared so relaxed
when he'd observed him from the forest. As
if he didn't have a care in the world. That
made the kidnapping of his girlfriend even
better.

When McCoy got home, he'd find an
empty cabin and a note. Billy Jo wished he

could be there to see his face. Now the bastard would sweat and feel dread, just as Talbot had in prison. His mother's plan was perfect.

Let the half-breed son of a bitch get scared. Real scared. Chuckling, Talbot held the gun on the redhead.

"You get any ideas about trying to escape, and I'll put a bullet through your brain. Got that?"

Kelly tried to settle her breathing, but adrenaline was running full tilt through her body. She tried to think. Tried to find a way to escape. It was impossible. The doors were locked.

Talbot was sweating like a pig next to her, with beads across his forehead, soaking into his damp strands of thin hair. The look in his eyes was one of sinister pleasure. She remembered his sneer from childhood, even more malignant now as an adult. And she was their prisoner.

What were they going to do to her? Sky was his target. They had to be using her to get to him, somehow. One thing Kelly did know: Talbot was fully capable of killing her. He'd killed before.

Sitting back, she closed her eyes. Oh, God, what was she going to do? How could she warn Sky? Once they knew she was missing, her parents would go crazy. And her father, who was a superspy by trade, would turn the world upside down to try to locate her. That gave Kelly a little solace, but not much. She had no idea what Talbot and his mother had in store for her. And Sky's plan to face off with Billy Jo at his own house was now in shambles.

Heart thudding with grief, fear and anxiety, Kelly stared around her. They were approaching the paved road at the outskirts of Philipsburg.

"Get that blindfold on her," Lena told her son.

Within a minute, Talbot had pulled a bandanna out of the canvas bag and tied it tightly around Kelly's head, so she couldn't see a thing. She wouldn't know where they were taking her. While trying to listen for any sounds, Kelly concentrated on the movements of the sedan, attempting to remember all the turns they took. If she knew where they were taking her, she might have a chance of escape. And having grown up in Philipsburg, she knew the streets intimately. Tuning in to the sounds of the tires, Kelly realized her life might well depend upon doing so. She pushed back the scream that threatened to rip from her throat. Billy Jo was loose! Sky didn't know

that. Now Talbot would go after him, and
Sky wouldn't have a chance. . . .

CHAPTER
TWENTY-ONE

Sky frowned. It was barely 3:00 p.m. and he couldn't find Kelly anywhere. After parking the truck in the driveway, he'd hefted the UPS box into the living room and called out for her. No answer. Thinking she was out in the mews with the raptors, Sky had gone there. He didn't yell or raise his voice in case it would startle his birds. There was only one way in and out of the enclosure, and Kelly was nowhere to be found.

He settled the tan cowboy hat back on his head, and saw the sun go behind puffy cumulus clouds hanging over the mountains. Kelly couldn't have gone far. Sky went in the back door to the kitchen. He spotted a message on the table, and relief fanned through him. She'd left him a note. Of course, she knew how worried he was about Talbot, even though it was three and half weeks away from his release date. Scooping up the paper, he read it.

If you want to see your girlfriend alive, meet me in Anaconda, at the corner of Lake Jackson and Miller Avenue, 10:00 a.m. on May seventh with a million dollars in a bag. Come alone or she's dead.

Sky's whole world tilted. May seventh was only four days away. He stared disbelievingly at the hand-scrawled note, then, his mind exploding with shock, dropped it back on the table. Sky scanned the room, looking for signs of a struggle. *Nothing.* As he raced through each part of the cabin, the silence hammered him like bombs going off inside his chest. Anguished, he ran to the kitchen phone. He dialed Morgan Trayhern's office, his fingers shaking. What would he say to Kelly's father?

"Perseus, Morgan speaking."

"Morgan, this is Sky." He rasped, "Kelly . . . she's been kidnapped. There's a note here on the kitchen table. I need your help."

"What does it say?"

As calmly as he could, Sky told Morgan everything, including details of when he'd left the cabin, the errands he'd run and what time he'd returned home. His voice was tight with emotions he couldn't even begin to stuff back down inside him. The love he had for Kelly mushroomed within his heart and tears burned his eyes.

"Have you touched the note?"

Belatedly, Sky realized his fingerprints were on the paper. "Damn, yes, I did."

"Don't touch it again, whatever you do. I'm grabbing a GPS phone. That way, I won't lose my connection with you. I'm having my chief of staff, Mike Houston, assist me. Now read the note to me."

Hearing the grim determination in Morgan's voice, Sky took a deep breath and slowly read it. How terrible Morgan must be feeling. And Laura, Kelly's mom, would have to be told. Both of them had been kidnapped by drug dealers years before, and suffered terribly while being held captive and after being rescued. Now, their beloved daughter had been snatched. Sky ached for them all, as well as himself.

"It has to be connected to Talbot, but he's still in prison," Sky stated.

"Maybe Talbot hired someone?"

Sky looked around the still cabin. Kelly was like sunlight to his world. Now, it was dark. And threatening. "I guess he could have," he admitted hesitantly. Why had he thought Talbot would do his own dirty work?

Because he had last time. Even if Sky

couldn't prove it, he sensed Talbot was in on this.

"Who were Talbot's friends, before he went to prison?"

Sky named two men. "Lester Conway and Butch North."

"I'll put tracers on them immediately. In the meantime, I'll have my son give a quick call to the prison. We want to get someone from our Seattle office out there to interrogate Talbot immediately. I know that bastard has something to do with this."

Feeling Morgan's tight fury, Sky couldn't disagree. "I think you're right." The words came out in a rasp. Even though his gut told him the truth, he didn't want to believe Talbot was in on this. The man had already killed the two people Sky loved most in the world. Now he could kill Kelly, the love of his life. *Oh, Great Spirit . . .* He squeezed his eyes shut, unable to deal with the possibility.

"Whatever you do, Sky, stay where you are. Don't move around. We're bringing a forensics expert with us. If there are any signs left by the intruder, such as footprints or hair, she'll find them. The less you walk around, the better off we'll be, and maybe we'll catch a break and find something."

"Are you going to call the police? The FBI?"

"Not yet. We can handle this on our own. We deal with KNRs — kidnap and ransom cases — all the time in other countries. Damn. Are you okay?"

"Yes, sir, I am."

But Kelly wasn't okay. Where was she? Had she put up a fight? Sky's mind revolved around all the horrifying possibilities. He gripped the phone so hard his knuckles ached.

"Listen, just stay on guard. We'll be there in twenty minutes."

"Do you think they know by now?" Billy Jo asked his mother in a quiet voice. They were having coffee at the kitchen table of their rental home on the outskirts of Philipsburg. The clock on the wall read 4:30 p.m. The rental was a good place to hide their victim. Luckily, Lena had come up with some more money to make it happen.

"Sure they have." Lena gave a hacking cough after taking a deep drag of her cigarette. She moved a fresh pack of smokes around on the table and squinted toward the padlocked basement door. "All we have to do is wait. We've covered our tracks. Now it's their turn to make a move."

"Do you think they'll trace the note?" Talbot worried about his mother. She was looking tired and strained. He felt completely stressed out and jumpy himself. Every time a car went down the street, he got up to see who it was. If the vehicle was unfamiliar, he unholstered his pistol and waited. Talbot feared the sheriff or feds finding something that would lead to them, and then sending a SWAT team to jump them. His mother seemed to think they were completely safe, because they weren't at their homestead, but a rented house she'd found weeks earlier. Even if the law started to hunt them, they'd find one of their cars there and the other gone. Everyone would think they were out of town. Lena had left a note on the door saying, Be back in two weeks from a well-deserved vacation. Billy Jo would never feel safe no matter where they were hiding out.

"You wore gloves when you wrote that note. They won't find fingerprints. Stop worrying. We're hiding her right under their noses. They'll never find her." Lena puffed contentedly on the cigarette, a smug smile curving her lips.

"I've never kidnapped anyone before," he muttered anxiously. "Isn't there such a thing as handwriting experts, Ma? I wish we'd printed something up on that library computer and used it instead."

"And have it on that computer, where police could possibly find it?" she demanded angrily. "Stop worrying!"

Wiping his brow, he felt another bout of shakiness and fever coming on, thanks to his AIDS symptoms. Getting up, he went over and grabbed his next dose of pills. He filled a glass with tepid water and, gulping unsteadily, washed them down.

"Kidnapping is straightforward," Lena assured him. "You saw how easy it was, son. That Trayhern girl fell for it like the stupid bitch she is. She suspected nothing. I made sure she didn't leave any 'hints' behind when we took her away. That cabin is clean as a whistle." His mom gave him a steely look. "Why don't you go lie down, son. You're looking peaked. You did a lot today and you're stressed out over it all."

He hesitated at the counter. "What about her?"

Lena checked her watch. "You take a nap. I'll wake you up at six. You can help me by standing guard at the cellar door when I take her down something to eat. She's got water and a bathroom pail down there, so she's set."

"I don't like the idea of leaving her hands

free. I think we should keep her tied up."

Lena shrugged. "Why? The cellar has no windows. There's only one way out and that's through this door." She jabbed a finger toward it. "It's padlocked. There's nothing down there except that cot, blanket and pillow. No, she'll stay put, so stop your worrying. You need your strength for tomorrow's gig."

Billy Jo nodded, feeling very weary. The rental was a small two-story house at the end of a lane. There were no homes on the street, the nearest a mile away, and that was reassuring. He didn't want any snooping neighbors or prying eyes. He and his mother had pulled the car to the side of the house facing the forest before unloading the girl. No one had seen them. He didn't like doing things in daylight hours, but it couldn't be helped.

The two-bedroom house came furnished, which was good. The bed in his room was old, the mattress sagging beneath his weight, the springs creaking. Too exhausted to care, Talbot stretched out on it, mentally reviewing the drill on his symptoms. He'd sleep for a couple of hours, wake up drenched in sweat, take a shower, pull on a set of clean clothes and feel halfway decent. At least his disease had a cycle, and he knew it by heart.

Draping his arm across his eyes, he relaxed his trembling muscles. He hated not having his full strength. Still, he was free. No more bars. No more clanging doors opening and closing. No more constant noise from men talking up and down the cell block.

Sighing, he felt the fingers of sleep pulling him deeper. Talbot's last thoughts were about McCoy. He wished he could be there to see the bastard suffer.

CHAPTER
TWENTY-TWO

Kelly's heart banged violently in her breast. She heard thumping and scraping as the lock was opened on the door at the top of the stairs. One dim bulb shed some light into her dark, damp prison. The odor of garbage, of fecal matter, assailed her nostrils.

The door yawned open and light flooded down the stairwell. Holding up her hand, she shaded her eyes, unused to the sudden brightness. Since her watch had been taken away, she had no idea what time it was.

"Now, girlie, you just stay sittin' on that cot," Lena called out hoarsely, a tray in her hands. "My son has the Glock. If you think about getting up, you'll be dead, you hear me?"

Lena's smoker's voice grated on Kelly's nerves. "Yes, I hear you," she called back. Wiping her eyes, she saw the woman coming slowly down the creaky wooden stairs. She had a cigarette hanging out of her mouth. Billy Jo followed right behind her, with the gun in his hand.

That door was her only escape. Kelly had spent hours trying to find another way out of this awful, smelly basement, to no avail. Her gaze cut back to Talbot. Why was he sweating? Perspiration dotted his broad brow and his hair clung to his pasty scalp.

Lena placed the tray on a wooden stand next to the cot. She straightened up and drilled Kelly with an assessing look. "You're a smart girlie. Now, eat." She pointed to a bucket in the corner. "Son, give me the gun. Then take that pail and dump it into our toilet." She reached for the weapon and pointed it at Kelly. "You stay where you are."

Kelly watched as Talbot bumbled by her. His mother held the Glock steady on her, with such a chilling, no-nonsense look on her face that Kelly sat unmoving.

"May I speak?" she asked in a quiet tone.

Chortling, Lena took a drag of her cigarette and then shoved it into the corner of her mouth. "Sure you can, girlie. Won't do you any good, though."

"Why have you kidnapped me? What have I done to you?"

A slow grin stretched across Lena's mouth. "Yore rich and a bitch. You were Miss High-and-Mighty in school. You helped put my boy in prison. That's enough reasons."

Hands clasped, Kelly watched Talbot move by her like a plodding ox. Something was wrong with him. He was pale and sickly, despite his bulk and height. Talbot climbed the stairs slowly and then disappeared, pail in hand.

Kelly retrained her focus on Lena, who held the pistol with both hands, pointing the barrel at her head. "What can I do to get out of here?" she asked the woman, trying to keep the terror out of her tone.

"Nothing, girlie. Yore a pawn whether you like it or not."

"A pawn?" Kelly played dumb. The look of triumph on Lena's face was clear. Maybe she could appeal to the woman's ego.

"Shore are. We're after that bastard McCoy. He's our real target, but I figured we'd mix things up for the cops and him by kidnapping you." She grinned. "Ever play chess, girlie?"

"Yes, I have," Kelly admitted, clasping her hands between her thighs.

"It's an old, country trick," Lena gloated as she saw her son reappear at the stairwell. "Wild animals make fake trails all the time to throw off bloodhounds tryin' to track 'em down. That's what we've done. We've got McCoy thinkin' yore kidnapped. He'll never realize my son is setting up to kill *him*." She snickered.

Placing a steel grip on her emotions, Kelly watched Talbot make his way down the creaking stairs, which groaned beneath his bulk. The man wiped his brow twice before he reached the bottom. What was making him sweat like that?

Her attention veered back to Lena's statement. "Your son is going to kill Sky?" she repeated in apparent disbelief, meeting the woman's narrowed blue eyes.

"That's right."

Despite her resolve to remain calm and cool, and to act naive, anguish arced through Kelly. "When?"

Talbot laughed outright as he walked past and dropped the emptied pail next to her cot. "Like we're gonna tell you? Get real."

Panic ate at Kelly. She cringed inwardly as Billy Jo stepped a little closer to her. Too close. She felt the heat from his body, smelled the sour stench of his sweat. Nostrils flaring, she looked up and saw interest in his eyes. Suddenly, she realized that he could rape her. *Oh, God, no!* Swallowing convulsively, Kelly shrank deep within herself.

"Son," Lena snapped, "get outta here!

Let's go eat our dinner and leave her to her vittles."

With a grunt, Talbot complied, obediently moving away, and Kelly breathed easier for a moment. She gave Lena a quick glance. The woman was smiling at her — a smile that made a feeling of nausea churn in her gut.

"Eat your supper, girlie."

After they left, Kelly heard a chain scraping on the other side of the door and the snap of the padlock. And then no more sounds. She eyed the tray, which held a sandwich along with some potato chips. Whether she wanted to or not, she had to keep up her strength. Luckily, there was a gallon jug of water nearby. She psyched herself up to eat, but her overriding fear for Sky made it difficult. What were the Talbots planning?

Kelly studied the stairs. They were noisy as hell. No way could she climb up them without alerting her captors. Or could she? They had to sleep at some point. Maybe the stairway led to the kitchen or another room? She had no idea, since she'd been blindfolded when they'd arrived.

Going to the tray, she picked up the peanut butter sandwich and forced it down. She kept her eyes on the door as she ate.

Light was coming through the cracks. The more she studied the area, the more she realized how old and dilapidated the house was. The scent of mold was strong, and whoever lived here had had cats — the basement smelled like a litter box. Cobwebs were visible wherever the dim light made an inroad into the darkness. Water leaked in through the redbrick walls.

How could she escape with just one exit? Kelly had memorized the turns the car had made after leaving the dirt road, but she wasn't exactly sure where she was. Sounds were muted in the small basement, and only once in a while did Kelly hear a truck or larger vehicle pass. Her watch and cell phone had been confiscated.

Sitting on the cot, Kelly picked up the plastic jug of water and drank deeply. It was so dark down in this dank hole. There seemed to be some furniture stacked in one corner, however. She peered toward the heap of dirty, dust-ladened cabinets, several drawers of which were partly open, and a broken table.

Was there anything in those drawers? Kelly quickly got up. She'd been so stunned and in shock that she hadn't completely explored the contents of her cell while she'd been looking for an exit. She could see the floor joist and the nails driven through from the floorboards above. Brushing away cobwebs, she managed to make her way over to the furniture.

A sudden panicked desire to escape crashed over her like a tidal wave. She had to get out of here. The look of sexual interest in Talbot's eyes had scared her almost as much as Lena Talbot's statement that they were setting a trap so they could kill Sky. Grimly, Kelly forced herself to calm down.

Groping her way to the dim corner, she reached out and began examining a cabinet there, trying not to sneeze from the dust. When she dipped her hand into one of the open drawers, her fingertips touched cloth. Old clothing? Kelly scooped up a stack and carried it to her cot, where the light was better. To her disgust, the men's T-shirts and moth-eaten plaid wool shirts smelled of mold and were covered with mouse droppings. Whoever had stored this stuff down here had done so a long time ago.

Wrinkling her nose, Kelly returned the clothes to the drawer. She didn't want the Talbots to know she was poking around. Crouching, she felt for the next drawer, which was closed. It was stuck, likely swollen from moisture, and she had to try hard before it finally inched open.

Footsteps sounded above her just then, and Kelly froze. She heard voices, too muted for her to tell what the Talbots were discussing, unfortunately. Were they about to come down here again? Kelly dusted off her hands and made her way back to the cot, shivering with fear and cold. There was only one ratty blanket, a green wool one. Pulling it about her shoulders, Kelly recalled that early May in the Rockies could be brutally chilly. In this damp cellar, she would have to try to protect herself against the temperature drop as night descended. Maybe those plaid shirts would be useful, after all, or she could find a sweater or jacket somewhere in those drawers. As she listened to the intermittent footsteps overhead, she decided to lie low and wait. With her captors eating dinner, Kelly sensed that it must be around 6:00 or 7:00 p.m.

Her thoughts swung back to Sky and her family. Did they know of her disappearance yet? They must. She knew her father would tear up heaven and hell to find her.

Biting down on her lip, Kelly realized she couldn't wait for rescue. Talbot was going to kill the man she loved.

Hot tears flooded her eyes and she fought back a sob. Why hadn't she told Sky she loved him more often? Now, she might never get another chance. . . .

Sky sat in the living room while Morgan, Mike Houston and the forensics expert, Patty Solare, finished combing the cabin. They were going over the place in minute detail, looking for clues. As they'd worked, Sky had fed his raptors their dinner, and he'd just returned to the cabin.

Had the Perseus team found anything? He squirmed impatiently, desperate for news. The kitchen was off-limits to him while Patty used a lightweight vacuum on the table and around it, searching for evidence.

Morgan gave him a grim look as he walked back into the living room, his shoes encased in special paper coverings to avoid contaminating the scene. The cell phone in his hand rang and he flipped it open.

Sky heard Kelly's dad grunt and then speak in low tones. His square face became very dark, his gray eyes taking on a stormy quality as he ended the call. Morgan came around the couch and sat down next to Sky.

"Bad news," he told him. "My son just got off the phone with the federal penitentiary in Washington State. Did you know they released Billy Jo Talbot on April first?"

An explosion of disbelief coursed through Sky. "What?"

"Yes," Morgan barked, glancing toward the open door. "He was given a medical release. Talbot has AIDS, Sky. He's dying from the disease. His lawyer argued that since that was the case, they could let him out a couple months earlier, and, dammit, they did."

Sky wrestled with his shock. "They never called me to tell me they were releasing him! They said they would." He gulped in disbelief. "What the hell happened?"

"Take it easy," Morgan said heavily, clasping his shoulder. "Jason said the official blamed it on a major computer crash at the facility. They're still trying to identify what information was lost. That's why you weren't notified of Talbot's release update. Son of a bitch."

"So Talbot is behind this," Sky growled, his heart pounding violently in his chest. "He's kidnapped Kelly." He knew the bastard well. This was a hunting ploy: a distraction to set him up for a kill. And Talbot could kill Kelly as well . . . if he hadn't done so already.

"I'd bet my life on it, too," Morgan snarled. He raised his hand and gestured for Mike Houston to come into the living room.

Sky sat there numbly, trying to think

despite his shock. His mind whirled at the staggering information. Vaguely, he heard Morgan telling Houston the news. Talbot had kidnapped Kelly. And he had AIDS! What if he raped her? Infected her with the deadly disease? Groaning inwardly, Sky switched his thoughts from the nightmarish possibilities, as Morgan swung his attention back to him.

"Jason is working on info regarding two of Talbot's buddies from school. He'll have more for us in about an hour."

"Okay," Sky rasped. He gave both grim-faced men a searching appraisal. "Where is Talbot? Did the prison get an address for him?"

"They did," Morgan said. "And Mike and I are going over to his mother's home right now. Her place is the address he gave when he left prison."

"Lena Talbot . . ." Sky growled. "She's as evil as he is."

Nodding, Morgan stood and clipped the cell phone back onto his belt, beneath his dark suit coat. "Maybe more so, but she has no criminal record. She just made her son a convict." He glanced toward the kitchen, where Patty was finishing up. "Sky, I want you to stay here. I'll be back in touch with you once we arrive at Lena's place. I just hope they're there."

"I want to go with you. I'll confront Talbot myself."

Morgan shook his head. "Look, we don't know if the kidnapper who left that note is Talbot or not. Chances are good it is. But what if they call here? You want to be around to answer. Sometimes in a kidnapping, the note will say one thing, but the kidnappers will call later and give you new instructions. You have to be here just in case. I'm sorry, but you can't come with us."

Sky cursed softly. "That makes sense." He looked around, suddenly noting how dark the cabin was. Night was falling and he hadn't turned on many of the lights in the living room.

Darkness was stealing inside him, too — into his heart, his panicked spirit. Was Kelly safe? Was she even alive? Acid burned in his throat and he fought back the urge to go find Talbot and kill him on the spot. There were so many questions, and none could be answered.

Without a doubt the Trayherns were reeling from this just as much as he was. Sky thought yet again about how Morgan and Laura had been kidnapped by that South American drug cartel. Their ordeal had been horrific, and Laura had been raped. Kelly had told Sky of their nightmarish experience, and how it still haunted the whole family. Could such a tragedy happen all over again?

"Have you wondered if Kelly's kidnapping might be by someone who wants to get to you, Morgan?" he demanded, thinking out loud.

"It's possible," the older man muttered.

"Anything's possible at this point, Sky," Mike Houston told him quietly. "We haven't ruled out that possibility at all. Perseus is continually fighting drug lords all over the world. It's our job to get back the kidnapped victims they've taken for ransom." He grimaced. "So, yeah, we're a player in this, too."

"We'll know more in a while," Morgan stated heavily, heading for the door. "Mike, let's go visit the Talbots . . ."

Sky so badly wanted to go with them, but knew he had to remain behind. The door shutting with finality sent a shudder through him. Getting up, he went to turn on various lamps around the living room. The forensics expert had already dusted them for fingerprints and vacuumed around each. Sky didn't know what the hell she could find, but hoped it was something. Anything.

"I'm done, Sky," Patty called from the kitchen. She smiled gamely and pushed her blond bangs off her brow. "You can come in and make yourself some coffee. It's past dinnertime. Are you hungry?" She quickly put her small vacuum into its carrying case and then tucked the plastic bags she'd tagged into her grip.

Sky shoved his hands into the pockets of his jeans as he entered the kitchen. Patty Solare was about five foot six inches tall, with short blond hair and sparkling blue eyes. Though she was dressed casually in jeans and a cap-sleeved T-shirt with a bright yellow sunflower embroidered on the front, she seemed highly professional.

"I'm not hungry," he muttered. "Thanks for doing all of this."

She smiled sadly and picked up her equipment, ready to leave. "Don't thank me yet. I'm taking this back to our lab, and I pray I'll find something. I'll give you a call if I do. Take care, Sky. And hang in there."

The cabin became deathly quiet after she left. Sky felt as if a raptor were clawing at his chest and ripping out his aching heart. Sitting down at the table, he scrubbed his hand across his face and tried to think. The vision of Kelly's face, those soft lips pulled into a smile, made him want to cry. Lips he'd tasted. Lips that had responded with the same ardor he felt for her.

Oh, Great Spirit, was that the last thing they would ever share? Would he see her alive again? Right now, all Sky wanted was Kelly. He couldn't even react to the fact that Talbot was out of prison and hunting him. All Sky cared about was her. He loved Kelly! Oh, how he loved her. Feeling miserable, he removed his hands from his face and stared dully at the kitchen sink. Kelly should be there now, helping him fix dinner.

Talbot had done this. But why go after Kelly? Good hunters employed distractions. And Talbot was a fine hunter. . . . Sky's mind whirled, searching for plausible answers to the enigma. Maybe this *was* another hit against Morgan and his family by a drug cartel? One targeting Kelly this time?

Numbness tunneled through him. Sky had no one he could call, to talk about his loss. All he had was an empty house, and an empty heart pining away for Kelly. Like a red-tailed hawk, which mated for life, he felt her loss keenly. She was his mate. But someone had come and kidnapped her, and his life was torn apart.

CHAPTER
TWENTY-THREE

"Not a damn thing," Morgan muttered to Mike Houston as they sat outside the Talbot house. He'd gotten a search warrant, and had enlisted the help of the local police chief and the FBI. Luckily, since Morgan was in the security industry, he knew all the organizations that worked on kidnapping cases.

He glared at the empty house. With the warrant in hand, they had gone through the home, room by room. The note on the door saying they were on vacation was a ruse, he was sure.

"What I can't figure is why Lena's car is still there," Houston murmured, making notes on his clipboard. "I saw food still on the table, and there's evidence of Billy Jo living with her until very recently. It's as if they suddenly got up and left. Without their car."

Frowning, Morgan looked at the clouds,

and rays of late afternoon sunlight lancing through them. The Talbot house sat at the edge of the tourist town, in a section where blue-collar workers lived. Hand on the wheel, he mouthed, "But they disappeared. That's the key. Lena's purse is gone. We found no wallet of Billy Jo's. They're staying somewhere else."

"I'm running rental lists for this part of the state," Houston said. "Maybe they rented a vehicle?"

"Must have. Why else would they leave her car in the driveway, if they are behind this kidnapping?"

Mike shrugged. "We need to think like they do. It's the only way to try to get a lead on them."

"So they rented a car and kidnapped Kelly?" Morgan suggested. "To what end? To hold her hostage for a million dollars? I'm hoping Patty has found fingerprints on that note by now." He knew his best forensics specialist at Perseus would call the minute she found anything. Patty was just as upset over Kelly's disappearance as anyone.

He knew he should put in a call to Laura, to keep her updated. Morgan ached over how this was tearing her up. He felt helpless, unable to shield his wife from the pain.

He couldn't even protect himself from his terror and anxiety over their daughter's disappearance.

It was nearly impossible to think clearly in this situation. Morgan was more than glad to have Houston along, because he would.

The cell phone rang and Morgan flipped it open.

"Hi, Patty. Did you find something?"

"Yes, I did. There was nothing on the note. It was free of fingerprints. But I went into our archives and dug out the case file on Billy Jo Talbot. Remember that you were involved in the trial that put him into prison?"

"Yes," Morgan said. "What did you find?" His heart pounded with hope.

"When I compared Billy Jo Talbot's handwriting on some papers he'd signed during his trial, and the note on Sky's kitchen table, they seemed to match. I'm not a handwriting expert, so I've faxed the samples to Wanda Stedman, who is. She lives in Sacramento. If it is Talbot's writing, then we have him, and we know for sure he's involved in this kidnapping somehow."

"Good work," Morgan said. "How soon do you think we'll hear from Wanda?"

"Very shortly. She knows Kelly's been kidnapped, and she's putting everything else aside to study the writing samples I just faxed to her. I'll give you a call the moment I hear from her."

"Excellent, Patty. Thank you. Did you scrounge up anything else?"

"Yes, a gray hair. I'm running it right now . . . We know Talbot doesn't have gray hair, and I'll call Sky to ask if he's had any visitors the past two weeks. It could have come from a friend."

Nodding, Morgan smiled briefly. "Sounds good, Patty. Any fingerprints anywhere?"

"Not so far. I dusted all the doorjambs, windowsills, the refrigerator and the table where the note was placed, and found nothing. I'm still going over the contents that I sucked up with my vac. I'll talk to you soon."

Snapping the phone closed, Morgan told Houston what Patty had found. Mike's green eyes narrowed speculatively.

"If Patty can see a similarity in the writing, I'd bet my life that it is Talbot, and that confirms that he's involved."

"And if he's involved, would his mother be in on it?" Morgan wondered out loud. "She has no criminal record."

Houston snorted. "No, but she raised a kid who sure as hell has one. They say apples don't drop far from the tree." Jabbing his finger toward the Talbot home, he said, "And I wouldn't put anything past the family at this point. Do you recall Talbot's mother from the trial?"

"She was pretty quiet. Like a mouse, but an angry one. She sat behind her son, and when it came time for her to get up on the stand, she lied like hell. She tried to convince the jury that Billy Jo was with her at the time of the murders."

"She did lie," Houston agreed, "but no one could prove it." He cut Morgan a quick look. "My gut tells me that Lena Talbot is in on this KNR, Morgan."

Wearily, he nodded, then started up the car. "I should get back to Sky. I'm sure he's going wild, wondering if we found anything. And we've got to put our heads together on all this."

Sky gripped the edge of the table as Morgan shared the latest information with him. Then he squeezed his eyes shut. "Talbot's mother is as cold as a robot. She's more than capable of being in on this with Billy Jo."

"And you're positive you've had no one here with gray hair visiting you recently?"

With a shake of his head, Sky said, "No, sir. No one. I feel it's Lena Talbot. Maybe she and her son came here and knocked on our door. Kelly would know Billy Jo, though. We went to school with him. She'd recognize him in a heartbeat and would never let him into the cabin."

"But what if Lena came to the door alone? Maybe Kelly let her in, not knowing who she was?"

"That's possible," Sky said tensely. "She probably never met Talbot's mother. The day Kelly testified at the first trial, I remember Lena being out sick with the flu."

"Damn," Morgan growled, standing up and restlessly buttoning his suit coat. "We protected Kelly from the trial by not allowing her to see TV news reports on it, or read the local newspaper, both of which would have run pictures of Lena Talbot. Kelly was just a little kid and was upset enough. We didn't want her seeing that stuff." Grumbling, Morgan said, "There's no way she would recognize Lena Talbot." He nailed Sky with a dark look. "Do you have any idea what their plan might have been? They've left everything at Lena's home. Her car is there, too."

Sky lifted his head. "Lena's a cunning fox in all of this. Everyone has underestimated her importance. I'll bet she's the mastermind behind Kelly's kidnapping. Billy Jo is a dumb ox in comparison. He must be the muscle and she's the brain. I've got to think they rented or stole a car, to cover their tracks. Maybe they've rented another house? She might even do it right under our noses."

"That's a possibility," Morgan agreed. "Mike is running a list of all vehicle rentals the past month here in western Montana. I hope Lena Talbot was stupid enough to use her own name to sign for one if they did. Or her son's name. Maybe she even used her new address . . ."

Sky stood up and looked out the kitchen window. It was getting close to evening now. "I don't think she'd be that stupid. Billy Jo is, but not Lena."

"You're probably right." Morgan gave Sky another searching look. The younger man stood with his hands on the counter, staring toward the enclosures where his raptors lived. Poor guy had to be suffering. "I'll provide security here at the cabin for you from now on. You need to stay here, in case they get in touch, but you have to sleep, enough to keep your head about you in the coming days. I'll send one of my men up here to keep an eye on things."

Sky turned. He rested his hips against the kitchen counter and folded his arms across his chest. "I'll be okay here, Morgan. I have all kinds of warning systems in place. Take that guy and put him on the case to find Kelly."

Uncertain, Morgan studied him. "You know, Talbot swore to kill you. He's out there, Sky. You aren't safe."

"I'll take my chances. I need to care for my raptors, and I don't want to leave this place or them open to that murdering bastard. I've got a pistol and I know how to use it."

Morgan couldn't argue with Sky's grim determination. "Okay. I'm heading home then. The police have wiretapped your telephone so that if anyone calls, they'll trace it. Just try to keep the caller on the line long enough for them to do so."

"I will," he promised, and watched Kelly's father leave. With a frustrated growl, Sky turned back to the window, gripping the counter once more. His heart hurt so damn much he could barely take in a breath. His mind churned, transfixed on Kelly. Was she all right? Was she hurt? He didn't want to think what Talbot might do to her.

Sky rubbed his eyes, as if trying to erase the frightening images in his head. Kelly was a pawn in this terrible dance between himself and Talbot. Sky would willingly give

his life for hers. He loved her, unequivocally.

Hanging his head, he berated himself for
never telling Kelly what she meant to him,
what she'd always meant to him.

The house was quiet. Kelly silently tiptoed
away from the cot, toward the corner where
the dusty furniture was stashed. For over an
hour she'd heard no footsteps on the floor
above her, no voices. Feeling as sleepy as
she did, she figured it had to be late. Settling on her knees in front of the old cabinet,
she managed to open the second drawer.
Her groping fingers met more fabric; this
was probably someone's bedroom set, and
all she'd find was clothes.

The basement was quite chilly now, and
Kelly hoped to at least locate something to
wear from the dusty drawers. Anything.
Feeling in the darkness, she angled her
fingers deeper into the drawer, which would
open only about four inches. Suddenly they
touched something cold. *Metal.* Frowning,
Kelly managed to pull the object forward
through the mass of clothes.

She got up and moved back to the cot to
see what it was. In the dim light, she realized it was a screwdriver about six inches
long, the Phillips-head type. The yellow

plastic handle was badly cracked, but the metal was sturdy. Kelly studied it hopefully. This was a weapon!

She again noticed light leaking around the door at the top of the stairs, which she knew was chained shut. Was it possible to use this screwdriver to take off the hinges? Her heart leaped with sudden hope.

Rising, Kelly recalled how old and creaky the steps were. She took her time getting up them, testing each one slowly, very slowly, and placing her weight carefully. If the wood started to protest, she froze. And then, after minutes went by, she would ease her foot onto it with hardly another sound.

Kelly had no idea how long it took her to get to the top of the stairs. With her pulse pumping with adrenaline, her nerves a jittery mess, it felt like hours.

If the Talbots caught her, she would suffer, maybe even die, she knew. Finally reaching the landing, she felt for the door hinges, deciding to work on the lowest one first, the one she could see best in the faint light. The rectangular metal plate was fastened on with four screws. Would the Phillips head fit them? Wiping her mouth nervously, Kelly got down on her knees to find out.

Her hands were shaking. How desperately she wanted to escape! As she eased the screwdriver into place, she found her heart thudding. *Yes!* The metal cross fit into the matching slot in the screw! Releasing a silent moan of relief, Kelly got to work, turning them as swiftly and quietly as she could, until at last four screws lay on the landing between her knees. *So far, so good.*

It was only then she realized her forehead was covered with sweat. Straightening her spine, she wiped it away with the back of her hand. Two more hinges to go. Eight screws. And then she could lift the door off the hinges and slip out. Out to freedom?

Kelly cautioned herself not to even think that yet. She had to unfasten two more hinges and do it silently. Rising up on her knees, she fitted the screwdriver into place, forcing herself to work slowly and breathe steadily. All the while, her hearing was keyed to the other side of the door. There were no sounds, that she could discern. It had to be around midnight, perhaps early morning. Were the Talbots asleep? Kelly tried to calm her apprehension as she worked.

One more hinge to go! She stretched upward. After wiping one sweaty palm on her trousers, she went back to work.

Done! A shaky breath whispered between her thinned lips as she finally slid the screwdriver into the back pocket of her jeans. With her fingers, she worked gently but firmly to dislocate each hinge from the wood. They were rusted and had been in place for a long time. It took Kelly another age to ease each one free.

Wiping her face again, she finally stood back. The door was in the frame, still in place. She would have to grasp the middle hinge and lift, then as quietly as she could, pull the door toward her. A wave of anxiety washed through her, leaving her dizzy.

This was like being held captive by the Taliban, she thought numbly. The Talbots were the enemy, and they wanted her to remain a prisoner.

But she had to escape! She was in an unknown place, unsure of her location, although she was fairly certain it wasn't far from Philipsburg. Compressing her lips, she steeled herself and set to work, her left hand on the freed hinge and her other one pressed to the panel. *Oh, God, please let me get this door open without a sound!*

The moment she applied strength, the door moved. Kelly's heart leaped with joy — until a creak broke the stillness. Freezing, she held the door and hinge in place, her hands shaking. For five endless minutes, she didn't move and barely breathed. With no sound coming from the other side of the door, she finally pulled on it again. It came easily. Quietly. Hope soared through Kelly as she swung it open, inches at a time.

Light streamed toward her, hurting her eyes. If the Talbots came to check on her right now, they'd find the door ajar, see her moving it. A sense of urgency shot through her as she angled the heavy panel. Finally, there was a wide enough opening for her to slip through. Propping the door against the wall in the stairwell, Kelly pulled the screwdriver from her back pocket and grasped it in her right hand. It was her only defense.

Peering cautiously through the doorway, she found herself looking into a kitchen. There was a loaf of bread on the counter, a gallon jug of water and a pack of cigarettes. Heart pounding so hard she was sure it would wake the dead, she tiptoed into the kitchen. The clock hanging on the wall read 3:00 a.m.

Ears straining to catch the slightest noise, she turned and listened. The other lights in the house had been doused. Somewhere down a hall, she heard snoring. It had to be Talbot. Kelly quickly searched the kitchen. There was a back door to her left. *Good!* Moving quietly, she checked to make sure it had no alarm attached. Nothing she could see, anyway. . . .

She rapidly scanned the room again, wishing for a cell phone. She couldn't risk staying in the house to search for one, though. No, she had to get out now.

Kelly slowly twisted the brass doorknob, but found the door stuck. Grimly, she worked with it, sweat stinging her eyes. She had to escape.

There!

The door yawned open with a squeak. Kelly pushed the screen door outward, stepped through and pulled it shut behind her, as stealthily as she could. The night was cool. It felt so good to breathe in fresh, clean air! She quickly oriented herself, finding herself in the backyard, with huge pine trees not far away. Moonlight shining through their limbs scattered its milky glow on the needle-covered earth.

Padding down the stairs, Kelly quickly made her way into the grove of trees. They would hide her. A dog began barking nearby. A neighbor? Would the barking wake up the Talbots? Jerking her head left, then right, she jogged through the dark woods. With every step she felt a little more of the dread slip from her tense shoulders.

Moving away from the house, she noticed there wasn't a car in front. Peering down the tree line, she saw lights from house about a mile away, down a dark ribbon of road. There were no homes nearby where she could call for help. *Nothing.* Kelly glanced up to see scudding clouds covering the moon. The humidity was high and she could smell rain in the air.

Did she dare step out onto the road and jog to that house in the distance? It had a streetlight nearby, but seemed mostly dark, its occupants asleep. Raindrops started pelting down on her and they felt good. They reminded her that she was alive. And free!

And then terror struck Kelly and she halted abruptly. What if Billy Jo had taken the car and driven back up to Sky's cabin? Talbot had sworn to murder him.

The fear galvanized her, and she started to race down the slope. No longer did she care if the Talbots discovered her gone, or saw her running away. She had to get to that house in the distance. She had to call the cabin, and then her parents.

She had to warn Sky that Billy Jo Talbot was stalking him!

CHAPTER
TWENTY-FOUR

Sky jerked awake. Adrenaline surged through him and he quickly sat up from the couch, where he'd been dozing. Night-lights positioned around the main rooms gave him just enough of a glow to see. What had he heard?

He automatically reached for the pistol he'd tucked beneath the sofa pillow, then held his breath and listened.

Was someone trying to jimmy a lock and get into the cabin? Was someone already in the house? Terror sizzled through him as he hunched there in the murky grayness.

With his fingers wrapped around the cold pistol, he waited, keying his hearing. *Nothing.* He scanned every inch of space he could see from the couch. The shadows took on menacing shapes, but in the end, it was only his imagination fueling his fear.

Had he dreamed the sound?

And then Sky realized that none of the

motion sensor lights outside had been tripped. He stood and padded silently to the kitchen window, where he looked out toward the mews.

No, there was no disturbance outside, except for some angry storm clouds. A light rain was falling, and off in the distance, he saw some cloud-to-cloud lightning.

Rubbing his eyes, he leaned against the kitchen counter and frowned. Maybe the sound that awakened him had been thunder. Otherwise, everything seemed quiet.

He glanced at his watch. It was 2:30 a.m. Again, he looked toward the enclosures that housed his beloved raptors. The shadows were deep because the rainclouds hid the moon. The shower grew heavier, temporarily blurring the scene.

Sky moved around the house, checking every window. They were all locked, so the only way Talbot could get in was if he broke a pane of glass, and Sky was sure he'd hear that.

Everything was fine. Going back to the living room, he allowed himself to relax. Sliding the pistol beneath the couch pillow, he sat down. The adrenaline began to dissipate, and he found himself feeling exhausted. His heart stopped pounding so hard and his thoughts returned to Kelly.

Oh, Great Spirit, how he loved her. It had been hell getting to sleep at all since her kidnapping. The fact that Talbot and his mother had her made Sky sick.

Logic warred with pure terror over her fate. She was ex-military. She'd fought in a war and knew how to survive; every officer was given survival training. And yet, because Sky loved her, none of that knowledge made him feel any better.

Restless despite his exhaustion, he walked to the kitchen and poured himself a glass of water. The rain had stopped, he noted. At least for the moment. He could see a few scraps of moonlight sifting down between breaks in the clouds.

The drink of water cooled his hot, queasy gut. Setting the glass aside, he finally decided he must have been dreaming when he heard the sound.

Turning, he went back to the couch and lay down. Would sleep come? Dropping his arm across his eyes once again, he tried to shut off his mind, quash his vivid imagination, and get to sleep. The last thing he remembered was praying to the Great Spirit for Kelly's safety. Would his fierce, undying love for her make any difference?

Billy Jo sat patiently just outside the mews.

It was half past two in the morning. He'd just shot out the motion sensor light nearest the cages. Grinning despite the rain dripping down his face, he crouched there, waiting.

Sure enough, Sky McCoy appeared at the kitchen window. Talbot knew he was invisible, but he could sure as hell see his enemy. The noise of the .22 pistol he'd used to put out the light had probably awakened him. Talbot had expected that. He shifted slightly, readjusting his position in the grove of trees so he had just the right angle to see and not be seen. Oh, he could have shot McCoy through the window, but that was too easy. No, Billy Jo wanted more. He wanted the bastard to writhe, to worry himself sick about his girlfriend. There was savage pleasure in letting McCoy suffer, for as long as he decreed. Talbot also prided himself on his superior stalking and hunting skills. The sense of control over McCoy made him feel ten times more powerful.

The thunder and lightning were moving off to the east, the worst of the storm now past. Talbot felt gleeful and invincible. For once, healthwise, he was feeling damn good. Having AIDS was like riding a roller coaster. There were days when he was weak as a kitten and others where he'd feel almost normal. Luckily, the past two days he was on a high, and Billy Jo was grateful. It made his stalking easy.

As he sat in the shadows, the trees dripping around him, he chortled inwardly. He'd left his mother back at the house, snoring, at 1:00 a.m. She was tired from all the day's activities, kidnapping Kelly Trayhern. Lena knew he'd be leaving to go after McCoy. She'd wanted Billy Jo to awaken her before he left, but he hadn't had the heart to do that. Knowing that Kelly Trayhern was safely locked away in the basement, he had left his mother to get some badly needed sleep.

Looking at his wristwatch, he removed the nylon cover to peer at the dials. It was 2:45 a.m., and it appeared that McCoy had gone back to bed. Time to move. Time to set the trap . . .

Was he dreaming again? Sky moaned and turned on his side, face buried in the pillow. He smelled smoke. It had to be a nightmare. And yet, as he tried to push the odor away, he couldn't erase it.

The smell increased in intensity. Finally, Sky jerked awake, disoriented. Darkness surrounded him except for the night-lights. *Smoke!* Leaping up, he turned, and his shock gave way to horror. The dancing light of flames came in through the kitchen window.

"No!" he groaned, and raced through the kitchen toward the exit. The mews were on fire! Sky nearly tore the door off its hinges as he yanked it open.

Immediately, he noticed flames leaping up from the farthest mew, where Luna lived. Sky's entire world stilled as he raced down the sidewalk. The motion sensor lights were on, likely because of the flickering blaze. In his sock feet, he tore around the outside of the enclosure complex to reach Luna's cage.

What had happened? Had a bolt of lightning struck? Panting, he slid in the mud and the wet pine needles, mindless of the fact he was wearing only a pair of jeans. He had to rescue Luna!

The flames gave him plenty of light as he approached. Luna was flying around in a panic. The fire was at the far end, eating up the wooden walls and engulfing the corrugated steel roofing. The odor of heated metal mingled with the wood smoke. Choking and coughing, Sky called to the owl. "Luna! It's all right. I'll rescue you!"

He got to the door, the flames licking toward him. The wind had picked up and was carrying the fire straight down through the enclosure to the flapping, floundering owl.

Sky hissed in pain when he touched the door latch, burning his fingers on the hot metal as he jerked it open. He leaped into the mew and ran for Luna, who seemed half-crazed, trying to escape the flames. This was no time for patience or gentleness. Sky lunged upward, grasping the owl's long wings, and wrapped her in his arms.

Luna bit him and hissed. Sky didn't even feel her large yellow beak tear the skin on his hand. Turning, he ran for the exit, followed by flames. Eyes tearing, coughing badly, Sky saw his chance. With a grunt, he threw Luna out the open door.

Instantly, the owl flapped her mighty wings and disappeared up into the firs.

Saved!

Gasping for breath, Sky dived out the door behind her, flames singeing him as he did so. There was no time to waste! Each mew was separate, designed that way in case of fire. But the wind was strengthening and the smoke was drifting into the cages of his Harris hawks, Bo and Bella. Sky could hear them calling out in alarm and flapping their wings.

He had to release them, as well. The other mews were far enough away that the fire wouldn't leap to them and put the raptors in jeopardy. As he crunched across the gravel, Sky used the fire to light his way toward the Harris hawks. His hands shook so badly he could barely manage to open the latch on Bella's, but he kept his whole focus on saving her.

The Harris hawks, Bella and Bo, flew out of the door just as soon as Sky hauled it open. Sky watched the pair as they, too, flew to the nearest trees and disappeared.

Wiping the sweat off his face, he felt a huge relief. At least his raptors nearest the fire would be safe. Tomorrow morning, at dawn, he would call them back, and they'd come. He had a few empty mews on the other side where he could place them. His mind gyrated. *Had* lightning struck the enclosures? How had this fire started?

The flames spat and roared, fanned by the wind as another thunderstorm advanced. In a few minutes, it would start raining again. Running back toward the garage, where he kept a hose, Sky felt pain in his feet from stepping on rocks and gravel. He didn't care. He had just enough light to find it, turn on the faucet and haul the hose back toward the conflagration.

Already, the flames were starting to die down. The mews were made mostly of lightweight steel, with only two walls composed of wood and other flammable material. Stopping nearby, Sky turned on the water and directed the spray at the flames. He was so focused on putting them out, so they couldn't spread to any of the other mews, that he didn't hear the pop of a rifle.

A hot, burning sensation slammed into his right upper arm. Shocked, but not realizing he'd been shot, Sky turned his head and saw blood on his biceps. And then reality crashed into him.

Talbot!

His mind sheered violently. Sky leaped behind the now smoldering mews, which were encased with thick, grayish smoke. He landed hard on the gravel, the stones biting savagely into his flesh. Billy Jo had set the fire, Sky realized. The bastard had lured him out here to kill him.

Cursing, Sky scrambled to his feet. He knew his mews better than Talbot, who had to be hiding in the stand of trees where the raptors had flown to safety. Breathing in gasps, Sky headed toward the other end of the complex. He had to get to the house. He'd stupidly forgotten to pick up his pistol from the couch.

As he ducked and darted, hiding behind each mew he came to, Sky's concern for his animals grew. His attention shifted continually, from listening for sounds to watching for movement. The motion sensor lights remained on. Talbot probably had the kitchen door covered, but there was no telling what exactly he was watching, how much he could see.

The wound in Sky's arm continued to burn. He felt a warm trickle of blood flowing down to his fingers. But he couldn't stop.

He decided to race through the shadows along one side of the cabin. Knowing that the kitchen door was a likely target, Sky dug his toes into the slippery pine needles as he fled around the back of the house.

Another shot sounded.

Wood chips off the cabin wall exploded near Sky's head.

Wincing, he felt the splinters gouge his cheek and the side of his neck. Dropping to his hands and knees, he crawled along the side of the house, out of sight of Talbot, who had to be following him.

Gasping, Sky made it around the corner of the cabin. He had to get to his pistol! He could hear the phone ringing in the living room inside. Quickly leaping to his feet, he balled his fist and slammed it into the nearest window, shattering the glass. Reaching inside, he unlatched it and then shoved it upward.

Moving shakily, the adrenaline pouring through him, he fell into the living room. *Get the pistol!* It was his only protection.

The phone rang incessantly.

He lunged for the sofa, fingers outstretched, and grabbed the pistol. Sitting up, breathing hard, he found his hands were shaking as he groped for the release.

Now the gun was ready to fire. Sky kept low as he eased around the couch.

The sensor lights lit up the whole place as if it were daylight. He wouldn't dare answer the damn phone; he could be a target if he tried to do so. No, he had to find the GPS phone Perseus had given him, and punch speed dial to Morgan Trayhern's emergency number, to let him know Talbot had arrived. They had agreed that if Sky ever called it, Morgan would know something was wrong at the cabin, and to get help there as soon as possible.

Groping frantically, Sky finally located the GPS device, which had ended up under the edge of the couch.

And then he heard the back door crash inward.

Talbot!

The shattering of glass was deafening as

the door caved beneath Billy Jo's weight and rage. Fumbling with the phone, Sky hunkered down behind the couch, hopefully out of sight. He groaned. The damn GPS was taking its own sweet time to turn on and lock on to a satellite signal.

"McCoy!" Talbot roared, standing in the kitchen, rifle in hand. "Where are you, you son of a bitch? I know you're in here. Show yourself, you goddamn coward!"

Sky winced. His nemesis was only ten feet away. With a hiss of frustration, Sky dropped the GPS. It was too slow in activating, dammit! He'd have to handle Talbot on his own.

Suddenly, bullets exploded through the living room. Sky flattened himself against the floor, pistol in hand as Talbot sprayed the area with rifle fire.

"Show yourself, you friggin' coward!" Talbot screamed.

Holding his breath, Sky rose to his knees and peeked around the corner of the couch. Talbot was backlit by the sensor lights outside.

Sky knew he wasn't the best shot in the world, especially at this angle. But he fired several times, the gun bucking in his hand.

Talbot let out a shout and leaped to the other side of the kitchen where the wall offered protection.

It gave him time enough. Sky surged to his feet and, in two strides, launched himself through the window he'd entered. If Talbot wanted a fight, he'd give it to him — but on Sky's terms.

Scraping his skin against the wooden frame, Sky tumbled out. He'd forgotten the GPS phone, but it wouldn't help now. This was all going down in a matter of moments, and he couldn't wait for assistance. Jumping to his feet, he sprinted around the cabin. No one, not even Morgan Trayhern, could get here soon enough to save his hide. Sky would either live or die in the next few minutes. A cold rage of revenge flowed through him as he reached the corner, where he could see the broken kitchen door hanging on a hinge. Talbot would probably come out that way, he knew.

Sky waited. Nothing happened. To make his back less of a target, he knelt down in the shadows. A fir tree near the corner of the house gave excellent protection and blocked the sensor light from revealing him. Where was Talbot? Had he wounded him?

Uneasy, Sky cocked his ears. Thunder rolled nearby, masking all possible sound. *Damn.* And then lightning lit the sky overhead. Suddenly, the sensor lights were doused. All of them. Sky knew that lightning could affect them. A bright light would make them go out, just as sunlight did. *Double damn.*

In the sudden darkness Sky could hear Luna's plaintive calls coming from the evergreen grove. The young eagle-owl was obviously frightened, and wanted her "parent" to protect her. But there was nothing Sky could do right now about Luna.

To steady his breathing, he opened his mouth, drawing in more air. Talbot was a consummate hunter so Sky kept checking over his shoulder, as well as peering toward the kitchen door.

Another minute passed. Still no movement. Frustrated, he wondered if he'd hit Talbot, if the man was lying in the kitchen, bleeding. Should he go look? Sky didn't want to go back into the cabin; it was too cramped and had too many places for Talbot to hide. No, he wanted the fight out in the open, where he had a chance.

He got to his feet, keeping flat against the wall, pistol raised and ready to fire. He had to go toward that gaping door and find out. One way or another . . .

Heart thudding in his chest, Sky saw more lightning flashes. The sensor lights remained off; the darkness swallowed him up again. Thunder caromed off the mountain behind him, shaking the ground. The wind whipped up as he slipped slowly around the corner. Sky's throat ached with tension. Fear clawed at him.

"Hold it right there, you bastard."

He froze. Jerking his head to the left, he saw Talbot come out of the shadows. Sky realized he must have gotten out of the house through the window, sneaked around the cabin and used the mews as a hiding place until Sky showed up.

"Don't move," Talbot snarled, smiling as he held up the rifle.

Raising both hands, Sky felt his spirit die within him. Talbot was twenty feet away, aiming the barrel of the rifle directly at his chest.

"Drop the pistol. Now."

Hearing the glee in Talbot's deep voice, Sky hesitated.

"I'll shoot you right where you stand if you don't."

Sky knew he'd kill him anyway. He was too far away from him to use his karate. Could he get off a shot? He knew Talbot's finger was on the trigger. Weighing the options, he sucked in a breath. He had to take the chance! Without the pistol, he was dead anyway.

"You don't leave me any choice," Sky snarled.

Talbot raised the rifle higher and sighted down the barrel. "Do it or —"

Out of the night, Luna flew toward them. Just as she did in her training exercises, she sailed soundlessly, upon hearing Sky's voice.

Sky gasped as the European eagle-owl suddenly appeared out of the trees and swooped down toward Talbot. Her large claws were outstretched and aimed right at his face.

Stunned by Luna's unexpected appearance, Talbot swung the rifle away for a split second as the owl whooshed by him.

It was Sky's one and only chance!

Lifting the pistol, he fired once, twice, three times. Luna swept on past him, causing a rush of air across his face, and disappeared into the night.

Sky's bullets hit Talbot in the chest and abdomen. The shots knocked him backward; the rifle fell out of his hands. He gave a cry of surprise as he fell to the ground.

Luna flapped by once more, called frantically, and Sky saw her land in a Douglas fir above her smoking enclosure. Racing forward, he quickly picked up the rifle so Talbot couldn't reach it.

Then, rasping for air, he hunkered over

him, while Talbot rolled onto his back, groaning. Weakly, he reached for his chest, perhaps trying to stop the bleeding. Just then the motion sensor lights flashed on, revealing the whole garish, shocking scene. The ex-con was pasty-looking, his eyes wild and rolling, spittle drooling out of the corner of his mouth as he tried to breathe.

"You — you —" he choked.

"You're going to die like you lived, Billy Jo," Sky whispered hoarsely. Blood stained the man's clothing. Sky knew the second shot was lodged near his heart, and that he wouldn't last long. And Sky was not going to try to save the murderer.

"I . . . hate . . . you . . ." Talbot suddenly spat up blood mixed with white foamy bubbles. His laugh came out a harsh bark. Lifting his hand, he jabbed it at Sky. "I get the last laugh, you bastard," he said in a choking gasp. And then he tried to spit at Sky. If nothing else, he would try to infect him with his AIDS virus before he died.

"What are you talking about?" Sky demanded, dodging the spittle, which landed harmlessly nearby. He leaned closer, glaring at him.

Talbot's laughter was hideous as he tried to breathe. Closing his eyes and dropping his hands, he rasped, "I got your girl. She's dead. Ma had orders to kill her tonight while I came over here to do you in. I might die, but the bitch is already dead . . ." A last breath of air exploded from him, along with a spurt of blood that covered his chin and neck.

Stunned, Sky straightened. Numbed by Talbot's last words, he turned and ran toward the kitchen, just as rain began to fall again, heavy and hard. The phone had stopped ringing. Switching on the lights, Sky hurried toward it.

"Sky!"

Jerking up, he stared across the living room. Kelly stood there, wet and muddy, her face flushed and eyes filled with tears.

"Kelly!"

"Oh, Sky! I was so afraid you were dead!" She rushed forward, her arms wide.

CHAPTER
TWENTY-FIVE

"I thought you were dead," Sky whispered, his voice cracking. He opened his arms and Kelly flew toward him. The moment their hot, sweaty bodies met, he groaned and crushed her against him. Kelly wrapped her arms around his waist, and Sky inhaled her feminine scent. She was trembling, shaking with sobs as he kissed her mussed red hair, her tearstained cheek and finally, her parted lips.

Hungrily, Sky claimed her wet mouth with his. His world exploded as she eagerly returned his kiss. Nothing else mattered. He'd survived and Kelly was alive. Suddenly, Sky felt tears leaking from his eyes. Tears of joy. Tears of relief. Her entire body leaned against him in silent trust, and she murmured his name, over and over. Sky couldn't get enough of Kelly — her mouth, her tongue, her taste and fragrance. Nostrils flaring, he absorbed every scent, every molecule of her firm, wonderfully curved body as it pressed against him.

"Oh, God," Kelly quavered, tearing her mouth from his, "I thought I'd lost you, Sky. I — I was kidnapped. The Talbots took me. I fell for a stupid ruse right here at the cabin."

"It's all right, all right," he rasped, touching her hair, her damp cheek, and drowning in her anguished green gaze. "We're both alive. It's going to be okay . . ." He gulped hard, tears burning in his eyes.

With a moan, Kelly threw her arms around his broad shoulders, feeling his flesh, warm and sweaty. "Oh, Sky! I love you so much . . . so much it hurts," she sobbed, pressing kisses across his neck, his jaw, and finally, his mouth. Kelly felt starved for his touch, desperate and needy after her escape from her basement prison.

Slowly, Sky felt himself settling to earth with the woman of his dreams, who was now alive and safe in his arms. The lights within the cabin seemed to symbolize new hope, new life. He clung to Kelly's sweet, wet mouth like a man who had been ready to die, but had been given a last-second reprieve. Sky realized how close he had come to dying.

"I love you, woman of my heart," he

rasped against her trembling mouth. "I love you with every breath I'll ever take, from this moment forward . . ." He deepened the kiss as the promise whispered between them.

Kelly's sobs abated. She kept touching Sky's bare body, his muscles hard and sleek beneath her searching palms. "I just can't get enough of you, Sky. I came so close to losing you." She looked up and glanced around the kitchen, at the door hanging by one hinge. "What happened? Where's Talbot? I know he was coming here to kill you."

Cradling her in his arms, Sky said, "He's dead. He won't hurt us anymore. Listen, how did *you* get here? I couldn't call your father or anyone, because things happened too fast. Have you contacted law enforcement? Your parents?"

Drawing in a ragged sigh, Kelly looked at the broken window, the glass shards scattered across the floor, shining like cut diamonds in the lamplight. In as few words as possible, she told him what had happened. "Once I got out of that house, I ran a mile down the road to the nearest neighbor. I kept banging on the door until the owner, an elderly farmer, answered. He let me in, and I kept calling here, Sky, for the longest time."

"I heard the phone ringing, but couldn't answer it," he told her apologetically. "Talbot was trying to kill me."

Kelly shuddered. "I knew something was wrong when you didn't answer. I asked Mr. Foster, the owner of the farm, if I could borrow his pickup. Thank goodness he knew my dad. Otherwise, I don't think he'd have entrusted me with his truck." Kelly made a motion toward the door. "I drove here as fast as I could."

"Did you have a cell phone on you?"

Shaking her head, she said, "No. The Talbots took it away from me. I never found it after I escaped from the basement. I did ask Mr. Foster to call my father, and he said he would. I'm sure Dad will be here any minute."

Sky frowned and eased Kelly away from him. "We need to call the police." He reached for the phone, which had been knocked on the floor when a bullet struck the table it had been resting on. Picking it up, he scowled. "No dial tone."

"Where's your GPS phone?" Kelly asked, looking around. She knew her father had given them one shortly before she'd been kidnapped.

Sky grimaced. "I had it here, on the same table with the landline." Getting down on his hands and knees, he searched through the wood splinters and glass on that end of the chewed-up couch. Six bullet holes now perforated the sofa.

"Here it is," he muttered, pulling the object from beneath the couch. He sat back on his heels and saw that part of it was blown off. "No GPS." He held it up to Kelly. "Talbot was shooting at me from the kitchen like a crazy man. Bullets flew all over the place. One must have hit this unit." Sky threw the useless satellite phone on the couch, the cotton padding of which was hanging out like pieces of popped corn through rips in the leather.

"Let's hope Mr. Foster called Dad," Kelly said. "I feel . . . naked being without a phone." She scanned the sad-looking, torn-up cabin, which mirrored how she felt. "Where's Talbot?"

"Out back near the mews."

Rubbing her face, Kelly began to settle down from her adrenaline rush. Her heartbeat slowed and she felt shaky and exhausted. Then she saw the blood on Sky's arm. "You're hurt!" She gently touched the torn flesh.

"Talbot winged me, is all," Sky groused. "I'll be okay . . ."

"I'll go get a wet cloth, towels and antiseptic. You don't need to get an infection on top of everything else that's happened here." As she turned, she caught a whiff of smoke. "Was there a fire here, Sky?"

He nodded and told her what had happened. Seeing her eyes widen with worry again, he held up his hand. "My raptors are fine. Luna and the two Harris hawks will spend the night in the nearby firs. They've been up there before and it's familiar territory to them." Looking at his watch, he saw it was 4:00 a.m. "At dawn, we'll call them down. They'll be real hungry, and it won't be a problem retrieving them."

"Good," Kelly whispered, relieved. "They aren't hurt. That's so important."

He smiled wearily. "Luna saved my life. She was flying around, chirping and trying to get to me. She flew near Talbot's head, and it startled him enough for me to get off the first shot."

"Bless Luna," Kelly declared, choking back her horror. How close Sky had come to dying! "The poor owl was confused by all the noise, the fire and chaos."

"She was. I don't know why she flew to Talbot instead of me. She has excellent night vision and could see me as clearly as you and I see one another."

"Maybe she realized you were in danger?

I'm just glad she did fly at Talbot's face."

"I am, too," Sky said. He sat down, feeling weary, his arm aching where the bullet had creased his flesh.

"Hang on, I'll get the medical kit," Kelly called, and disappeared down the hall to the bathroom.

Quiet descended upon the disheveled cabin. It was beginning to sink in that the ordeal was all over. Talbot was dead. He would no longer continue to haunt Sky, to be a threat to Kelly or himself. It was almost too good to be true.

Sky sighed raggedly, widened his legs and planted his elbows on his thighs. He rubbed his face, which was gritty and smeared with blood from the shrapnel splinters. He closed his eyes. It was over. Really over . . .

"There you are!"

Sky snapped up his head, then stared. In the open doorway stood Lena Talbot, a pistol in her hands. And it was pointed at him. His heart contracted when he saw the hatred on the woman's pinched, wrinkled face. Her eyes were narrowed and filled with rage. The pistol in her grip didn't waver.

"Where is he? Where's my son?"

Her gravelly voice seemed to rip across his raw, sensitized nerve endings. Trying not to glance down the hall, he desperately hoped Kelly wouldn't emerge from the bathroom yet. She didn't know Lena Talbot was here. Fear arced through Sky. He held up his hands. "He's out back."

"What did you do to him?" she snarled, taking two steps into the room. Glass crunched beneath her feet.

Mind whirling, Sky knew he had to buy time. Was Morgan on his way? Sky hadn't seen any headlights out front. Opening his mouth and then closing it, he hesitated. He saw the cold, lethal look in the woman's glittering eyes. "I — He's out back." Sky spoke loudly, hoping Kelly would hear what was going on, and keep hidden.

"Alive?"

Sky noted the sudden wobble in Lena's voice, the hope pouring out despite her hatred of him. "Yes, he's alive." That was an outright lie, but he had to do something. Anything to keep Kelly from walking back in here. Talbot's mother was angry and kept brushing the trigger of the pistol. If Kelly reappeared suddenly, Sky was afraid Lena would fire first and ask questions later.

"Get up and take me to him, you half-breed son of a bitch."

Sky rose to his feet, keeping his hands in the air. Though his mind kept catapulting from one plan to another, his first priority was to keep Kelly safe. He'd take a bullet for her.

Throat stiff with tension, he said, "Come on, I'll escort you out there. It's not far." He turned and said, "I've already called an ambulance. It's on its way."

He saw Lena's face suddenly crumple. "My son's going to be okay?"

"Yes," Sky assured her. He moved into the kitchen, the glass shards cutting into his socks. He didn't feel the pain. He knew as soon as he stepped outside that motion sensor lights would flash on. Luckily, Talbot was partially hidden by the first mew, and Lena would have a tough time knowing whether he was alive or dead until she got close.

"Hurry up!" she snarled, following on his heels.

Just get outside. The night air brushed Sky's sweating skin. The rain had stopped, the thunderstorm having moved on down the valley toward Philipsburg. The lights flashed on, casting his shadow down the concrete sidewalk that led to the mews. Lena came up behind him, poking the barrel of the gun into his back.

"Where is he? Where's my son? I don't see him, dammit!"

"He's over there," Sky told her, trying to

sound reassuring and confident, while his heart slammed into his chest and adrenaline nearly choked him. Trying to breathe, trying to think, he led her along the slick, wet sidewalk. Up in a tree on the other side of the mews, Luna started to call for him. The owl must have spotted him walking toward the mews, and Sky hoped she would stay put. What was he going to do when Lena found her son dead? She'd shoot him.

Lena Talbot tried to peer around the tall, lean half-breed. Cursing, she jabbed him again with the barrel of the gun. Anxiety clawed through her. Billy Jo was alive! Oh, why had he left her sleeping when he'd driven off to find McCoy? He was supposed to have awakened her. And worse, Kelly Trayhern had escaped, while she'd slept through it all.

Lena had no idea where the girl had gone. But once she realized their plan had been blown, she'd called a cab and gone home, climbed into her own car and driven straight up to the cabin to help her son tackle McCoy. Tears filled Lena's eyes as she stepped cautiously off the sidewalk and onto the gravel around the mews. She saw her son's legs sticking out from behind the nearest cage.

"Get outta of my way!" she ordered Mc-

Coy. Waving her hand, she said, "Stand over there!" In her rush to get to Billy Jo, she stumbled in the heavy gravel. The pistol went off.

Sky, who had his back to her when the gun exploded close to his ear, automatically ducked. A bullet struck the light steel post of one of the mews, sending sparks flying. Jerking around, he saw Lena staggering forward, her left hand stretched out to stop herself from falling. This was his chance!

As he spun on his heel to use his karate, Sky realized that Lena was stumbling away from him. Her right arm flew up in the air as she tried to rebalance, but she was too far away for him to make a grab for the pistol.

Behind him, Kelly screamed out a warning.

And then Luna came flying toward Sky.

Lena had just righted herself when it happened. A flurry of feathers, of wings, slapped at her face. She yelped and fired the pistol again and again.

And then she felt the crush of a big body slamming into her. With a grunt she flew off her feet. The pistol was yanked from her hand before she fell to the hard, unforgiving gravel.

Lena hit the ground with force. The half-breed had tackled her from behind, spun her around as she fell. Her vision wasn't as good as it used to be, especially in the glare of the yard lights, but something was attacking her. Something big and dark. She raised her hands to protect her face, yet no matter what she did, there were wings and feathers beating around her head. In shock, not understanding what was happening, she lay on her back, out of breath.

She stared upward and saw as McCoy grimly got to his feet, the pistol now in his hand. And to her right, just a few feet away, Lena noticed a huge, dark owl, its orange eyes trained on her.

Kelly raced forward, calling Sky's name. Just as she reached him, Luna flew up from the ground to Sky's arm. The frantic owl had finally gotten to her "parent" and was ruffling her feathers and calling to him for help.

"Sky!"

"I'm all right," he panted, keeping his gaze and the gun trained on Lena. The older woman slowly sat up, glaring at him.

Kelly stared in shock at Billy Jo's mother. "She's the one behind all of this," she growled. "I'll get some rope. Stay put."

Sky gladly stayed where he was. He smiled slightly as Luna made her baby sounds and ruffled her feathers once more. "You're okay, Luna. Everything is going to be okay now."

Lena Talbot gave a sudden cry. She'd spotted her son sagged against the wire mesh, head resting on his chest, unmoving. "No!" she shrieked.

Sky didn't try to stop her as she got to her knees and crawled to where Billy Jo lay in the shadows. Lena crumpled and, sobbing loudly, wrapped her arms around her dead son.

Maybe he should feel remorse for Talbot's death, but Sky didn't. This woman had raised a child to believe that might was right, that it was okay to use violence on others. Sky couldn't find any sympathy for Lena Talbot as she wailed and rocked her child in her arms, her cries filling the night.

Kelly came running back out with some cotton rope in her hand. She looked at Sky and then at Lena, crouched on the ground with Talbot.

"Should we leave her?"

"Yeah, she's occupied. But we'll watch her," he whispered, giving Kelly a searching look. "You okay?"

She managed a slight smile. "Pretty rattled, is all. I never expected her to show up."

Just then, headlights came up the road, the gleaming shafts bouncing off the trees near the cabin. "Someone's coming."

"Gotta be my dad." Kelly handed Sky the rope. "I'll go meet him. I don't think Lena's going anywhere."

Watching Kelly jog around the cabin, Sky forced himself to remain on guard over the sobbing woman. Lena was beside herself, rocking her son and wailing plaintively. How could she love a murderer? It was beyond Sky to understand the events, or even begin to cope with it emotionally. Could a parent still love a child who had slaughtered others? How?

With a shake of his head, Sky shifted Luna's weight on his forearm, where her large yellow toes were digging lightly into his flesh. She wasn't hurting him, thank goodness. Luna seemed to realize that, without a gauntlet on, he was unprotected.

Sky smiled into her large orange eyes. "I owe you my life, my friend. Thank you."

Luna responded with a slow blink and then closed her eyes. Sky knew she must be stressed out and exhausted. She had nearly lost her life in the fire, and then to be abandoned by him, left out in the thunderstorm, added to the owl's distress. When a bird imprinted on a human, the relationship would always be close.

As soon as Lena Talbot was in custody, and Billy Jo's body removed, Sky would put Luna in the unused mew, and she would feel safe and happy once more.

Looking up at the tall fir trees, Sky knew the Harris hawks must be sleeping, happy to be together, because they were social hawks and formed a lifelong pair bond. The chaos of this night would not be as stressful on them, because they had one another. He would call them down at dawn, with some meat on a gauntlet, then put them back into their enclosures, which had survived the fire.

The next hour was a blur of activity. Kelly came through the cabin with her parents. Morgan and Laura both seemed incredibly relieved, and Sky understood why. The glow on Kelly's face made his own heart mushroom with such fierce love for her that Sky couldn't help but grin back.

Behind them was Mike Houston, who looked grimly over the scene. Along with Houston were two FBI agents, the Philipsburg police chief and a sergeant, plus two paramedics from an ambulance service.

Within minutes, the police officer had handcuffed Lena Talbot, read her rights and taken her, still sobbing, out to the police cruiser parked in front of the cabin. The paramedics removed the body of her son, shaking their heads when Sky declined their offer of treatment. He was then able to put Luna into her new home while Kelly went and retrieved some choice bits of meat to feed to the owl.

Laura Trayhern had noticed Sky's bullet wound. She made him come back into the cabin after he'd finished taking care of the raptors, so she could attend to it. *Like daughter, like mother,* Sky mused, as the slender woman gripped his hand firmly and led him away.

In the shambles of the living room, Sky sat quietly while Laura washed and bandaged the crease made by the bullet, then his many cuts and bruises. The two FBI agents took his and Kelly's statements. The raptors were not forgotten in all the chaos. Kelly went out to feed them at dawn, and Sky followed. Lured in by their breakfast, Bella and Bo quickly came to them and were placed back in their mews.

Once the raptors were taken care of, Sky wanted Kelly at his side, and that's exactly where she stayed, gripping his unburned hand in hers. Morgan called a cleaning agency and left a message for them to get up there that day to take care of the cabin and yard. He left another message for a carpenter friend of his to repair the back door and replace the living-room window. Sky was amazed by the quiet efficiency of Kelly's family. He had to remind himself that the Trayherns had gone through a lot of high stress and trauma before. They knew how to get things done. Later, they would all collapse, but right now they kept busy.

It was well after sunrise when the FBI and police left, and so did the Trayherns. Laura and Morgan wanted Kelly and Sky to come home with them, but she refused. Kelly wanted to stay at the cabin despite the mess. She and Sky were still too keyed up from the night's terror and trauma to sleep. Instead, they would use the energy to clean up some of the mess in the kitchen, and she'd make them breakfast. Kelly explained that they needed to get back into their rut, which would give them a semblance of stability among the ruins.

Laura Trayhern understood, Sky realized, but Morgan didn't. He wanted his daughter safe. All their old kidnapping memories had resurfaced, and Sky saw the anguish in their eyes, heard it in their voices. Still, Kelly was able to assuage her dad's worry with a fierce hug and a kiss on his cheek. She promised they'd come down for dinner and spend the evening with them. That seemed to mollify

Morgan for now.

"Phew!" Kelly gave a low whistle as her parents' car finally drove off. Giving Sky a warm, wry look, she said, "What a night."

"Yeah," he replied, gripping her hand and giving it a squeeze. "How are you doing?"

"A mixed bag. I'm feeling relief, shock, realization and happiness. You?"

"The same." He gazed worriedly into her shadowed green eyes. "I know you've been dealing with PTSD, Kelly. I can't help wondering how all of this is affecting you."

She shrugged. "It hasn't helped, but then, when you walked into my life, Sky, I started to heal. You and your raptors gave me a peaceful sanctuary, and I was able to finally stop fighting it and let it all go."

"Until now," Sky said unhappily. Lifting his hand, he threaded his fingers through her tangled hair. It needed a good washing, and he'd like to do that for her. Then comb and brush it to gleaming life once again. He wanted to perform small, loving acts for Kelly. To show her just how much she meant to him. And judging from the terror he saw banked in her eyes, he knew the next few weeks, even months, were going to be devoted to her, and healing these latest wounds. He felt confident that he was the one to give her that nurturing, loving environment in which to heal.

"We'll get through this together . . ." Kelly sighed and closed her eyes as his palm came to rest against her cheek.

"Yes, we will," he promised her.

Kelly sank into his arms, snuggling close as they sat down on the couch. Somewhere across the road, a melodic robin was welcoming the new day, as the world grew brighter around them. "I'm whipped but wired, too. I want to sleep, but I can't," she murmured. "If I went to bed, I'd just lie there staring up at the ceiling."

He chuckled and pressed a kiss on her hair. "That's the adrenaline charge. It's going to take all day to come down from this, Kelly. By the time we go to your parents' house tonight, we'll probably be ready to drop."

"Nothing like a good, home-cooked meal after a hellish night like this." She moved her hand across his stomach. Once her mother had cleaned and bandaged his wounds, Sky had retrieved a white shirt from the closet in his bedroom and shrugged it on. He still wore the holey, dirty socks on his feet, a dark reminder of the night's trials. As her fingers glided across his firm, flat abdomen, she heard him groan. Smiling, she ran her palm across his chest.

"I love you," she told him, lifting her head and meeting his gaze, which smoldered with desire for her. It dissolved the terror a little.

"You are my life," Sky told her simply. Caressing her cheek, he added in a low tone, "I love you so much, Kelly, that my heart aches for you. You are my wind, my rain and my sunshine. . . ."

CHAPTER
TWENTY-SIX

"Is it really over?" Kelly asked Sky. They stood in the newly cleaned living room of the cabin. In the two days since the shoot-out, the sofa had been replaced, a new window installed and the kitchen door repaired. A cleaning crew had come in to help as well. She stood with her arm around Sky's waist and leaned against his strong, lean frame. The past couple of nights they had driven down to Morgan and Laura's home, and slept in separate bedrooms. It was the right thing to do, given it was her parents' house.

As she glanced up at Sky, she saw the corners of his mouth relax. They had spent the days cleaning up, sorting out, digging bullets out of the walls and filling the holes with plaster. It had been an emotionally arduous and stressful time, but a healing one.

Giving Kelly's shoulder a squeeze, Sky

said, "My head knows it is, but emotionally, I'm nowhere near working through all that happened." He couldn't stop watching her, almost as if he were afraid she'd disappear again.

Kelly's hair was soft and mussed. Every time he looked into her green eyes, more of his inner chaos and shock was soothed.

They had just put the finishing touches on the living room. The place smelled of fresh paint, a coat of which covered the new plaster and drywall. All evidence of the bullet holes had been erased.

"I know," Kelly said. "It's going to take a while, Sky. At least the cabin looks like home again. That's a comfort."

He nodded gratefully. He'd also spent several hours repairing Luna's mew. With new walls and timber posts in place, the eagle-owl was now back in her original home and happy once more. "Time. It's a luxury, isn't it? I was dreading June first, the date when Talbot was supposed to be released." Sky looked around the cabin. "Now I don't have to live under his shadow anymore." He smiled and leaned down and kissed Kelly's brow. "And I don't have to worry about you being hurt by him, either."

"I know." With a shake of her head, she said, "Lena Talbot is in jail. It means another trial, Sky. Are you ready to go through this once more?"

"Three's the magic number, isn't it? And you'll be with me this time. One last dance with the Talbots. Yes, I'm ready."

Kelly sighed. "My mom calls it karma. Who would guess that a school-yard bully from the sixth grade would shadow our lives, threaten and nearly kill us as adults? It's just too wild to grasp. At least we'll have one another to lean on for support."

"And your parents will be there — again — as they were in the first two trials."

"I know they will be. It's the last go-round, Sky. Lena's trial won't come up for at least a year, the court system is so backlogged with cases. And she's been denied bail, so she can't stalk us. That's good news."

Looking at his watch, Sky said, "Let's put all this behind us for now. How about a celebration? A picnic in the upper meadow, where we teach the raptors to hunt?"

Kelly hugged him fiercely and saw a glimmer of light enter his eyes. "Alone at last," she said, her voice husky with sudden emotion. How she wanted to love Sky. Fully. Completely. And from the promise in his smile, she could tell the feeling was mutual.

"Among other things," he teased. "Come

on, let's pack a lunch and take a hike. Everything's quiet around here. We can spend the afternoon up there, just watching the world go by."

Kelly enjoyed sitting by the small stream tumbling through the high meadow. Overhead, pine trees gave them shade from the May sunlight. It was warm without being hot. The stream, no more than six feet wide, gurgled happily past, amid young ferns unfurling their leaves.

Sky sat near her on the blanket. They'd finished off their peanut butter sandwiches, drank from their thermos of coffee and munched on day-old brownies from the Philipsburg bakery.

Sky was powerfully attractive in his white cowboy shirt, the sleeves rolled up to just below his elbows. Stone-washed jeans, nearly threadbare with age, showed off his long, powerful legs. She ached to touch those thighs, to explore them intimately. He'd taken off his boots and socks, leaving his bare feet exposed.

Kelly packed away the remnants of their lunch and stuffed them back into their day pack. She was happy just to share this time and space with him. But his eyes told her he had other things on his mind, and her entire body responded.

Just then the quiet was broken by the shrill cry of a hawk overhead. Sky looked up, spotting a red-tailed hawk soaring high above. He grinned. "There's our local red-tail hunting for lunch," he said.

"Yep, he's trolling his territory for a snake or rabbit." Kelly saw a second hawk spiraling just above him. "I like the fact that these birds mate for life."

"Yes, they're like Harris hawks," Sky agreed. He turned back to Kelly, absorbing her rapt features. The freckles stood out across her nose and cheeks, and her hair was glinting with gold highlights as a slight breeze moved the pine boughs above them. His gaze settled on her lips, which were lifted in a smile as she watched the circling hawks.

Maybe it was the pale pink T-shirt she wore, or those jeans that showed off her womanly hips and long legs. In any case, he felt more like a starving raptor himself at the moment than he ever had in his life. Ever since nearly losing her in the kidnapping, and then almost dying himself, Sky craved contact with Kelly. How badly he wanted to love her, to mate with her and make her his woman! He'd been waiting so long. And now . . .

"Come here," he growled, holding out his hand toward her. "I want to love you, Kelly. Right here. Right now. Is that what you want?" He peered into her luminous green eyes, and when he saw those gold flecks emerge, he had his answer.

Gripping his hand, Kelly rose to her knees and moved over to where he sat. "I want nothing more, Sky. You and me. That's the way it's always been. Even as little kids, we loved one another." Releasing his work-worn hand, she ran her fingers through his short, black hair, which glinted with blue highlights as the sun sifted through the pines above. "I want to lose myself in you, Sky . . ."

The shrill, whistled call of the red-tail echoed again across the meadow. For Sky, it was a sign of approval. Even though they were high on the mountainside, surrounded by a profusion of colorful wildflowers, Kelly's beauty made them pale in comparison. His scalp prickled pleasantly beneath her fingertips. "All I want, all I've ever wanted, is you, Kelly." He slid his hands upward and framed her face. "Beautiful woman of the earth, my woman . . ." And he pulled her down, down, down until their lips met.

The power of his mouth on hers melted

Kelly inside, and she moaned. The world, its sounds and scents, seemed to amplify as his lips rocked hers open, to gently engage her more thoroughly.

Her hands explored him — down his cheeks, to the column of his neck, finally reaching the buttons of his shirt. As she sipped and nipped at his lips, Kelly began to undress him. Lost in his simmering heat, in his masterful mouth, she found her breathing becoming unsteady, her heart beginning to pound.

She eased the shirt off his broad shoulders and helped him remove it. Their mouths separated and she sat back on her heels, smiling at Sky. Wordlessly, she spread her hands across his powerful chest. "You feel so good to me," she confessed, feeling his muscles leap and tighten wherever her fingertips grazed them. She heard Sky laugh softly, and she closed her eyes to memorize the shape and form of him. It was then that his hands left her face and trailed fire from her jawline down the length of her neck, to curve and cup her breasts. A sigh of pleasure escaped her parted lips.

"Oh, Sky . . ." She opened her eyes to meet his hooded gaze. The delicious sense of arousal as his thumbs caressed her taut nipples sent a sheet of heat rolling downward between her thighs. Lifting her hands from his bare chest, she grasped the hem of her T-shirt and pulled it up and over her head. Kelly wore nothing underneath. And when his hands settled warmly around her breasts once more, she dropped the shirt and leaned against him.

Without a word, she sought and found his mouth. Molding it beneath hers, she took him hungrily, her hands now moving down across his taut abdomen to the waistband of his jeans. With trembling fingers, she managed to open and unzip them, then thrust her hand beneath the fabric. She felt him tense, and when he groaned, she absorbed the sound into her aching, needy body.

Moments later, Sky was lying with her on the blanket. Settling beside her, he unbuttoned her jeans.

Kelly rolled onto her back, sliding her arms around his shoulders. Her breasts tingled, aching for his caress. Smiling up into his stormy blue eyes, she felt a haze of desire wash through her as his palm stroked across her naked abdomen and down to where her thighs joined.

A cry of utter pleasure escaped from her lips as his fingers sought and found her wet core. Arching into his hand, she relished the joy of sharing such intimacy with a man she had always loved. And now that love could be acted upon, could be shared. Mindlessly, Kelly responded to his caresses, until her world disintegrated into an ageless hunger and throbbing want.

His exploring fingers left her and he set about pulling off her jeans. Then she finally lay naked before him, her eyes barely open. As he divested himself of his own jeans and boxer shorts, Kelly gloried in seeing him naked for the first time in her life. "You are a gorgeous hunk of man," she whispered, opening her arms to him as he knelt above her once more. "Love me, Sky. Just love me . . ."

A rush of air escaped his taut lips as Sky settled over Kelly's warm, eager form. How firm and responsive she felt beneath him. He didn't want to hurt her, so he propped his weight on his elbows. "You are incredibly beautiful, Kelly. You feel so good," he told her, and leaned down to capture her smiling mouth. Drowning in her half-closed eyes, which gleamed with emerald and gold, he thrust forward as her thighs opened to receive him.

With a shiver of utter pleasure, Kelly felt Sky filling her. The shock was fiery, welcome, and her entire body glowed like molten lava, moving restlessly and heatedly with their rhythm. As he locked tightly into her, she arched and moaned. The moment her breasts grazed his firm chest, white-hot tingles radiated in all directions, like sunlight striking the mirrored surface of a lake. All thought spun away as she wildly met and matched his stride.

The fragrance of pine mingled with the musky scent of their lovemaking. A soft breeze caressed her sensitized flesh while she gripped Sky's lean hips with her thighs. There was such an incredible bonding on every level that she felt totally connected to him. And when her body exploded like a sunburst and she cried out, the sound was absorbed within Sky.

Rivulets of heat spread from her core outward, as if a stone had been thrown into a pond, rippling its quiet surface. The joyous release flowed through her, taking her to a spiraling place she'd never known before. Moving with Sky was like riding a shimmering rainbow across the blue vault above. And even as her first orgasm waned, another began to build. Kelly reveled in her partner's hardness, his hand beneath her hips prolonging the pleasure. Her heart expanded, burst open, and the love she felt for this man overwhelmed her. Like a sponge, she absorbed all this knowing, all these revelations into herself, and it did nothing but make her love even more fierce.

Like a raptor that had been caged all her life, Kelly was now free to fly with her mate. The joy of doing so matched the physical pleasure she experienced.

And then Sky tensed, growled and clenched his hand in her hair. Understanding that he had finally reached his own release, she ran her palms boldly across his hips to prolong the sensations for him, as well. There was such satisfaction in being able to share with one another, to give and take. His fingers gripped her and she opened her eyes to see the effects of their mating. Sky's eyes burned a dark blue, with a glittering light in their depths. They told Kelly he was truly hers in every way. His lips drew away from his teeth as he reached his climax, and his swift intake of breath made her spirits soar. Together. They were together as they had always been meant to be. Finally.

"You are a gift to me, woman," Sky murmured. He lay on his side a long time later, his arm beneath Kelly's neck, their naked bodies molded to one another. The breeze riffled across his damp skin as he lifted his hand and traced her mouth with his finger.

"Oh, no." Kelly laughed softly, caressing his cheek. "You're *mine!*"

Their laughter mingled with the rustle of wind through the pines that shaded them from the spring sunlight. Kelly leaned up, placed her lips against his and whispered, "Do you know how often I wanted to do this? It drove me crazy not to be able to run over to you and kiss you."

Teasing her lower lip with his tongue, he took her mouth and cherished it, relished the feel of her breasts pressed to his chest, her hips against his. Drawing back just enough to gaze into her love-filled emerald eyes, Sky responded, "As many times as I wanted to kiss you, I bet."

Kelly sighed. "We've always been in love, Sky. Do you realize that? I didn't at first, but after you let me stay with you those three months in the cabin, to get a grip on my life again, it hit me."

He stroked his fingers tenderly through her hair and watched the sunlight drift through the burnished strands. "I realized it."

Easing away, Kelly sat up and slipped on her shirt, then handed him his. Sky got to his feet and picked up his jeans as well as hers, then helped her up. She pulled on her jeans, then her socks and shoes, gazing over at him as he dressed, admiring his tousled hair, the deep blue of his eyes, which smoldered with desire he no longer had to hide. That made Kelly feel free in a way she never had before.

Sky took her hand and kissed the back of it, and the fragrance of jasmine drifted into his nostrils. He took the red velvet box from his knapsack and studied her face. "I want a life together. I want to marry you, Kelly." Leaning down, he caught her luminous gaze. "I love you, sweet earth woman. And I want to share my life with you. Is that what you want?" He handed her the box.

Kelly opened it and gasped. The engagement ring glinted in the sunlight. She lifted her hand and cupped Sky's cheek. "That sounds wonderful to me. And the ring is beautiful, Sky." She allowed him to slip it on her finger.

"Are you sure you aren't going to miss your exciting life of flying? Putting out wildfires around the country?"

Shaking her head, she said, "No, I'm through with shock and trauma, Sky. All I want is you — helping you with your raptors, living up here, being close to my parents and my family. That's what really counts. I'll be happy for the first time in a long time."

"We have the time now, Kelly," he said hoarsely. "Will you marry me?"

She glanced upward and met his hooded eyes. "In a heartbeat, Sky. As soon as you want."

Relief deep and broad sheeted through Sky. He absorbed Kelly's warm smile, her dappled gold-and-green gaze. She loved him! She always had. And she always would, no matter what tests were thrown at them in the future. They'd stood the greatest of all tests: life and death, and passed it — together. "How about if we clue your parents in? I know your mother too well. She's not going to just let us skip down to a preacher in Las Vegas and get hitched."

Kelly giggled. "You're right about that! And really, I'd love to have a nice, small wedding with close family and friends right here in Philipsburg. How about you?"

"The same," he agreed. Touching her blushing cheek, Sky said, "All I want to do is make you happy, Kelly. I want to wake up every morning with you at my side. That's all I'll ever need. We've gone through so much together."

"Mmm, I like the sound of that, Sky. Maybe it took me all these years to really know what I wanted for the rest of my life."

Embracing her gently, resting his jaw

against her hair, he said, "We're lucky we know at this age. A lot of people out there search their entire life and never realize what they're needing."

"Well, we've found one another," Kelly said, shutting her eyes. She hugged Sky close. "We'll go down in a little while and let Mom and Dad know the good news. I want to show off my ring. Mom will go bonkers over planning our wedding, and that's fine with me. She's the detail person." Kelly chortled softly. Pressing her cheek against Sky's chest, she added, "It's going to be such a happy event, especially compared to the horror of the past week. I know they'll be thrilled. And so will my brothers and sisters."

"I'm going to let my relatives know, too," Sky told her. "They won't come to the wedding because of their age, but it will be good news, after so much tragedy in our family. They'll be happy for us."

"Right now," Kelly whispered emotionally, "I just want this moment with you, Sky."

"You have it, my sweet earth woman." Kissing her hair, he added in a husky voice, "You'll have me forever. That's a promise."

ACKNOWLEDGMENT

This book could not have been birthed without the considerable help of Susan Hamilton of High Country Raptors, Flagstaff, Arizona. As a raptor rehabilitator, licensed in that state, she has an incredible background regarding raptors of all kinds, from owls to hawks and falcons. I want to thank her for giving me the time to understand her world of falconry, the habits and fascinating characters of the raptors themselves. Without her assistance, the information provided in this book would not be here.

You can visit Susan's Web site at: www.highcountryraptors.com and learn why our raptors are "green" and so important to maintain the balance in nature and our environment. I have written on Susan, called *Susan's Friends,* which can be seen at: www.blurb.com/bookstore/detail/113359.

She goes around the state educating schoolchildren of all ages, giving talks to organizations and clubs to let people know that raptors are vital to the earth's health.

Thank you, Susan.

The Flagstaff Arboretum and Botanical Garden has hired Susan's raptor programs. Thank you for allowing Susan and her wonderful raptors to be a part of your overall efforts to teach people that there must be balance with nature and ourselves. More about their nature programs and Susan's daily raptor education can be found at:

www.thearb.org

ABOUT THE AUTHOR

As a homeopath, **Lindsay McKenna** writes books that introduce people to alternative medicine. Living in twenty-two places in seven states during the first eighteen years of her life provided her with a backdrop for her fictional writing. A U.S. Navy veteran, she was a meteorologist while serving her country. Coming from an Eastern Cherokee heritage, she likes to write about Native Americans and introduce people to the world as she lives it. When she was nine, her father introduced her to healing concepts that she utilizes to this day. Continuing to capture the beauty of our earth, Lindsay is an amateur photographer and can always be found hiking in nature, recording our natural world. She can be reached at tales fromechocanyon.blogspot.com or www .medicinegarden.com. As always, she loves to hear from her readers at mink82841@ mypacks.net.

We hope you have enjoyed this Large Print book. Other Thorndike, Wheeler, Kennebec, and Chivers Press Large Print books are available at your library or directly from the publishers.

For information about current and upcoming titles, please call or write, without obligation, to:

Publisher
Thorndike Press
295 Kennedy Memorial Drive
Waterville, ME 04901
Tel. (800) 223-1244

or visit our Web site at:

http://gale.cengage.com/thorndike

OR

Chivers Large Print
published by BBC Audiobooks Ltd
St James House, The Square
Lower Bristol Road
Bath BA2 3SB
England
Tel. +44(0) 800 136919
email: bbcaudiobooks@bbc.co.uk
www.bbcaudiobooks.co.uk

All our Large Print titles are designed for easy reading, and all our books are made to last.